A Gift in December

JENNY GLADWELL

A Gift in December

HODDER

First published in Great Britain in 2019 by Hodder & Stoughton
An Hachette UK company

This paperback edition published in 2019

1

A CIP catalogue record for this title is available from the British Library

Paperback ISBN 978 1 529 30268 4
eBook ISBN 978 1 529 30269 1

Typeset in Plantin Light by Hewer Text UK Ltd, Edinburgh
Printed and bound in Great Britain by Clays Ltd, Elcograf S.p.A.

Hodder & Stoughton policy is to use papers that are natural, renewable and recyclable products and made from wood grown in sustainable forests. The logging and manufacturing processes are expected to conform to the environmental regulations of the country of origin.

Hodder & Stoughton Ltd
Carmelite House
50 Victoria Embankment
London EC4Y 0DZ

www.hodder.co.uk

For Alex

Nybergsund, Norway, 11th April 1940

The snow was falling.

The young soldier stood by the truck smoking, his dark eyes fixed on the huddle of men. The silence bothered him far more than the bombs. He took a last drag of his cigarette and threw it away. His mouth tasted sour.

At last, some decision seemed to have been reached and the men turned and began to walk towards him. They were wrapped in thick coats and mufflers and walked hurriedly through the snow. One of the men was his superior officer. The others he knew were cabinet ministers, their faces impassive but strained. And the fifth man was King Haakon.

So, the soldier thought, this was it: they were leaving. After weeks of discussion, of prevarication, of negotiation, King Haakon was leaving his people and his country. A decision born in these strange times not out of cowardice but sheer, stubborn courage. The unlikely monarch, who no one had believed was up to much, might be braver than they had all thought. Refusing to endorse a puppet ruler, he was now an enemy of the Nazi regime and every moment that he remained here meant danger for him and for the people of Nybergsund.

The soldier knew the plan, such as it was. They were to strike for Molde, the centre of Norwegian resistance, and then the Swedish border – and then after that, God alone knew. The king thought he could form a government from afar. From England, perhaps. Norway's chance to draw a line in the sand. To strike a blow for democracy and freedom.

If they made it out alive.

The border had never seemed so close and yet so far.

The figures drew closer and the soldier straightened. His breath was a cloud in the air. Snow fell thickly now, mantling his shoulders. His eyes met those of his superior.

'The king is leaving now,' the officer said, as he drew near. 'Are you ready?'

'Yes, sir,' the soldier said.

'Please, Your Majesty.' The officer guided the king towards the car.

The soldier was used to the king's face, after this past week – it was just a face now, like any other. Rather gaunt, made haggard by weeks of worry, with a large moustache and heavy eyebrows.

In these last moments, the soldier found himself looking not at his officer or his king but at the woman who stood behind them. He had to look now, he realised, as he might never see her again. Had to drink in that face – the fierce cheekbones, navy eyes, thick, dark hair that sprang off her forehead in waves. Imprint it on his memory so that he might never forget.

His officer rested a hand briefly on his shoulder as the king was ushered into the truck. 'Our country is relying on you,' he said. 'The king is no soldier,' he added drily. 'Do what you must to get him to the border.'

The soldier nodded.

And then the woman was taking a step towards him through the darkness, holding out her hand for him to shake. He took it, felt her pulse beating beneath her glove. Quickly, he pulled her towards him and for the briefest of seconds her cold cheek was pressed against his own.

'Take care of yourself,' she muttered, her voice hoarse in his ear.

'And you.'

'I will write.'

And then he was running away from her, scrambling into the car, where the two men sat in silence. Foot to the floor, ploughing through the snow, he watched through the rear window until she was gone, swallowed up by the endless white.

Dear Thomas,

This will be the last letter that I write.

I thought at first that I should not mind, but after all it is hard, writing and getting no reply. What goes through your mind when you get one of my letters? Does your heart leap?

You know it's over – I don't need to tell you so. But I am writing one last time because I think I should like someone to know how clever I have been. I managed, didn't I? So I thought you might like to have this memento. 'Well done, Marit,' I should like you to say.

You are the keeper of my secret and perhaps you might see it told.

Do that for me. And maybe one other thing. Come back one day. Come back to where we spent that last night, before our lives completely changed. Afterwards, you can go off and live a nice respectable life with your nice respectable girl. But come back to me, just once.

Your Marit

I

London, November 2017

The snow was falling.

In her tiny flat on a quiet street in Stoke Newington, Jane Brook sat on her window seat looking out at the fat snowflakes drifting down from the sky. Snow for the next week; snow for Christmas, maybe. It brought her no joy. Snow was not for watching out of the window, alone. Snow was for enjoying *with* someone. With Simon, for instance.

She thought of that week last winter when snow had fallen and she and Simon had been happy. He persuaded her to spontaneously take the week off work, unheard of for her. They sat with coffee in the Turkish café near her flat, talking, drunk on the newness of it all, giddy at their secret romance. Their eyes would meet across the table and they would burst out laughing at nothing at all. Every touch was a spark.

He brought out a sense of fun in her she had forgotten was there. Where she was calm and ordered, he was chaotic and spontaneous. She discovered the joy of lying in, of curling up in bed together, drowsy and warm. They spent long afternoons in the pub. She would buy a big stack of newspapers for research and they would read and drink, gossip about other journalists, share packets of crisps, and leave pleasantly tipsy.

Cheeks pink and eyes bright, they would stumble back to her flat through drifts of snow, clutching at each other as they slipped and skidded. Simon's scarf wrapped round her neck, smelling of him, her gloved hand in his. Lazy evenings on the sofa, her feet in Simon's lap, drinking expensive whisky he brought over and watching old films that he loved. *It's a Wonderful Life* at Christmas. *The Apartment*, his favourite, on New Year's Eve. Simon laughed at her when she cried at the end.

'I thought you were meant to be tough,' he teased.

The snow was coming down more heavily now. Jane breathed on the window and drew a jaunty, smiling face that she dashed out just as quickly. A burst of laughter carried down the street and a child in waterproofs and wellies staggered past, the snow nearly up to his waist. A couple followed, a man and woman with their arms wrapped round each other. Jane closed her eyes and leaned her forehead against the glass.

With Simon, she had understood how wonderful sharing her life with someone could be. She had opened up her neat, ordered world to him and things would never be the same again.

Her best friends, Margot and Kate, had taken her for dinner the other night, to a restaurant in town that they loved. They had poured her a large glass of red wine, ordered her steak, spinach and mashed potatoes. Margot was pregnant, in her third trimester, and Kate, her partner, was casually solicitous, rubbing the small of Margot's back. Talk, despite their best efforts, turned to birth plans and childcare, maternity leave, mortgages and kitchen fitters. Jane listened to their chat, charting the gentle, loving beats of a relationship, and felt misery rise up in her. They listened to her woes, eyes sympathetic, but Jane knew she would have to help herself out of her gloom.

She could no longer stay here, perched by the window, watching the snow fall. Her feet and hands were cold. She hadn't eaten properly for days. Right now, she needed to take a shower, wash her hair. Throw out the old food in the fridge. At the last count, it had contained a lump of old cheese, half a jar of pesto and a wilted lettuce.

Because tomorrow, she'd be gone, off on a work trip to Norway of all places. She groaned. Norway.

That only meant more bloody snow.

Her boss, Nadine, had suggested the assignment. 'Suggested' was euphemistic: Nadine issued orders, not suggestions.

She breezed out of her office yesterday and dropped the press release onto Jane's desk – thick cream paper, elegant, swirling font, full-colour photos of fir trees in the snow and blazing log fires.

'I'm sending you to Norway to watch the Trafalgar Square Christmas tree being cut down,' Nadine said. 'A very *lavish* press trip.'

'You want me to write about a tree?' Jane asked, incredulous.

She had been at the *London Courier* nearly ten years. From the start, she had hero-worshipped Nadine, who had white-blonde hair cut short, wore trouser suits and trainers and no make-up, and ran her paper with calm efficiency.

Nadine also had something that Jane had come to understand was rare in the industry: integrity. The *Courier* was respected for its impartial reporting – and was newsworthy itself at the moment, thanks to Jane's recent breaking of a dramatic immigration scandal that exposed corruption at the heart of the government.

She had hoped that her next story would be something just as juicy.

Jane glanced at the glossy release. 'This looks like a puff piece,' she said, and one of Nadine's elegant eyebrows rose. 'I just thought,' Jane continued, more diplomatically, 'that I might be better off staying here. I want to start something new. I've got loads of ideas . . .'

Nadine looked at Jane over her glasses for a long moment, something curious and unfamiliar in her expression.

'I want you to take a break,' she said at last. 'You've worked hard, and I've seen more experienced journalists than you burn out after a big story like that. Plus, I have a feeling that things haven't exactly been easy for you here.'

That was Nadine being diplomatic in turn and *not* mentioning Simon.

'You should take a holiday,' she went on. 'That's what anyone else would do after the month you've had. But since there's no chance of that happening, yes; I'm sending you to Norway to write about a tree. It's the next best thing.'

Jane picked up the press release and began to read.

The global social-media spotlight will be on Norway this November as a select group of bloggers and journalists join us for a magical journey into the past . . .

Since 1947, the city of Oslo has presented a Christmas tree to the city of London every year, in gratitude for its assistance during the Second World War.

In 1940, in the midst of the occupation, King Haakon of Norway refused to install a Nazi sympathiser as the head of government. Miraculously, he escaped German bombs and established a temporary government in London. Norway worked tirelessly against the Nazi regime for the remainder of the war. Each year, a magnificent Christmas tree – known as the 'Queen of the Forest' – is carefully chosen from the forests outside Oslo and transported, by boat and lorry, back to London. This gift to Londoners from the Norwegians forms a central part of the city's Christmas decorations and is integral to many festive events throughout the season.

Jane paused to protest and Nadine raised a hand. 'Just keep reading.'

This year, the Norwegian Tourist Board, Luxury Travel *magazine and a selection of top fashion and lifestyle brands are sponsoring a lavish trip for our guests through the stunning Norwegian landscape to see the chosen tree cut down. Guests will stay in Norway's top hotels and sample the country's finest cuisine and Christmas traditions. The trip will culminate in a winter ball before returning home to see the tree installed in Trafalgar Square.*

A symbol of peace for our time, shared with the world.

'I'm sending Andersen too,' said Nadine. She raised her voice. 'Do you hear that, Ben?'

Ben Andersen, a freelance photographer, who was known for being irrepressibly cheerful despite covering a succession of bleak war zones, raised his head.

'I just got back,' he said mildly. 'I've been away for six months. I haven't even unpacked yet.'

It was as close to a complaint as Ben would ever make.

'Think of this as a nice change of pace,' Nadine cackled. 'You're too nice to say no. It's perfect – you're actually Norwegian, right?'

'I am,' said Ben. His face brightened. 'I guess we'll be there for the Christmas markets.'

Nadine beamed. 'That's the spirit. Take a leaf out of Ben's book, Jane. Now then, if you're both happy . . .'

'I just don't understand what the *story* is,' Jane muttered, scanning the paper. 'Also, I hate Christmas.'

'Well, Scrooge,' Ben replied, 'if anything can convert you, it'll be a few weeks in Norway. It's where Christmas was practically invented.'

'Just stop,' Jane told him. 'Christmas was invented by department stores in a bid to sell people more stuff they don't need.'

'Christmas as we know it was invented by Dickens,' Nadine said, sat next to her, absently tapping out an email on her phone, already thinking about something else. 'It's a feel-good story. That doesn't make it worthless.' Ben nodded vigorously and Jane shot him a dirty look. 'Our readers need a bit of sentiment – something to remind them that people are essentially good. A positive story about European solidarity and collaboration might be just the ticket.'

'Exactly!' said Ben.

Jane allowed herself a very small smile.

'Besides,' Nadine added, 'how many fancy holidays normally land in your lap when you're writing for a boring old broadsheet? Think log fires and hampers and hot tubs. I had to fight Chrissy from Travel for it.'

Jane leaped in as Nadine took a swallow of coffee.

'Chrissy from Travel is *exactly* who should be covering this—'

'Finally, and most importantly, you'll avoid this place in the run-up to Christmas,' Nadine continued. 'Think of it, Jane. No office parties. No average pub lunch where we have to fork out thirty quid to wear paper hats.'

'Even if those hats look great on you,' Ben said. 'Even if you were born to wear those hats.'

Jane groaned. 'Christmas isn't for ages,' she said weakly. 'And you're already putting me off it.'

'It'll come around sooner than you think. But at least you'll be relaxed after a few weeks in Norway,' Nadine said, standing and smoothing down her trousers.

The sly glances from the rest of the team as Simon and I avoid each other, thought Jane.

'Fine,' she said. 'I'll take it. Like you're giving me any choice.'

'Good,' Nadine said briskly. 'I'll loop you in with the PR now. She's called Natasha. Watch out for her – she's already annoying me.' She gave Jane the ghost of a wink. 'Ben, it's your mission to make Jane enjoy herself. I want her back more cheerful than Scrooge on Christmas morning.'

'Ho, ho, ho,' Jane said mirthlessly, slumping down in her seat.

Jane had always prided herself on not getting too involved when it came to men. Her hard-won job as a reporter for the prominent, award-winning *London Courier* brought her a joy so fierce that she could only acknowledge it with a sort of superstitious caution. Even after a disheartening day, she still had to pinch herself that this was her, with her patchy education, working alongside some of the best journalists in the country. She had hit her stride at the *Courier*, found something she loved doing and thrown herself into her work.

And then Simon Layton had joined the *London Courier* just over a year ago as arts and culture reporter. 'Sitting in a dark room watching films – what's not to like?' he said to her.

Jane hadn't paid him much attention at first – average height, curling dark hair, a lilting Irish accent – but suddenly he was everywhere. Teasing her in the kitchen, asking her opinion with flattering frequency on his work. Stopping by her desk with tempting little nuggets of office gossip, making her laugh. Arguing with her about politics, which, as she told him, he knew nothing about. Coffee, exactly how she liked it – strong, with a lot of milk – on her desk every morning. Waiting for her, ever so casually, at the end of the day so that they could walk out together.

He became, she wasn't quite sure how, part of the fabric of her life.

So this is what it's like to have an office crush, Jane thought. Someone you made an effort for. She was constantly aware of Simon's presence – when he was in the room, she would surreptitiously apply lip balm, fluff up her hair, sit straighter. She chose her outfits and applied her perfume in the morning with extra care. He was one of those people who was friendly to everyone: she had no idea whether she was special to him or not. The uncertainty made their flirtation – if that was what it was – extra exciting.

She found out he had just split up with his long-term university girlfriend, Emily.

'She wanted the whole two-point-four-children thing,' he told Jane one day by the coffee point. 'You know – big ugly house in suburbia, big ugly car. Good schools. Holidays in Center Parcs.' He shrugged. 'It's not for me. Not just yet anyway.' He grinned, his eyes lighting up his face.

Jane had stalked Emily on Facebook as soon as she was back at her desk. Wholesome – a sweet face, long, shiny dark hair, freckles across her nose, and very white, even teeth. Jane skimmed through the photos of her and Simon – camping, hill-walking, beaming at the camera over pints – then shut down the page and smiled.

The tension, real or imagined, had bubbled away for weeks. And then finally, after Nadine's birthday drinks last November, they found themselves alone and slightly tipsy on a corner of Lamb's Conduit Street. It was a perfect London night, clear and cold, Christmas lights twinkling and their breath clouding in the frosty air. Simon's hand on her arm, pulling her to a halt. Jane's heart beating so hard she thought it might burst as he leaned towards her, and then their mouths fitting together, just right.

After that, they were inseparable. They kept it quiet at work, but everyone knew. For nearly a year, everything was perfect.

Or almost perfect.

Looking back, Jane had to admit that there were cracks. When she had introduced him to Margot and Kate, he couldn't have been more charming, but she sensed an unusual reserve on their part. Kate laughed at his jokes, but Margot seemed distant. She didn't talk much, which for Margot was a red flag. She mostly leaned back and watched Simon through half-lidded eyes.

Jane began their group WhatsApp the next morning with an excited 'Well??????' Kate had been effusive – 'He's gorgeous! That accent!' – but Margot was strangely muted.

'Didn't you like him?' Jane asked her the next time they met, over fish pie in their usual midweek dinner spot. 'I feel like you guys didn't like him.'

'Oh, we liked him,' Margot said. She was in the middle of IVF and the strain was showing, although the signs – the faintest furrow in her perfect forehead, the bluish shadows under her eyes – would have been imperceptible to most. She took a thoughtful swallow of her sparkling water. 'He's handsome and charming, which I'm sure he knows.' She leaned forward, her face serious. 'He seemed a bit cross about how late you were coming home from work.'

'Oh,' said Jane, waving her hand. 'He just worries about how hard I work.'

'And he said you should be getting the drinks because you make more money. That felt kind of bitter.'

'That was a joke! He's not threatened by me, if that's what you think.'

Margot nodded, clearly appeasing her. 'OK. I mean, you know him best. The only thing that matters to me is – is he nice to you?'

'Of course he is!' Jane exclaimed. Margot was way too protective of her, she thought. She knew what she was doing.

And it was true – Simon *was* nice to her. He adored her. They even spent Christmas Day together because his family were in Spain for a wedding and he hadn't enough holiday allowance left to go. Since her mum died, Jane spent it with Margot and Kate, but Margot airily waved off her apologies. 'There will be plenty more Christmases,' she said. 'Enjoy yourself.'

Jane agonised over what to give him for this first Christmas but chanced on a battered first edition of *Moonfleet* in a charity shop, his favourite book as a boy. And he had given her a ridiculously expensive pink bobble hat, something Jane would never have bought in a million years.

'One hundred per cent cashmere,' he said proudly, when she unwrapped it. 'Try it on.'

She pulled it on and he laughed at her doubtful expression. 'You look adorable in it. Like a very serious elf. It's not a crime to have nice things, you know. You should see how overboard my parents go at Christmas.'

'Do you miss your family?' she asked, snuggling next to him on the sofa, still wearing the hat.

'They're all right, but they're not a patch on you.' He kissed the tip of her nose. 'You'll meet them all next Christmas,' he said confidently, and she glowed.

The months rolled by and Jane counted them off with glee. Finally, after years of rubbish men, she was in an adult, functional relationship. Weekend trips to the seaside and dinners with friends. A drawer in his flat for her to keep her underwear and a hairdryer.

And then Jane had hit on her big story – an immigration cover-up that struck at the heart of the government itself. She had known she was onto something huge right from the start. This was it, her career-defining moment. And she was going to nail it.

She put the story together piece by painstaking piece over a six-month period, knowing that it had to be rock solid. She worked long into the night. Things with Simon took a back seat, and at first he was understanding about the cancelled dates and missed calls. Then she noticed him becoming slightly grumpy and distant. Rather cold when they spoke on the phone.

She would have to make it up to him, she thought vaguely, as soon as this was over. But she hadn't thought very much about it – she'd been working too hard. And then she had emerged, dazed and exhausted, with the story of the year in the bag.

The day it broke, she entered the office to a round of very British, yet warmly enthusiastic applause. Nadine went so far as to squeeze her arm. 'This will be front page on every paper for the next month,' she said. 'Scandal of the decade. And we were there first, thanks to you.'

Jane's phone started ringing then and it didn't stop all morning. Talk of her winning prizes had begun. It was only after lunch when, still flushed with excitement and triumph, she noticed the email sitting towards the top of her neglected inbox. It was from Simon, marked 'high importance'. *Please read this*, was the subject line.

A wave of love and affection rushed over her. Simon, who had been at her side so patiently these last hectic months, just waiting for her to come up for air.

And now she could breathe again.

She beamed.

He must be out watching films today. He was probably going to suggest taking her out for dinner to celebrate after work, somewhere typically Simon, over-the-top and decadent.

She clicked on the email. And suddenly everything around her became muffled, as though she were underwater.

Jane,

I'm emailing you at work because I can't think of any other way to get your attention these days. You only seem interested in work. So here goes.

I can't do this anymore. You've barely spoken to me in months. The last time I persuaded you to come out for dinner, you spent the whole night on your phone fact-checking. I know you've been busy, and I know this story is important, but I matter too. And right now, I feel invisible.

I'm sorry. I've reached my limit. I really hope we can still be friends. For the record, I think you're an amazing woman. I just can't come second to a good story anymore.

I'll come by the flat this morning when you're at work and clear out my stuff. To be honest, I doubt you'll even notice.

Love always,

Simon

Jane stared at the screen, a chill sweeping through her whole body. Even the tips of her fingers went cold. Dimly, she felt a pang of fury that he had dared to ruin this moment for her, but it was lost in her confusion and misery.

She was still numb moments later when she became vaguely aware of Nadine calling her name and the sound of a champagne cork popping.

She went home that evening to a flat that felt bare without Simon's towering piles of books, the jumble of cycling gear by the front door, the cookbooks full of outrageously complicated recipes, the expensive coffee maker. Her beloved flat seemed now empty and rather cold.

It didn't take her long to find out that Simon had moved on – or, rather, had moved *backwards*. In fact, it took Jane the investigative journalist precisely two hours before she went on Emily's Facebook page and saw her with Simon's arms wrapped round her, and the caption *Maybe it was always meant to be.*

Margot came over straight away, carrying a bottle of wine in one hand and one of gin in the other.

'I thought you could choose, depending on how bad you're feeling,' she said sympathetically, sinking onto Jane's sofa. She gazed at her bump slightly regretfully. 'This is *all* for you.'

'You were right all along,' said Jane. She held up her phone and brandished Emily's profile at Margot. 'He's gone back to his ex.' She laughed bitterly. 'I guess it'll be fine so long as she doesn't have to work long hours.'

Margot seized the phone. 'Give me this. Until you're of sound mind, I'm removing Facebook, Twitter and Instagram. All the torture devices. And I'm blocking his number.' She glanced over. 'OK?'

Jane nodded miserably. 'OK.'

'There.' Margot handed back the phone. 'And now, I'm

going to find some ice because I think it'll have to be the gin.'

After sobbing into her pillow for a few nights, Jane attempted to pull herself together. But something had changed. Her well-ordered life had been knocked off course when she let Simon in and now she didn't know how to get it back on track. Job offers poured in, including a coveted foreign correspondent post at the *Washington News*, but Jane turned them all down. She needed to stay where she was safe.

She tried acting as cheerfully as she could, but Margot wasn't fooled.

'I *know* you,' Margot told her one afternoon over tea, when Jane had been trying to smile so hard her face hurt. 'And you can pretend you're fine to everyone in the world, but I want the truth.' With her dirty-blonde hair, perfect rose-petal skin and blue eyes fringed with thick lashes, Margot's beauty could still take Jane's breath away. Even now, with a raging cold and in the grip of pregnancy insomnia, she looked gorgeous.

The waiter came over to take their order.

'We'll have a pot of Earl Grey tea for two, one raspberry millefeuille and two forks.' Margot handed the menu back, drew a packet of tissues from her handbag and blew her nose vigorously. 'I swear pregnancy is making me catch every bloody cold going.'

'Now.' She laid a firm hand on Jane's. 'Break-ups suck, Jane, and they especially suck if you're a control freak, which, let's face it, you are. But I'm telling you that this *will* get better. Think how many times you've rescued me from one disaster or another.'

A single tear trickled down Jane's cheek and she caught it with her finger. 'Like when you forgot your speech at

Fiona's wedding and made us sing the Spice Girls' "Two Become One" instead,' she said, smiling faintly. 'Or when you told that girl in Cornwall you were a competitive surfer and nearly drowned. Or when you borrowed the dog that was tied up outside the supermarket for a fancy-dress competition and I had to get you from the police station. Or—'

'That was a long time ago,' Margot said, shifting back while the waiter set down a fat pot of tea and two china cups. 'Anyway, the point is that I was always getting into bad situations and you were always getting me out of them. Look at everything you've been through these last few years. You lost your mum. You broke the story of the year. No one is tougher than you. And let me tell you that Simon, of all people, is not worth the heartache. He's gone back to his boring ex so they can move to the boring suburbs and have boring babies. Is that *really* what you want?'

'Yes. No. Sort of,' Jane said.

'Come on, Jane,' said Margot. 'You used to have fun. Not as much fun as me, but fun. You can have fun again.'

Jane sighed.

The waiter brought the cake, all pastry and raspberries and puffy cream. Jane's stomach turned.

'I'm not hungry,' she said.

Margot looked at her thoughtfully.

'You know, as much of an arse as Simon is, he did serve one purpose. He reminded you that it's not a bad thing to enjoy yourself.' She pushed the plate towards Jane. 'Now eat the bloody cake.'

Still hovering by the window, Jane glanced down at her delicate cup, half filled with tea that was now stone cold. She missed Simon, ached for him. He had cleared out his stuff, but still she kept stumbling across fragments of him, which were gradually filling a charity-shop bag by her front door. He was too messy, too impulsive and generous, to have left her life without a trace. The cup was yet another reminder – of a day by the seaside and him buying her the cup at a little antique shop. '*Pretty, just like you*,' he had said.

With sudden force she put it down on the window ledge. Enough of this wallowing. She was going to go outside and buy some food. Then she would come home and make coffee. And she was going to drink it out of a proper mug, not a stupid china teacup.

This Norway trip was coming at just the right time. She would get some distance from Simon, turn in a few thousand words on a Christmas tree and come back refreshed for the new year.

And one other thing.

She would avoid all men.

2

Jane staggered her way through the snow to the shops, bought a loaf of cheap sliced white bread, milk and some coffee, and marched back again, relishing the bite of the wind against her face. Once home, she heated the coffee on the hob and made a grilled cheese sandwich, the food of her childhood, filling her mouth with the comforting taste of grease and salt. '*If you don't take care of yourself, no one else will*' – her mother's voice, coming unbidden into her head. Aileen, who had died five Novembers ago and who would have poured scorn on the idea of crying over a man.

Jane's flight to Oslo was early the next morning. The PR agency had sent over a suitcase for her to use, gifted by one of the sponsors, tasteful dusky pink with an inbuilt USB charger. She was good at packing and her hand reached for the outfits without thinking, automatically smoothing and folding, rolling and tucking. Simple clothes, practicality over style. White shirts, dark trousers, jeans, thick, warm jumpers, thermals, several pairs of woollen socks, a swimming costume for the spa (a one-piece, obviously). No skirts or dresses – she had long ago decided that they didn't suit her.

She reached for the little pouch that contained her toiletries, and for her phone charger, headphones and eye mask. Her warm, charcoal-grey winter coat and scarf. The process felt calming. She checked her handbag for what she thought of as on-the-job essentials – mints, a pen, more warm socks, business cards, notebook, lip balm, hairbands, an extra charger. She slipped a guidebook to Norway in too and downloaded a recent popular history of Norway's involvement in the Second World War. If there was one thing she had learned from Nadine, it was to take every job seriously. She hesitated over the incongruous pink bobble hat, turning it over in her hands.

Her phone buzzed. Margot. She picked up and tried to sound cheerful.

'Hey! How are you feeling?'

'Bored. Whoever said I should take early maternity leave was an idiot. How's the packing going?'

Jane surveyed her neatly packed bags. 'You know me,' she said. 'Military precision as always. Dreading this trip, though.'

'It sounds amazing. I would kill for all of it.'

'I just . . .' Jane chewed her nail. 'It's not really my thing, you know. Plus, I should be working on a new story, not spending a fortnight stuck in a swanky hotel with Ben from work, who is never not happy and never not talking.'

'Rubbish,' said Margot, and Jane could feel a lecture coming on. 'This is exactly what you need. Some fun. Are there any hot men going?'

With the phone wedged under her ear, Jane shook the passenger list out of her travel documents and scanned it: *Sandra Riley*, a food critic; *Nick Green*, a tabloid journalist for the *Daily Post*; *Ben Andersen*, photographer with the *Courier* and the happiest man in the world.

And then the bloggers: *Lucy Partridge*, travel writer and fashion blogger; *Lena Thorpe*, yoga teacher and sustainability blogger; *Frederica Moss*, interior design and lifestyle. Jane had no idea who they were, but the itinerary described in glowing terms their credentials as influencers, their international reach and work with various brands and charities – none of which meant anything to Jane.

There was another name on the list – *Thomas Erikson.* Next to him, it just said, *Visitor of importance.*

'There are a couple of men,' Jane said at last. 'But I've no idea if they're hot or not. Besides, I'm off romance for ever, remember?'

'About that,' said Margot. 'I've been thinking. You want to exorcise this Simon relationship, am I right?'

'More than anything,' said Jane emphatically.

'OK, well, I had a brainwave at three a.m. As I said, Simon was useless, but he did remind you how to let your hair down. He made you silly again, and you need to hang on to that. And I've figured out how.'

'I'm listening,' said Jane cautiously.

'You need to sleep with someone in Norway. Someone hot.'

'Oh, please, Margot, that is such a cliché,' groaned Jane. 'Can't I eat ice cream for a month and mourn this properly like a normal person?'

'You've done that already,' said Margot. 'When did you break up with Simon?'

'Like, a few weeks ago.'

'One month ago, to the *day*,' Margot said. She had a forensic memory for dates.

'But I read that it takes exactly half the relationship to mourn it properly and—'

'Rubbish,' said Margot crisply. 'That's an equation for losers. Have you packed any sexy underwear?'

'I bought a new pack of M&S pants.'

'Jesus. Hang on – what about the bra-and-pants set I made you buy last summer?'

'Not those,' Jane protested. 'You have to hand-wash them. Who has time to hand-wash *underwear*?'

'Those.' Margot's voice was steely.

'All right, all right.' Jane rooted around in her drawer for the filmy and insubstantial articles that Margot had persuaded her to buy for a friend's wedding. 'Found them,' she said.

'Right. Put them in the case. Get on that plane, go to Norway and make some bad – no, make that *good* decisions, do you hear? I don't want you to come back until you do.'

There was a long pause.

'You really think it'll help me stop thinking about Simon?' Jane said at last.

'I guarantee it.'

Jane sighed. 'I guess it can't hurt.'

'That's my girl,' said Margot, satisfied. 'And don't think I won't be monitoring you. Daily updates, OK?'

'Daily updates,' agreed Jane.

'I have to go now. I've got a midwife appointment. But you can do this. I don't want Sensible Jane on this trip. I want Badly Behaved Jane, Jane from uni, before she sobered up and became super ambitious and battered by love. She's in there somewhere. You just have to let her out.'

'I'll do my best,' Jane said. She hung up and stared down at the flimsy pieces of fabric that Margot thought constituted underwear, then opened her suitcase and slipped them inside. As she'd told Margot, it couldn't hurt.

Her gaze fell again on the bobble hat. She stared at it – soft and sugar pink. Decadent, silly and cheerful. Simon all over.

On impulse, she snatched it up and stuffed it into the charity-shop bag that was waiting by the door.

Simon Layton would *not* be coming with her on this trip.

3

The taxi arrived at Gatwick at 4.40 a.m., a clear hour and a half before Jane had to board her flight. She checked in with practised ease and found the gate number. They were all going to be sitting together on the flight. An enforced Christmas holiday was one thing, but did it have to be with so many people?

Jane walked through the airport in a daze of early morning exhaustion, not helped by the tinny Christmas music that hummed in her ears and her month-old sleep debt. She paused to look at herself in a mirror as she walked past.

'*A face with the shutters down*' was how Simon had described it when they had first spent the night together. '*You always have your guard up.*' His hand, brushing her cheek. '*But you look so lovely when you smile.*'

Tears came, but Jane lifted her chin and blinked them back. She was working. Her heart might be broken, but she would not let it show.

At the gate, Jane recognised the bloggers immediately. A trio of young women, frantically tapping on their phones. They were all clutching eco coffee cups, were all swathed in thick, blanket-like scarves, and they were all beautiful. Something about them – the sheen to their skin amid the grey, exhausted pallor of the other passengers, their bright lipstick and artfully tousled hair, their elaborate layers of clothing – set them apart. As Jane watched, one of them, a beauty with red lipstick and an Afro, lifted her phone, held her coffee cup to her lips without drinking and took a photo. Then a second photo. A third. A fourth . . .

'Hi,' came a brisk, aristocratic voice at Jane's elbow and she turned. 'Are you one of the Oslo party? I'm Natasha Barnes. We've spoken on email. I'm looking after PR this trip.'

Natasha looked about Jane's age, tall and blonde, dressed in fur-lined boots, a jumper with a vaguely Nordic pattern and jeans that were at once frayed, distressed and high-waisted. Her hair tumbled about her shoulders, and her face was immaculately made up.

'Hi. Yes, I'm Jane Brook, from the *Courier*.'

Natasha nodded, looking not at Jane but at her phone.

'That's all of us, then.' She had a cut-glass accent and the sort of intimidating good looks that made Jane immediately defensive. 'These are the bloggers, Lucy, Lena and Freddie' – she nodded at the trio of girls on their phones – 'and the traditional press. That's you, Nick Green over there from the *Daily Post*, Sandra Riley from the *Gourmand*, photographer Ben Andersen and Philip Donnelly, who's writing a piece for *Rural Living*.'

Jane glanced over. Sandra was bundled up in a thick puffa coat and had her eyes closed. Nick, pale with stubble and glasses, was flicking through a paper. Ben, his dark hair rumpled, wearing a navy pea coat and jeans, was drinking coffee and yawning.

'I know Sandra and Nick a bit. And that's Ben from work,' said Jane, waving at him.

He raised his coffee cup to her in salute and beamed. *Never not cheerful*, she thought, *even on a dawn flight*.

'Hang on,' Jane said, her tired brain clicking into gear. 'Did you say Philip *Donnelly*? From the TV? He wasn't on the list, was he?'

Natasha was still tapping away on her phone. 'I know, right? Wants to get back to his journo roots. His people only confirmed last minute.' She leaned closer to Jane. 'That's him over there. In the sunglasses. He'll be handy if the plane crashes and we have to survive in the forest.'

Jane stared at the figure slumped gracefully in the plastic seat. Philip Donnelly was a genuine celebrity, a former travel journalist who had carved out a more glamorous career presenting *Survival of the Fittest*, a TV programme that involved a group of celebrities living for a fortnight in inhospitable terrain. The success of the programme had long depended on Philip Donnelly's taciturn persona – laconic and handsome, with flinty blue eyes, rumpled T-shirt and iconic battered leather jacket. As well as effortlessly building fires and scaling ravines, he spoke passionately about the environment and preserving indigenous cultures, though most people only watched it for the entertainment of seeing pampered celebrities roughing it. The show had been a ratings winner for years.

And then it had all come crashing down. Philip had been caught having an affair with his co-presenter, Donna Marks. She left her husband – and small children – for him, and there had been a significant public backlash. Philip was blasted by the press for being a homewrecker.

Now, Jane took in the long legs and square jaw. *Sunglasses in the airport*, she thought grimly: *classic celeb*. She wondered if he was asleep behind them.

She sat down, took out her phone and texted Margot.

At the airport with some children who are supposedly lifestyle bloggers. And Philip Donnelly off *Survival of the Fittest* is on this trip too. He's wearing his sunglasses inside the airport.

A pause and then her phone buzzed in reply:

Excellent – this was all I was hoping for and more.

Then:

If you don't manage to kiss Philip Donnelly in a hot tub, then don't come home at all.

Jane snorted.

He's a notorious shagger!

Margot's replies came in quick succession.

Fine. If you don't *shag* him in a hot tub, then.

Remember, it's the only way to get Simon out of your system.

Safe flight.

Jane snorted again and stuck her phone into her bag. She looked over at the rest of the group. The bloggers were now posing for a joint selfie, all pouting mouths and perfect hair. If Philip Donnelly was as much of a ladies' man as the tabloids suggested, there were far better prospects than her on this trip.

It was Jane's first time in business class. She received a hot towel gratefully, declined champagne in favour of a glass of sparkling water and lay back, luxuriating in the revelation of comfortable seats and lavish leg room. Around her, the bloggers were putting on eye masks, rubbing lavender-scented aromatherapy oil on their wrists and snuggling under cashmere blankets with the ease of practised travellers. Jane peered into the complimentary bag of in-flight goodies and, in the spirit of trying new things, tentatively sprayed some 'relaxing facial mist' onto her face. It stung her eyes and she coughed.

The blogger sitting next to her, Lucy, seemed happy not to talk, instead tying her hair into a gorgeously messy topknot, pouring out a glass of thick green juice and then burying herself in a psychological thriller that Jane had seen advertised at every Tube stop she'd used in the last fortnight. Jane put on her headphones and cued up the Norwegian-history audiobook on her phone. It was called *A King's Impossible Choice*, and, to her amusement, it was narrated by none other than Philip Donnelly, which felt surreal given the man himself was seated only a few feet away, sunglasses still firmly in place.

Jane leaned her head back and let the story wash over her. It was the same story as in the press release but in more detail, all described in Philip's languid tones.

April 1940 and Norway was being held hostage.

German troops had invaded Norway. They demanded the king install Vidkun Quisling, a Nazi puppet, as prime minister.

The Norwegian government, however, had other ideas. The king and his cabinet escaped to safety in the little village of Nybergsund, close to the border. It was to be a very temporary haven.

For now, with time running out, the king's choice was stark. Either accept a government headed up by Quisling or risk the full force of the Nazi Army on his beloved country.

After a long and terrible night of the soul, King Haakon told his cabinet that he could not in conscience accept a Nazi as prime minister. They agreed.

The wrath of the German Army was immediate and brutal. Nybergsund was bombed. The king and his cabinet barely escaped with their lives, sheltering in the nearby forest as the bombs rained down amid the snow.

Escape seemed impossible. And yet the king, along with the crown prince and the majority of his government, achieved just that.

They were helped over the mountains by secret agents working with the Norwegian resistance and across the border, eventually reaching London. There, they established a government in unoccupied territory, and for the remainder of the war this exiled government led their country and the Norwegian war effort from London.

They would not return home for another five years.

Jane shook her head as she listened, wondering how she would have acted in those extreme circumstances. Would she have shown an iota of the bravery and stubbornness of the Norwegian royal family and cabinet, or would she have just tried to survive?

Her thoughts were interrupted by the captain, announcing they were circling over the city of Oslo.

'Ladies and gentlemen, we are about to start our descent into Oslo,' she said. 'You are lucky to see it in the run-up to Christmas. As you may know, Norway's winters are the longest and darkest in all of Europe, and November marks the beginning of the twilight days. You're in for a wintery treat!'

Jane leaned over to look out of the window, feeling a flicker of excitement. She could see the city lights twinkling below.

She grinned, imagining what she would be doing right now in London – trudging out of the Underground, hot, sweaty and irritable, to spend the rest of the day staring at her screen and avoiding Simon.

Instead, she was descending over an unknown city, rich with history, for a luxurious all-expenses-paid trip. And her only challenge was to do something outrageous.

Perhaps, in Norway, land of the midnight sun – or in November, the everlasting night – it would be easier than she thought.

4

As the group were driven through the city's streets, Jane felt her tired eyes grow wide with wonder. The sky had a strange, bluish quality that spoke of twilight, and lights burned in the windows of every house. Shoppers and tourists, wrapped in layers of heavy scarves, hurried through the snowy streets. Braziers glowed at each corner as vendors touted bags of hot sweet chestnuts, and strings of fairy lights hung from lamp-posts and the bare branches of trees. It was a magical, snowy, night-time Christmas tableau and yet it was barely midday.

They wandered, dazed, around the stalls on the docks, looking at reindeer skins and wooden ornaments.

'Who fancies a drink?' Ben asked, and Jane nodded along with the rest of them.

'*Glogg for alle, vær så snill*,' he said to a stall-holder selling hot apple wine, and she ladled out a mugful for each of them.

'I didn't realise we had a translator as well as a photographer,' said Natasha, taking her mug. 'How useful.'

The bloggers posed for photos clutching their mugs, cheeks glowing under their woolly hats, hair blowing artfully in the faint breeze.

Back in the car, Jane's stomach growled and Ben handed her a Snickers bar.

'You're very well equipped,' she said, taking it gratefully.

'They never factor in proper meals,' he said, ripping the wrapper off another chocolate bar.

She peered into his camera bag. 'A first-aid kit? How dangerous is this press trip going to be?'

He nodded at her own bag. 'At least we won't run out of socks.'

'I've pulled too many all-nighters with cold feet,' she said with feeling.

'Next stop,' Natasha said, pressing her fingers to her temples, 'the hotel.'

They drove to the outskirts of the city, where they finally rolled through an ornate gateway down a long gravel drive lined with trees.

The hotel was vast, like a chateau from a fairy story, a grey brick building covered with elegant ironwork. Jane got out of the car and was surprised to find the sounds of the traffic were muffled and the bustle of the city felt very far away.

She watched the others stretching their legs. Sandra and Nick had clearly identified each other as kindred spirits. They were stood together, looking tired and grumpy. The bloggers trailed behind, holding their phones up for signal. Ben was sizing up the hotel for potential shots.

'Where's Philip Donnelly?' Jane asked Nick.

'Didn't you notice?' he said. 'He gets his own car. That's Z-list TV stars for you. The more insecure they are, the more demanding they turn out to be.'

Sandra chuckled, drawing her expensive-looking embroidered scarf closer about her. 'Doesn't like to be tied down, then? Pretty revealing, given his love life.'

'I wonder why he's here,' Jane said. 'It seems a bit small-fry, doesn't it?'

'Probably doesn't want to pass up the free trip,' Sandra said tartly, as a large black car crunched down the drive a little faster than was necessary. 'Here's the pound-shop Tom Cruise now.'

Philip climbed out, still wearing his sunglasses. He looked, in his battered leather jacket and jeans, the very image of a tough adventurer.

Ben zipped up his camera bag. 'He's really tall, isn't he?' he said.

'You're tall,' Jane said kindly. 'I think it's just the muscles that make him seem bigger.'

'Or the ego,' muttered Ben.

A stout man with a white moustache came hurrying out of the hotel to meet them.

'Come in, come in,' he said, guiding them up the steps and into a vast reception area, a cavernous, cathedral-like space. Marble statues lined the hall, contrasting with the abstract paintings, which provided blooms of colour against the forest-green walls, and an imposing staircase stretched ahead of them.

'Welcome to the Grand Hotel, where old meets new in modern Oslo. For tonight, there are no other guests: the whole hotel is yours. So, if you will spare a moment to check in, we will have you settled in no time.'

Jane was shown to her suite by a young man with a mop of blond hair. He waited as she walked around slowly, taking it all in. The walls were inky blue, and the bed, with its pristine white sheets and golden headboard, was heaped with pillows and thick sheepskin rugs.

Poinsettias filled every spare surface. Brass lamps cast a gentle glow across the room, with its elegant mid-century furniture and framed abstract prints, which marched round the walls, breaking up the dark space. Faded antique rugs covered the smooth floorboards. A grey sofa piled with mustard-yellow cushions and sheepskin throws completed the sense of luxury.

There was a hamper on the table, filled with fruit, teas, biscuits and chocolate, as well as a sleek metal coffee maker. Flannel pyjamas were folded neatly on the pillow, towelling robes hung by the bed, and best of all, there was a pair of cosy fleece-lined slippers just waiting to be put on. A fire burned softly in the grate, perfuming the air with woodsmoke.

'The Wi-Fi code is on the desk. The television is Apple,' the man continued cheerfully. 'You have a private balcony, of course.'

'Great,' said Jane, feeling somewhat awed. She opened the window and breathed deeply, taking in the smell of snow and pine trees. In the distance, she could see mountains, studded with fir trees.

'Is that where we're going tomorrow?' she asked, pointing.

He joined her. 'That's right,' he said. His English was flawless. 'That's the forest of Oslomarka, where the Christmas tree will be chosen. The foresters call her the "Queen of the Forest". The committee choose four trees, and tomorrow they will narrow their choice down to one.'

'I can't believe it's so close,' Jane said softly. 'All that wilderness.'

'It *is* wild out there,' the man agreed, grinning. 'There are wolves.'

'No!' said Jane, startled, and he laughed.

'At least two of them. They're famous. But don't worry – the foresters will look after you. Here.' He handed her the key card for the room, along with a thick piece of cream paper covered in elegant, swirling type. 'Your itinerary. You will meet the others in the bar at five.' When Jane opened her mouth to protest, he went on smoothly, 'Our mixologist has created a special cocktail, inspired by the Queen of the Forest. And you definitely don't want to miss dinner . . .'

With that, he left, the door clicking shut behind him. Jane glanced longingly at the fleece-lined slippers and the bed, and then at her watch. Four o'clock – she had an hour before they had to meet, and she intended to make the most of it.

She took a photo of the suite for Margot and sent it, along with a caption:

Is this hygge enough for you?

A string of angry red-faced emojis followed, and a picture of the view from the top deck of a bus: London, choked with traffic. Then:

Have you checked out the closet yet?

Jane walked over to the wardrobe and opened it. There was a large cream cardboard bag hanging inside, and within that, something wrapped in pale green tissue paper that rustled promisingly. Jane peeled back the paper and her breath caught.

It was a deceptively simple red crêpe dress, short-sleeved, with a neat collar and delicate buttons all the way down. But the colour – a rich flame-red – made it daring. There was a little card pinned to the bag and Jane opened the envelope.

I know you'll wear jeans tonight, but just try this on. Red is YOUR colour!

And wear your hair up – no hiding behind that fringe. Remember, you left Sensible Jane behind in London.

Jane half smiled, half grimaced at Margot's attempt to play fairy godmother.

The bathroom was as large as Jane's London flat, with a roll-top bath and two sinks. There was also a washbag stuffed full of expensive products, a plate of dark chocolate truffles and a mini bottle of champagne on ice, with a label in swirling script: *Drink me in the bath.*

Now *there* was an instruction she was happy to follow.

Forty minutes later, pleasantly drowsy from the hot water and champagne, Jane surveyed the dress that was lying on the bed. Cautiously she held it up against herself and looked in the mirror. The material was gossamer-thin, and there was a slit all the way up to the thigh. She hesitated, then folded it carefully away in the green tissue.

Instead, she pulled on a pair of jeans and a warm grey sweater, put on a little mascara and, in deference to Margot's instructions, pulled her hair up into an approximation of one of the bloggers' glamorous topknot. She surveyed herself in the mirror. Oh well – Margot couldn't expect her to have a complete personality transplant overnight.

She drank a glass of water, squared her shoulders and walked out into the corridor.

5

The scene that greeted Jane as she entered the rooftop bar took her breath away – long, sage-green sofas, low tables dotted with little tea lights, the murmur of voices and music playing quietly. Braziers burned, raising the temperature of the bar area to one of cosy warmth even as her breath formed a cloud in the cold air. The views of the city on one side, all twinkling lights in the gloom, and the fjord stretching murkily ahead on the other, were eerily beautiful.

Natasha was chatting to the barman, wearing a cobalt-blue dress with a slashed neckline. The three bloggers were sharing a sofa. Of Philip or Sandra there was no sign, but Ben and Nick were on another sofa, drinking beer.

'Jane,' called Ben, waving to her. 'Come here and talk to us.' He shifted up for her.

She dropped down next to him and accepted an amber-coloured cocktail from a waiter that smelled faintly, and not unpleasantly, of pine and was garnished with what appeared to be twigs spray-painted gold.

'The Queen of the Forest cocktail,' he murmured. 'With gin made from foraged Norwegian botanicals.'

Nick shook his head at it. 'Whiffy, if you ask me. I'll stick to lager.'

Ben clinked glasses with her. 'You look nice. How's your room? This place is amazing, isn't it?'

'Pretty amazing, yes. I could get used to this.' She turned to Nick. He always seemed like a decent man and she wondered how he was coping at the *Post*, which had become so toxic in the last few years. 'How are things with you, Nick? How's the *Post*?'

He shook his head. 'Let's just say I struggle with my conscience on a daily basis. I'm tempted to chuck it all in.'

'That bad?'

He shrugged. 'It's a job, isn't it? How many of us love our jobs?'

'I do,' Ben said.

Nick gave him a dirty look. 'Apart from *you*.'

'Jane does too.'

Jane nodded. 'It's true.'

'That's just the prizes talking,' said Nick mournfully. 'I was surprised to see you here, in fact,' he added, peering at her through his thick glasses. 'Christmas trees symbolising international harmony. Bit fluffy for you, isn't it?'

'I couldn't pass up the glamorous company,' Jane said. 'The chance to rub shoulders with a genuine Z-list celeb? Sign me up.'

'I wonder who you could mean,' came a drawling voice from their left, and Jane looked up to see Philip Donnelly dropping into the seat opposite her, stretching his long legs out in front of him. His hair was damp, and he smelled of soap and clean laundry. Jane blushed.

Philip set down a cocktail also crammed full of leaves and twigs on the low table and nodded briefly at Ben, who gave him an amused smile. Then he frowned at Nick, who seemed to sink a little in his seat.

'Don't I know you from somewhere?' Philip asked, his blue eyes suddenly steely. 'Aren't you the one who went through my bins at three a.m.?'

'That's entirely possible,' said Nick meekly. He glanced at his watch. 'Is that the time? Better go and call the wife before dinner.' He rose and walked off hastily.

Philip glanced at Ben with barely disguised boredom. 'And you're a photographer?'

'That's right,' said Ben.

'I probably know you too, then,' said Philip sourly.

'Doubt it. Not my sort of thing,' said Ben. He glanced over to the bar. Sandra had just swept in, looking resplendent in green velvet. 'I'm going to get another drink and say hi to Sandra. You want anything, Jane?'

'I'm going to stick with this, thanks,' she said, eyeing her drink. 'If I can get past the foliage.'

Ben loped off to the bar and immediately launched into conversation with Sandra, drawing in Natasha, who was soon laughing. Jane smiled, watching them. If anyone could pierce Natasha's cool façade, it would be Ben.

'I noticed you on the plane,' said Philip. 'You looked very serious.'

'I was listening to an audiobook,' said Jane. 'It's about Norway during the war. *A King's Impossible Choice*. I think you did the reading.'

'Ah yes.' He ran a hand through his damp hair. 'Fascinating, the Norwegian war effort.' He leaned forward. 'I'd be happy to tell you a bit more about it.'

'Erm,' said Jane, suppressing a smile. 'I'm only halfway through. Don't spoil the suspense.'

'I see,' said Philip. He grinned and looked suddenly more boyish. 'That's rigorous prep for visiting a Christmas tree. Unless you're hoping to write an explosive exposé of the blogging world?' He smirked. 'I'd begin with their ad campaign for this travesty of a cocktail.'

Jane looked at him more closely. Without the sunglasses,

she could see that he *was* handsome, as handsome as he appeared on the television, but with something bitter about the mouth. His cheeks were flushed slightly, perhaps also from champagne drunk in the bath.

'I'm a journalist. I like to be prepared,' she said.

'Like the Scouts,' he said. He took a large swallow of his drink and spluttered.

'It's quite a serious drink, isn't it?' she said sympathetically. There was something endearing about seeing the immaculate and handsome Philip Donnelly with his eyes streaming.

'That's one word for it,' he said, coughing. He wiped his eyes. 'Smiling suits you, by the way.'

Jane felt her stomach drop. That was what Simon always said.

'Oh no. Have I upset you?' Philip asked, looking at her thoughtfully. 'What's wrong?'

'I'm just tired,' she said. 'Long day. What brings you on this trip, anyway? Are you really writing an article for *Rural Living*?' She couldn't keep the note of incredulity out of her voice.

He shrugged. 'I can still just about string a sentence together, thanks very much.' His tone was light, but there was rancour underneath.

Uh-oh. Massive ego alert, Jane thought.

'I just meant, why now?' she asked innocently.

'I thought I could do with a change,' Philip said. Something in his voice shut down any further questions. Then he said, his tone light again, 'And what brings Jane Brook, investigative journalist extraordinaire, out to Norway to write about a Christmas tree?'

Jane hesitated. The truth – that her boss felt sorry for her after an excruciatingly painful break-up – was far too embarrassing to reveal.

'I thought I could do with a change,' she said, throwing his own words back at him.

Their gazes locked. Feeling suddenly awkward, Jane reached for her drink, but he caught her wrist lightly.

'No more of that muck,' he said softly. 'Let me get you a real drink. One without any foliage in it.'

Philip's idea of a real drink turned out to be shots of vodka, the delicate glasses frosted, on a little tray. They arrived with slices of black rye bread spread thickly with butter.

'This is very fine vodka,' the waiter explained, as he set down the tray, 'so we don't pollute it with tonic. You can sip it or drink it all down at once.'

'Down at once,' Philip said to Jane, smiling wolfishly. 'We'll be eating soon. How much damage could we possibly do?'

Jane couldn't remember the last time she'd done a shot. The icy liquid slipped down her throat, quick silver-fast, followed by warmth. She gasped. It was like a plunge in the sea. Her chest felt as if it was on fire.

'That looks good,' said Lucy, the blogger who had sat next to her on the flight. 'I'm still picking pine needles out of my teeth.'

'It's a proper drink, not a pretty drink,' said Philip.

Lucy smiled at him in return.

'I think I can handle it,' she said.

She was beautiful, Jane thought, enviously, and she glanced over to see whether Philip was looking appreciative. To her surprise, he was looking at her.

Natasha sank onto the sofa next to them, looking flushed and radiant. 'Everyone getting to know each other via the medium of alcohol?' she asked. 'That's what I like to see.'

'Jane and I have been sampling the purest vodka known to man,' said Philip. 'She didn't even flinch.'

Jane flushed and caught herself revelling in being the one who had Philip Donnelly's attention. *Idiot*, she told herself. *He's a professional flirt.*

'Aren't you both hardcore. Dinner is served,' Natasha said, and although she was talking to them all, she too was smiling at Philip. 'I hope you're in the mood for reindeer.'

Jane all but gasped as she walked into the dining room. It was even lovelier than her bedroom. The walls were still deep blue, but the dark, polished wooden floorboards were covered in thick reindeer-skin rugs. A long wooden table was draped with white linen and set with tall candles and branches of Norwegian pine. The air smelled of Christmas – the Christmas of storybooks and old paintings and carols. There was a large fire crackling in the grate, casting great shadows up the wall, and a Christmas tree in the corner, ablaze with lights. Jane found that Philip was sitting to her left.

'What a nice surprise,' he said, so smoothly that she looked at him with suspicion.

'Did you meddle with the seating plan?' she asked.

'Why on earth would I do that?' he answered.

The waitress appeared at Jane's side, serving slices of smoked salmon, cured with dill and sugar, and sprinkled with capers, along with more of the nutty rye bread. There was a long-stemmed wine glass by her plate, which the sommelier filled with a pale yellow wine. It tasted cool and crisp, and utterly delicious.

'Ah, come on.' Philip leaned back in his chair, watching her in amusement. 'I can tell what you're thinking, you and everyone else here. Philip Donnelly, third-rate TV presenter, favourite of the gossip mags and washed-up journalist, takes an easy assignment to try and claw back his reputation. That and he probably fancied a cushy trip. Wants to flirt with all those gorgeous twenty-something bloggers. Is that right?'

Jane smiled. He'd nailed it. 'It doesn't matter what I think.' She took another swallow of the wine. 'You don't need my approval.'

'Of course I don't,' he said affably. 'I'm just making small talk. Who else have I got to talk to?'

She narrowed her eyes at him. 'Any one of those gorgeous twenty-something bloggers for a start.'

Philip gave the bloggers a swift, appraising glance. 'I'm sure they're very sweet girls.' He leaned forward and a lock of dirty-blond hair fell in front of his eyes. 'But I've always had a thing for ice maidens.'

Jane laughed. She couldn't help it. 'Sorry,' she said, as he looked at her in surprise. 'It's just – are you always this obvious?'

It was true. He reminded her of someone, and that someone, she realised, was Simon. Smart, cocky, handsome – a lethal combination.

'In what way am I obvious?' he asked, looking put out.

'Well, for one thing, pretending that you're all that discerning in your conquests . . .'

He raised an eyebrow. 'My *conquests*?' he said.

'Oh, come on,' Jane said, resting her chin on her hands. 'You're a famous womaniser. The last affair sounded . . . explosive.'

'Yeah,' said Philip, his jaw tightening and his blue eyes clouding over. 'It was.'

Jane felt guilty. She had clearly struck a nerve. Philip Donnelly's love life might be a joke to the rest of the world, but just because he reminded her of Simon didn't mean she had to take out her post-break-up rage on him. She was relieved when another course arrived.

'Halibut,' the waitress murmured, 'with snow crab.' White fish, surrounded by a pale yellow, frothy sauce, studded with chives.

Philip wasn't eating, though. He was swirling the wine round his glass and looking rather thoughtful.

'You're right, by the way,' he said, unexpectedly. He glanced up and there was something frank and disarming in his gaze. 'I'm everything you think, I'm afraid. I don't have much of a reputation to salvage. But I used to be a fairly decent writer and I'd like to try to be that again.' His eyes met hers. 'And I know I don't need your approval, Jane, but for some reason that I can't put my finger on, I'd like to have it.'

She felt herself flushing again. 'It's none of my business.'

'Absolutely none,' he agreed amiably. 'And this is none of mine, but I'll ask anyway. For the second time, why are *you* here in Norway, Jane?'

'I told you,' she said. The waitress was back, this time with side dishes – a tangle of watercress covered with toasted almonds and a jug of bright green sauce that tasted how she had imagined grass might taste. 'I fancied a change.' She shrugged. 'And this was sold to me as a Christmas experience of a lifetime.'

'Well, you're certainly a long way from the news desk,' Philip said, looking restlessly around the room. 'Never liked Christmas myself. I imagine you have to come from a happy family to enjoy it, and how many of those are there?'

'I'm not sure,' Jane said, thinking about Christmas at home. The little tree, dragged out year after year and decorated with care by her and her mum, the pair of them giggling and squabbling over who got to pin the glittery angel on the top. The wild excitement of the lumpy pillowcase heavy at the foot of her bed in the morning. Tearing it open and finding it full of books and chocolate money and jelly beans to be eaten on the sofa. Reading her new Enid Blytons, eating her chocolate, listening to Christmas songs on the radio. The treat of being allowed to lie on her stomach in front of the television afterwards, while her mother washed up.

A happy Christmas? *Yes*, she thought. Her mum had tried her best, and that had meant everything. All of their little traditions – leaving out a carrot for the reindeer, that would be found chewed to a stump in the morning, pouring Father Christmas a glass of Baileys because he didn't like sherry, the special breakfast of mince pies and chocolate, laying out the best china – had burrowed their way into Jane's heart. It was the reason she hadn't been able to bear Christmas since her mother had gone.

What had Philip's Christmases been like? she wondered. She glanced at him.

'Here,' he said, his voice cheerful once more. 'Let's have some more of this free wine, which really isn't bad given how expensive it is in Norway. Since we're on this ridiculous trip, we might as well make the most of it.' He grinned at her and raised his glass in a mock toast. 'To Christmas. May it be better this year.'

She knocked her glass lightly against his. 'To Christmas,' she echoed, trying to match his easy tone. Last Christmas – sitting round a little tree with Simon in her pyjamas and thick socks, wearing her ridiculous new bobble hat, drinking sherry and unwrapping their silly gifts – she had felt warm, happy and loved. This year, she would probably be waking up in Margot and Kate's spare room, third-wheeling yet again at their Christmas lunch. Except that this time, there would also be a baby.

As the thought crossed her mind, Philip's eyes met hers, briefly, and she was surprised to see sympathy in his gaze. They were silent a moment, an oasis of stillness in the buzzing room. Philip's hand was resting by her plate, and, so briefly that Jane was unsure if it was an accident or not, his fingers gently brushed hers.

As the wine started flowing, the chatter in the room rose. Everyone was in a good mood, first-night excitement kicking in, combining with exhaustion and nerves to create a cheerful hysteria. Jane could feel her mood softening.

The food kept coming, course after course. Jane was sure that she would remember this dinner for as long as she lived. What on earth would Aileen have made of all this? *She'd tell me to enjoy it*, Jane thought, and just then she caught Philip's eye again and smiled.

During the lull in conversation, Jane noticed an elderly man who hadn't been on the flight or in the bar seated at the far end of the vast table. He was a handsome old man, she thought, in his eighties at least, with white hair and a distinguished face, beautifully dressed in a dinner jacket. He was gazing into the middle distance and sipping his wine. As Jane watched, his eyes met hers in the candlelight; he raised his glass in the very briefest of salutes before turning away to speak to Sandra at his left. Was that Thomas Erikson, the mysterious visitor of importance?

But she didn't get to wonder much because at Jane's elbow was Philip. Pouring her more wine, laughing at her jokes, teasing her for picking up the wrong fork from a bewildering array of cutlery.

He was definitely flirting with her. He was talking to everyone, but he returned to Jane as though drawn by an invisible magnet. And she found that she was enjoying his company. Underneath the obnoxious self-confidence, he was funny and charming, with little flashes of vulnerability.

After everyone had finished eating, Natasha tapped her glass with her fork and the room fell silent.

'We're playing a game,' announced Natasha. 'A little icebreaker. We all have to go round and say three things about ourselves, and one of them has to be something we don't know from the press pack.' She pointed at Sandra with an elegant, manicured finger. 'Go.'

'All right,' Sandra said, rather wearily. 'Food critic. Widow.' She gave Natasha a disapproving look. 'Introvert who would rather enjoy her food than play games. No offence.'

'None taken,' said Natasha. Her finger travelled to Nick.

'Dad,' he said, looking like he just wanted this to be over. 'Amateur wine expert. Journalist.'

'Are you sure about that last one?' said Philip coldly, and Nick ducked his head.

'Let's be friends,' Natasha admonished. 'We've got a fortnight of each other.'

Her gaze swept to Lucy.

'Instagrammer,' Lucy said. 'Cat owner.' She hesitated. 'Shy.'

Freddie laughed. 'OK. Instagrammer, obviously. I love old films. And I'm *not* shy, but icebreakers like this make me want to rip off my head.'

'Or tell everyone you're a polyamorous sociopath and see how *that* breaks the ice,' said Lena. 'OK, fine, my turn. I blog about yoga, smoothies and bondage.' She arched an elegant eyebrow. 'Only two of those are true.'

'We shall live in suspense,' said Natasha drily.

Her pointing finger reached Ben, who said promptly, 'I've got four sisters. I was born here in Norway. I love my job.'

Jane laughed. '*Four* sisters? Why aren't you more scarred?'

'I kept my head down,' Ben said gravely.

Natasha nodded at Philip. 'Go on, tough guy. You're not exempt just because we've seen you on telly.'

He smiled lazily. 'TV presenter. Nightmare reputation.' He shrugged. 'I'd like to write for a newspaper again.'

'Bet you won't like the pay cut,' muttered Nick.

Natasha turned to the elderly stranger, who smiled benignly.

'Thomas?'

'I was born in Oslo,' he said, in faintly-accented English. 'Father. Husband. Nothing very interesting, I'm afraid.'

'I don't believe it. I think you have a hundred dark secrets,' Natasha said. 'And we'll ferret them out. Too many journalists here for you to remain enigmatic.'

He smiled and rose. 'The secret is, I'm longing for my bed.' He raised a hand. 'I'll leave you young people to it. I shall see you all in the morning when we visit the tree.'

Natasha pointed at Jane as Thomas left the room. 'Last but not least.'

Jane hesitated. 'Journalist,' she said carefully. 'And, well, I love my job too.'

'That's two things,' Natasha said. 'Barely. Come on – something personal. Something we don't already know.'

'I want to travel,' Jane said, surprising herself. 'I want to leave London and work around the world.' She didn't think she'd ever put that thought into words before, but as she said it, she realised it was true.

'Well, I was hoping for something racier, but that'll do,' said Natasha. 'And now that we know each other inside and out, we all do a shot.'

'We didn't get to hear anything about *you*,' said Philip.

'That's because I'm in charge,' said Natasha. 'I make the rules.' She nodded at the shot glasses being lined up in front of them. 'Speaking of which, shut up and drink.'

Jane drank and the room around her lurched and dipped.

I'm not drunk, she reassured herself, but she was steadily approaching that territory. As the dessert course was brought in – dainty floating islands of meringue dotted with rose petals, almonds and fresh mint – she realised that the chatter, which had started up again, was now an indistinct blur of noise. She pushed back her chair and rose.

'I'm just going to the loo,' she said carefully, then swayed slightly.

'Need a hand?' Philip asked, and winked.

'I'm fine, thank you,' Jane said with dignity.

The bathroom was all white tiles, big vases of pink flowers and black-and-white photographs of grizzled Norwegian fishermen. There were plenty of mirrors for selfies, too, giving Jane the impression that she was accompanied by half a dozen other Janes.

She studied her face in one mirror with drunken intensity. She didn't look half bad.

Sober Jane would have avoided tacky, tabloid-fodder Philip Donnelly like the plague. Sober Jane would be back in her room right now with a herbal tea and a good book. But then, perhaps Sober Jane needed shaking up a bit. And maybe tonight was the night.

It seemed she *had* accepted Margot's challenge, after all.

Dinner was winding down as she took her seat. There were bowls of walnuts and dates on the table, and trays were brought in with little cups of strong-smelling espresso, and crystallised sugar to have with it. Jane had never been able to drink coffee black, but she took a scalding sip to sober herself up a bit.

'I was just wondering,' murmured Philip's voice in her ear, and a shiver went down her back, 'whether I could persuade you to come out and look at the moon with me. It's a lovely night, and you won't see the stars like this in London.'

She turned to him, her eyebrows raised. Her heart was beating fast in her chest, from more than just the coffee. 'Really?' she said, with a grin. 'Does that line usually work?'

'Oh, every time,' he assured her. He was looking at her through half-closed eyes. 'But genuinely, I can think of few nicer things right now than a walk in the moonlight with you.'

Jane held his gaze for a moment, then looked away at the room. The bloggers had abandoned their phones and were talking excitedly about the hotel's heated rooftop pool; Ben had gone, presumably to bed, and the old man too; Nick and Sandra were now engaged in drunken gossip in the corner. On the other side of Philip, Natasha was scrolling through her phone.

Jane turned back to Philip. He was watching her and smiling easily, but beneath the smile, there was something else. Something hopeful.

She took a deep breath. 'All right,' she said, and she was surprised by how calm she sounded. 'Some fresh air would be lovely.'

6

A set of glass doors led from the dining room out onto a verandah. Darkness had fallen during dinner, but still there was that strange half-light, at once eerie and magical. An eternal twilight hour, during which any sort of madness might happen.

Tea lights guided them down a flight of stone steps out into the garden, where little gravel paths snaked through the immaculately tended lawn and twinkling fairy lights were tangled in the bare branches of the trees. The air smelled of snow, but the sky was clear. It was cold out of the warm dining room and Jane shivered.

'Here,' said Philip, and she found herself draped in his suit jacket. She could smell his aftershave, lemony and expensive. She had thought the cold night air might sober her up, but instead she felt more drunk. The world was spinning around her.

'Have you been to Norway before?' she asked as they walked under a little copse of trees.

'I was here last year,' he said. 'To see the Northern Lights with someone who wanted to see them.'

'*Did* you see them?' she asked. He laughed, a short, derisive bark.

'No. We came all this way and we didn't see a thing.' He shrugged. 'I suppose you can't expect magic to happen on demand.'

'I suppose not,' she agreed. She lifted her face up to the sky and shivered. The delicate branches traced a stark canopy over her head.

Philip glanced at her. 'Are you all right?' he asked.

'I was thinking . . .' She hesitated, wondering whether he would laugh at her. 'There's something about this place that reminds me of folk stories. Maidens spirited away to snow caves, that sort of thing.'

He nodded, looking around. 'I wouldn't be surprised to see a troll coming out of the undergrowth to take you back to its lair.'

She grinned. 'I hope you wouldn't let it.'

'Oh, I wouldn't,' he reassured her. 'I would bop it on the head. I don't know if you know this, but I'm actually very brave.'

'I *do* know,' she said, teasingly. 'I've heard all about the *Survival of the Fittest* hero, Philip Donnelly. You've battled malaria, a crocodile attack . . .'

'Don't forget the celebrities,' he said softly. 'They were the scariest of all.'

They had walked in a lazy, accidental circle and now came to a stop at the front door of the hotel. Jane could see that most of the rooms were in darkness: it must be late.

'Well,' she said, and to her irritation her voice sounded small and nervous. 'I should get to bed. It's an early start tomorrow.'

'Ah yes. The famous tree. Well. Sweet dreams, Jane.'

She nodded. 'Thanks. And thanks for the, ah, stroll.'

'No problem,' he said, his voice low. 'It was very refreshing.'

She realised she was still wearing his jacket and made to lift it from her shoulders. 'Here, have this back.'

'Keep it.' He raised a hand and rested it on her shoulder, one finger gently grazing her collarbone. 'It suits you.'

'Thanks.' Still, she hesitated. Her feet were rooted to the ground. She could feel the warmth of his hand through the cloth. What, she wondered, was she waiting for?

And then she knew.

Philip took a step towards her and, when she didn't move away, lifted her chin very slowly upward. Jane's heart was pounding so hard she was surprised he couldn't hear it. He took another step and raised a hand to tuck a strand of hair behind her ear. As he did so, his fingers skimmed her cheek. He lowered his forehead towards hers, so that they were touching, then tilted his head; his lips softly brushed her neck, her jaw . . .

There was a creak as a window above them opened and bright light spilled out onto the drive. A penetrating voice spoke, in clipped, assured vowels. Natasha.

'And did you see them at dinner? He couldn't keep his eyes off her.'

'He's a total sleaze, though.' The other voice belonged to Lucy, of the stylish topknot and casual elegance.

'You're just jealous because he's gorgeous and he was all over her . . .'

'Absolutely. Why should she get all the fun?'

'It won't be fun when he ditches her, though. Did you hear what he did to Donna Marks? If ever anyone spelled trouble, it's him.'

Their voices carried with disastrous clarity on the still air. Jane felt as though someone had dashed cold water on her face. She pulled away from Philip, face burning, her gaze drawn inexorably upwards to the little balcony where the women were standing, wrapped in white robes.

'Oh my God,' Lucy hissed, her words still horribly audible. 'They're down there!' There was a burst of giggles and muffled shrieks, and then the balcony window banged shut.

Jane's limbs came unfrozen as embarrassment flooded through her. She thrust the jacket at Philip with an inarticulate sound, turned, shoved the door open, then hurried through the corridor and up the stairs.

In her room, she threw herself onto the bed, groaning. The room was spinning unbearably. She pulled the pillows over her head to drown out the humiliation.

How could she have been such an idiot?

7

When Jane awoke the next morning, everything was silent. With what felt like a tremendous effort, she raised her head.

She sat up and rubbed sleep from her eyes. It was strange not being able to tell what time it was from the quality of the light. She reached over and grabbed her phone: 7.15 a.m. Not nearly enough sleep, given her late-night stroll.

Oh God.

She dropped her phone and let her head fall back on the pillow. Last night came flooding back, along with the onset of a punishing hangover. Dinner flickered into her brain in humiliating flashes – shots of vodka, wine, countless plates of food.

More wine, stumbling drunkenly out into the garden with Philip.

That almost-kiss.

The laughing girls above who had witnessed it.

She walked over to the mirror on the wall. Dark shadows under her eyes, smudged mascara, matted hair and creases from the pillow embedded on her cheek.

She went to the window, opened it and leaned out, breathing in great lungfuls of fresh, icy air. The rest of the hotel was quiet: presumably everyone was still sleeping off the night before. She would have to face them all soon.

A shower would make her feel better.

She stumbled into the bathroom and sat on the edge of the enormous bath. *One drunken mistake*, she told herself, and she doubted anyone else had been all that sober.

She grabbed her phone and texted Margot, hoping that pregnancy insomnia would mean she was awake.

I got drunk on a litre of vodka and nearly kissed Philip Donnelly and everyone saw so I panicked and ran off. Now they all think I'm an idiot. And this is YOUR fault.

She put her phone on a ledge and turned on the shower, flipping through the settings until she found one that cascaded down like rainfall. She used an expensive-looking body wash, two different kinds of shampoo and then stepped out, wrapping herself in a thick robe. She moisturised her face vigorously, imagining herself expelling the vodka-wine toxins from her body. Then she dressed warmly in blue jeans, a thick navy jumper, socks and snow boots.

The bright-eyed beauty of last night had definitely gone, along with the vodka fumes.

Her phone buzzed as she was about to leave the room. Margot, ringing her back.

'Nice work!' she shrieked as Jane picked up. 'He looks like a good kisser. Is he?'

'We didn't even actually kiss,' said Jane piteously. 'My head hurts.'

'Nonsense – good vodka doesn't give you a hangover,' said Margot with authority. 'Why are you worried?'

'Because a blogger saw us, and the PR, and he's got a terrible reputation and it was mortifying.'

'So? They'll just be jealous. Now, this is a promising start, but remember I want you shagging Philip Donnelly in a hot tub before this trip is out.'

Jane groaned. 'Can I have breakfast first?'

'Certainly,' said Margot graciously.

'Thanks,' Jane muttered.

'One more thing,' said Margot. 'Do you think it would have been a good kiss?'

Jane paused, massaging her temples.

'I think so,' she said at last, remembering the heart-stopping moment when Philip's fingers had skimmed her jaw, his touch sending goosebumps down her spine. 'I feel like he probably knows what he's doing.'

'All right. In that case, carry on.'

As Jane left the room, her phone buzzed once more.

Last thing. DON'T GET ATTACHED.

Jane snorted. *Fat chance of that.*

The breakfast room was deserted except for the old man from dinner last night, Thomas Erikson.

'Good morning,' said Jane, slipping into one of the chairs.

'Good morning,' he said politely, and went back to buttering a roll.

The long table was covered in snowy-white linen, upon which were laid glass jugs of iced orange juice, baskets of delicious-looking pastries and china bowls full of red berries. There were platters of ham, fruit and hard cheese, and crystal bowls of cherry jam, glinting in the pale sunlight. Jane surveyed it all, her stomach grumbling uneasily.

'What can I get you?'

Jane glanced up to see the same man who had showed her to her room yesterday. He looked neat, cheerful and disgustingly awake.

'Just coffee, I think,' she said. 'I'm not sure I'm up to anything else.'

'Are you sure? We have eggs, sausages, bacon – an omelette?'

She swallowed quickly and he smiled.

'Try a *skillingsboller*,' he said persuasively. 'Cinnamon bun.'

She nodded weakly and poured herself a glass of juice with hands that shook slightly. The coffee came quickly, strong and hot, with plenty of steaming, frothed milk, and after drinking a cup, Jane started to feel better. The waiter then brought a basket of plump buns, dusted with icing sugar and wrapped in a tea towel. She dipped one into her coffee and nibbled a piece gingerly.

'It went on late, then, last night?' Thomas asked, looking at her over his coffee cup, and Jane nodded ruefully.

'You were smart to go to bed early.' She set down her own cup. 'We weren't properly introduced. Jane Brook.'

He reached over and shook her hand with a firm grip. 'Thomas Erikson,' he said. 'And I know who you are, Jane Brook. Your newspaper story reached us even here in Oslo.'

His English was good, flawless almost, but again she caught a trace of his Norwegian accent.

'You were at dinner last night.' She eyed him curiously. What on earth was this courtly old man doing with a motley crew of journalists and bloggers? 'And I read the press pack too. You're a "visitor of importance". Not a journalist, then?'

'No.' He shook his head. 'Not a journalist. I am a soldier in the Norwegian Army, or at least I was. My family are rather the big cheeses – a strange expression, no? – around here, and this year I was asked to help choose the tree. It is something of an honour. Besides' – his gaze drifted past Jane to the conservatory windows and the view of the mountains – 'I wanted to see the forest again.' He cleared his throat. 'Is this your first time in Norway?'

She nodded. 'It's a beautiful country,' she said.

'It is,' he said warmly. 'I am biased, of course. You will like where we are going today, to see the tree. Flåm, it is called. A little village at the end of Sognefjord, the deepest fjord in all the world. Legends have been born in that place. You will see my country at its most sublime – white waterfalls, the greenest of forests. People call winter in Norway the "dark time", but to me, it is the best time. The most magical. It is not true dark – there are all sorts of colours: the softest greys, the coolest blues.' He smiled at her. 'And the people . . . they change during the Christmas period. If they can seem reserved during the rest of the year, then Christmas is when the warmth shows. It is when we light fires, sing songs, tell stories, have parties. Let ourselves go a bit.' His eyes twinkled. 'We all need to let ourselves go sometimes.'

'Well, well,' came a voice from the doorway. Jane looked up to see Philip standing there, looking irritatingly well rested and immaculate in a freshly ironed shirt. Her heart flew into her throat.

Be cool, she told herself.

'Good morning,' he said, coming into the room and taking a seat opposite her. He nodded at Thomas, who had gone back to his breakfast. 'Did you sleep well, Jane?' His voice was low and teasing, and Jane felt a flicker of annoyance that he managed to make the most innocent query sound indecent.

'Fine, thanks,' she said shortly, draining her coffee cup. She heard voices in the hall and got quickly to her feet. The last thing she wanted after last night was for the others to see her cosily breakfasting with Philip. 'I've still got to pack a few things. I'll see you on the train.'

'There's no need to dash off,' he said. 'More coffee?'

'No, I'm going,' she said. 'I don't want anyone thinking . . .'

'Thinking what?' he asked, his brow furrowing.

She darted a panicked glance towards the door. 'That we – you know.'

He looked at her innocently.

'I don't want them thinking we came down to breakfast together, all right?' she hissed.

'Ah.' His voice was cool. 'Would that be so bad?'

'Yes, it would.' She snatched up her jumper from the back of her chair and sped out of the room, colliding with Ben in the doorway, yawning, and behind him Sandra, wearing what looked like at least two jumpers. Jane muttered a hasty 'Morning' and made for the safety of her room.

They were leaving for a different hotel today, deep in the forest of Oslomarka, where the tree was. She started to pack hurriedly, throwing clothes into the suitcase without her usual care. Amid her confusion and embarrassment, she couldn't stop thinking about the look on Philip's face as she had rushed from the breakfast room.

Was it her imagination or had he looked hurt?

The motion of the car taking them to the station made Jane feel nauseous all over again. She rolled down the window a crack, surreptitiously gulping down some fresh air. Freddie shot her an amused glance.

'Mint?' she offered, holding out a packet. Jane took one gratefully.

'Thanks. I'm just feeling a bit travel-sick,' she said, and Freddie smiled.

'You're not the only one feeling travel-sick this morning.'

They clambered out and trundled their suitcases onto the train platform.

'We're travelling on the *Golden Express* steam train,' Natasha was saying. She peered more closely at her itinerary. '*A painstakingly restored five-star excursion into the past.*' She looked up again. 'Well, it sounds like a good one anyway.'

'I can't wait for this,' whispered Lucy, her eyes fixed on the tracks ahead. 'It'll be like we're in *The Railway Children*.'

Jane watched as, with a great cloud of steam and a hiss, the famous train pulled into the station. The engine was an extraordinary creation, all shining brass and gleaming cherry-red paintwork. Porters wearing immaculate uniforms waited to take their luggage as the cloud of steam overwhelmed the platform, pooling around their legs and mingling with the fog and the half-light to create a bewitchingly old-world atmosphere.

When it cleared slightly, Jane saw Thomas, a striking silhouette against the smoke, and she caught her breath. He was wearing a greatcoat and muffler and looked for all the world as though he had been conjured up from the past.

'Are you all right?'

Jane turned to see Ben beside her. Sandra stood next to him in a black puffa coat, looking pained and shivering, and next to her was Nick, wearing a hideous purple fleece.

'I'm all right, yeah,' said Jane, eyeing Ben suspiciously and wondering how much he already knew. 'I just wanted to pack.'

'Is that why you dashed off?' asked Nick. 'Because I heard a rumour that *somebody* found a certain famous TV star pretty irresistible . . .'

'Oh God, don't,' Jane grimaced, blushing furiously. 'What happens on a press trip stays on a press trip! That's the rule.'

'Hey, we're just impressed,' Ben chipped in, tucking his scarf in more closely. Jane looked up at him, but he seemed to avoid her gaze. 'I went to bed early with a cuppa. Was it all those vodka shots?'

She groaned again and he laughed.

'Ah, come on. You're allowed to cut loose. I just didn't figure you for a Philip Donnelly conquest, that's all.'

'What do you know about him?' she asked. 'Is he as much of an arse as everyone says?'

'He's *worse*,' Sandra snapped. 'It's not entirely his fault, of course,' she added. 'Dreadful family. His mother's ghastly.'

'Is she?' asked Jane, startled by her venom.

'Awful. Minor aristocrat. Philip is just like her. Maximum self-loathing now he's gone down this Z-list celebrity route. Arrogant *and* insecure.' She gave Jane a disapproving look. 'God knows why that's so appealing to women.'

'Do you know them, then?' Jane asked. 'His family?'

'Vaguely.' Sandra gestured dismissively, as if it was a given that one *had* to know these people. 'I generally avoid the hunting and shooting scene, but I see them at weddings and so on. And I've been for tea once or twice at their estate. Draughty old place.' Her dark eyes flickered ominously. 'His mother was very rude. No manners at all. I'd take bets Philip's just as bad.'

Jane nodded thoughtfully.

'Come on, guys,' called Natasha, glancing at her watch. 'Save the chat for when we're on the train. We have a schedule to keep here.' They began to file obediently onto the train.

Jane was shown to her seat by a conductor wearing white gloves. *This is ridiculous*, she thought, as she sank back against the plush cushions in a pool of muted light from the old-fashioned lamp above. Ridiculous yet wonderful. Like the *Orient Express*.

There was so much space that they each had a table seat to themselves. Thomas was across the aisle from Jane, but he made no move to speak to her, instead taking out a slim book and opening it.

It was astonishingly comfortable. The walls were wood-panelled, creating the impression of a very luxurious library, and decorated with delicate ironwork. The seats were covered in rich red velvet, the tables were marble, set with silverware, and before Jane, on a white doily, was a small vase of purple Norwegian heather. The windows offered a panoramic view of the world outside, and art-deco stained-glass lamps punctuated the elegant gloom with their jewel-like colours. If it weren't for Jane's still-pounding head, she would have been in utter heaven.

An attendant appeared at her elbow and deftly set down a crystal bowl of crisp green pickles and a frosted glass of aquavit. Jane shuddered.

'While you wait for your lunch,' he said.

'Just some coffee, please,' she begged, and he nodded and disappeared immediately, clearly reading her anguished expression as the plea for help it was.

There was the piercing, thrilling sound of a train whistle, followed by a grinding sound and the train heaving into action. Jane looked out of the window as they left the station. It was lighter than yesterday, and she watched the suburban houses gradually change to lush green forest as they sped out of the city.

The attendant not only brought her some coffee but, as though reading her mind, a carafe of iced water, an enormous glass tumbler and a little plate of dry, salted crackers. Jane received them gratefully, then put on her headphones and tried to concentrate on her audiobook. She had reached the point of imminent Nazi invasion and King Haakon's stirring speech to his cabinet as he laid out the case for rejecting Nazi rule:

I am deeply affected by the responsibility I face if we are to reject Hitler's demand. The responsibility for the calamities that will befall my people and country is indeed so grave that I dread to take it. But my position is clear.

I cannot accept the German demands. It would conflict with all that I consider to be my duty as King of Norway . . .

The steward returned with a mound of creamy mushroom stroganoff and pillowy, herb-flecked dumplings. It looked delicious, but Jane shook her head regretfully.

Her head ached. She closed her eyes and rested her burning forehead on the cool glass of the window.

'Penny for them?'

The voice – quiet and ironic – made her jump. She looked round to see that Thomas had laid down his book and was watching her with interest.

'That's the expression, isn't it? "Penny for your thoughts." Another odd one, like most of your expressions.'

Jane laughed politely.

'You looked very serious,' Thomas said. 'I should say your thoughts were worth much more.'

She laughed again, properly this time. 'I was actually wondering whether I could ask the attendant for some chips.'

She glanced out of the window at the blur of white and green, and remembered what the man at the hotel had said. 'Is it true there are wolves in the forest?' she asked Thomas.

He nodded, his eyes twinkling. 'Indeed, there are rumoured to be two. But that might be rumours only – we Norwegians like a good story. Are you looking forward to seeing the tree – the Queen of the Forest?'

'Yes, of course,' Jane said. 'I like remembering the past.'

He nodded. 'Me too. In fact, it seems increasingly important to me that people *do* remember the past.'

'Or they will be doomed to repeat it?' she said.

'Yes.' He smiled. A little sadly, she thought. 'And the memories are good, sometimes. I was braver then, I think.'

Jane was quiet for a moment. She had placed him as in his mid-eighties at first, but it occurred to her that perhaps he was older – old enough to have fought in the Second World War. She wondered what form his bravery had taken, exactly.

'I've been listening to an audiobook about the king's choice in 1940,' she said tentatively. 'Whether to accept Nazi rule or flee.'

He nodded slowly. 'So long ago . . .'

Jane leaned forward. 'Were you in the army then?'

'I was,' he said. 'A boy of nineteen who could not wait for war to start so that I would have something to do.'

'There you are,' came a voice, and Jane looked up to see Ben making his way down the aisle. 'It's the next stop.' He caught sight of Thomas. 'Hello. Did you sleep well? *Sov du godt?*'

'*Når du blir gammel, er søvn vanskelig,*' Thomas replied, and Ben laughed.

'You seem spry enough to me,' he said.

'Now you're showing off, Andersen,' Jane teased.

'Andersen?' Thomas said, looking at Ben keenly. 'A local name.'

Ben nodded. 'My dad's Norwegian. I grew up not too far from where we're going, in fact.'

'Then you must have been fishing in the fjord at Otteroy,' said Thomas. 'And you must have swum that fjord as a boy and camped on the island – or you aren't a true local.'

'I did both,' Ben said. 'Every summer and some winters too. Do I pass?'

'Absolutely,' said Thomas.

'Will you see your parents while you're here?' Jane asked.

'No, they live in Scotland now,' said Ben vaguely. 'How's the head? I brought you this.' He held out a crumpled packet of aspirin.

Jane seized it gratefully. 'I'll never make fun of your first-aid kit again,' she said, swallowing a couple of tablets with a gulp of water. 'I feel rotten.'

'You drank too much?' asked Thomas solicitously.

'Let's just say, far too much,' said Jane. 'Behaved disgracefully.'

Thomas shrugged. 'Enjoy yourself! You are young. My late wife Ana and I used to go out dancing once a week. Even if we hated each other when we left the house, we always came back laughing.'

'I'm sorry about your wife,' said Jane, but he shook his head.

'She had a very happy life. She would never have wanted me to be sad. Although she had a lot to put up with, being married to a soldier – I was often away, fighting for king and country.' He glanced out of the window. 'I must get my things together. I move rather slowly these days. And wrap up warm, you two. The snow is picking up.'

8

Snow was indeed falling heavily as the train pulled into the station. Jane tightened the laces of her snow boots and drew her coat more closely about her. She got out, then stood with her luggage on the platform, watching as Lucy, Lena and Freddie tumbled out, shrieking in delight at the snow. Ben guided Sandra and then Thomas down the steps. Jane caught his eye and he mimed an exaggerated shiver for her.

'Bloody snow!' he called. 'You'd think we were in Norway or something!'

Philip and Natasha were the last to descend. Natasha was managing to make proper cold-weather gear look glamorous, as though she had spent many winters at ski resorts. Philip looked moody; Jane couldn't help meeting his eye across the platform and he turned away. She wished now that she had been a little less brusque at breakfast.

Unnecessarily defensive and prickly, Jane? a mocking little voice whispered in her head. *That's not like you.*

Large, blacked-out SUVs with four-wheel drive and snow tyres were waiting for them, and Jane found herself in one with Natasha, Freddie, Lena and Lucy.

'Only half an hour to the hotel,' Natasha said, pleased. 'We're going to be exactly on schedule, just how I like it.'

'Is there a hot tub?' asked Freddie. She was looking out of the window at the snow and applying lip balm.

'Yup,' said Natasha. 'There's an outdoor sauna, as well as

a spa.' She glanced at Jane and smirked. 'Just let us know if you and Philip need it for private use tonight, Jane.'

Behind her, in the back row, Lena and Lucy burst out laughing, and even Freddie snorted. Jane glared at them.

'I'm ignoring that,' she said. 'And changing the subject. Do you come on these sorts of trips a lot?' she asked Freddie. 'These blogger and influencer things?'

'Well, I was in Japan last week, but only for two days,' Freddie said. 'And before that, New York, then Portugal. Before that, let me see. I think it was Iceland . . .'

'Goodness,' said Jane, startled. 'That sounds exhausting. To me, I mean,' she added hastily. 'I like my bed.'

'Do you now,' murmured Freddie. 'I hope you've let Philip know.'

Jane scowled at her. 'Last night was a one-off.'

'Oh, don't say that,' said Lena, cackling from the back. 'Poor Philip. He'll feel so used.'

'It'll be a nice change for him, won't it?' said Natasha, and they burst out laughing again.

Jane rolled her eyes. 'I just don't quite get how all this' – she waved a hand around the car – 'taking selfies and everything, translates into income.'

'You wouldn't,' Freddie said, not unkindly. 'But believe me, you can't live off hotel gift baskets and monogrammed robes alone.' She jerked her head at Lena and Lucy behind her, now tapping away on their phones. 'It's advertising, just not as you know it.' She smiled. 'And now, if you don't mind, I have to post another one of those selfies, and woe betide me if I don't use the correct hashtag.'

Jane leaned back against the seat. Her hangover, and the unfamiliar landscape, had induced an almost tranquil state. After half an hour, though, she saw something that made her look twice – a succession of massive glass boxes which seemed to be floating in mid-air, looming uncannily out of the endless white landscape.

The hotel. Once out of the car, Jane could see that each box was in fact a room, floor to ceiling glass, suspended on wooden stilts.

'Wow.' She couldn't help being impressed and Natasha nodded, pleased.

'The Flyte Hotel,' she said. 'I've been obsessed with coming here ever since we started planning the trip. They've cleared the hotel just for us.'

'Robyn will be jealous,' murmured Nick, staring. 'She's probably at Bounce and Rhyme with the baby right now, drinking shit coffee.'

Sandra laughed hoarsely. 'For God's sake, don't tell her. It'll push her over the edge.'

Inside the lobby, all clean lines and pale wood, a chic woman in a white button-down shirt, pinstriped trousers and trainers came forward. Her hair was pulled back in a neat chignon, and her face was bare of any obvious make-up except for a dab of bright orange-red lipstick.

'Welcome to the Flyte Hotel. My name is Emma,' she said crisply. 'We have twelve rooms here, each with its own beautiful view.' She nodded to a younger man, wearing glasses with thick black frames, who came over at once. 'Jon and I will show you to your rooms.'

Jane's room was the last, and as she stepped through the door, she found herself letting out a breath she hadn't known she was holding in.

The space itself was relatively small, with only the most minimal of furniture – a wide bed with cream sheets, a little yellow lamp on a slate-coloured ledge and, in the corner, a writing desk and stool. But the most extraordinary thing was that every wall was a pane of glass. Jane was suspended above the ground in this glass cube by some astonishing feat of architectural magic. She felt as though she could step through those walls out into the thick snow right now and walk among the pines.

'Amazing,' she murmured. 'We're *in* the forest.'

Emma nodded, smiling.

'The outside and the inside becoming one,' she said. '"Heals the heart", we say in this country.'

'Heals the heart,' repeated Jane, and then bit her lip. If she could somehow return to London with a whole heart, then she would be happy.

Emma continued. 'You'll miss the green hills and blue skies of summer, but instead you'll see these woods at night, all lit up, the snow on the trees, and occasionally, just for a few minutes, the sun brushing the mountains with pink light. Enjoy it.'

Jane noticed a sheet of paper in the woman's hand. 'I bet there's an itinerary, though.'

'There certainly is.' Emma handed the slip of paper to Jane. 'A talk about fishing now, then cocktails before a four-course festive dinner in the hall tonight.' She ran her gaze over Jane's – presumably haggard – face. 'You do have time for a bath and a lie-down first, however.'

After she had gone, leaving the scent of blackcurrants behind her, Jane decided to unpack while she still had the energy. They were going to spend a few nights here, so she took the time to fold her jumpers into the drawers and hang up her shirts and trousers. Then she set up her laptop on the little desk. She had better start drafting something for Nadine.

There was a burst of laughter in the corridor – Lucy, Lena and Freddie, heading downstairs to explore. She remembered her conversation with Freddie in the car. Perhaps she could write about the bloggers' trip from the point of view of a trad print journalist. 'My Christmas Tree Adventure #itsallaboutthelikes.'

She began to type a rough outline, to see if there was anything to the idea. There'd be a lot of humour at the bloggers' expense, but with a bit of tinkering, it could be funny. She yawned. She could end on a moving message about the Christmas tree itself, symbol of international solidarity. A sprinkling of Christmas good cheer.

She yawned again and stretched. Her hangover had receded slightly, but her eyes still felt gritty, and Emma's suggestion of a bath and a lie-down sounded too good to pass up. She glanced at the itinerary. The speech about the fisheries was due to start in under an hour. *Don't want to be late for that*, she thought sarcastically.

After half an hour in the tub, Jane could feel her eyes drifting shut. She got out, wrapped herself in a thin, grey cotton robe and lay down on the bed. She felt marooned in the darkness, suspended in her glass cube of a room, aloft among the pine trees. Hovering above the earth, untethered and ungrounded.

Not herself.

She would close her eyes for a few minutes. Just a few minutes.

When Jane awoke, the room was dark. She stared into that darkness, slowly remembering where she was, and then realised what had woken her: a gentle tapping on the door.

She swung her legs to the floor and stood, groping for the bedside lamp before giving up and walking to the door in darkness.

Ben was standing outside, holding a tray.

'Hi,' he said.

'Oh God, I slept through dinner, didn't I?'

He nodded. 'And you missed that talk about fish. They're checking off every Norwegian cliché one by one.' He held out the tray. 'Dinner.'

'That's nice of you,' said Jane. 'Come in.'

'All right, just for a second. I'm running out of stuff to say.'

'I refuse to believe that is possible,' said Jane. 'You could happily talk to a stone. Can you find a light switch? This place is too minimalist even for me.'

He came into the room, deposited the tray on the table and reached for a switch, which flooded the room in muted, warm light. Jane imagined what they must look like from outside – two figures in a painting, suspended in the darkness, watched by unseen eyes in the forest.

'Just like mine,' Ben said, looking around. 'Unbelievable, isn't it? I never even knew this place was here.' He dropped onto the bed, stretching out his long legs. 'I suppose you have to be a rich tourist to know about it.'

Jane sat down at the table with her food. A piece of salmon, pickled cucumber, buttered rye bread and salad. She took a bite of the bread. 'Is Natasha cross with me?'

'Fuming,' said Ben. 'It's the most animated I've seen her. She didn't blink for about five minutes when she eventually realised you were missing the whole lot. She even raised an eyebrow.'

'That's it,' Jane said. 'I can't face her in the morning. I'm on the next flight out of here.'

Suddenly, she yawned, an enormous yawn that made her eyes water. 'Sorry! I don't know why I'm so tired.'

'It's this time of year,' Ben said, looking out at the night, dark and still beyond the glass walls. 'The darkness, or the half-light. I always forget how strange it is.' He cleared his throat. 'It's nice, isn't it? Us. Hanging out. Away from the office, I mean.'

Jane looked up in surprise.

'You're hardly ever *in* the office, Ben,' she said. 'You're hardly ever in the country.'

He sighed. 'Yeah, that's true. It can make things tricky.' He rumpled his hair. 'Maybe I should try and be in the same place for more than five minutes.'

She laughed. 'You couldn't do that. Imagine how bored you'd be. Besides, I'm just jealous. I'd love to travel.'

'Why don't you?' he asked. 'Don't tell me you haven't had the opportunity.'

Jane hesitated, thinking of the job offer from the *Washington News* she had turned down. 'I just don't think it's the right time,' she said at last.

'There's never a right time in our line of work,' he said. He glanced at his watch. 'I'll let you go back to bed. And don't worry about missing dinner and all that. No one cares apart from Natasha. The rest of them didn't even notice.'

She grinned. 'I'm glad I'm so memorable.'

He laughed. 'I didn't mean *that*.'

A knock at the still-open door caught their attention and they turned to see Philip Donnelly standing in the doorway. He wore a white shirt with the sleeves rolled up and was carrying a tray with a plate laden with food, two glasses and a bottle of wine. His eyes flickered between Jane and Ben, and his jaw tightened. Jane was furious to realise that her cheeks were burning.

'Evening,' Philip said, his voice cool. 'I thought you might be hungry, but' – his gaze took in the tray of food on the table – 'it looks like you've already been looked after.'

'Great minds think alike,' said Ben curtly. 'Well,' he said. 'I've got a bit of work to do – I'll see you guys in the morning.' The door clicked loudly shut behind him.

'That looked cosy,' said Philip, his voice still cold. 'What does he do again?'

'He's a photographer, actually,' Jane said awkwardly. 'A really good one. Ben Andersen. He just got back from six months in Aleppo.'

Philip scowled. 'Bloody do-gooders. How do you know him?'

'He's a mate from work. He was bringing me some food because I missed dinner.'

'Oh, sod him anyway,' said Philip, pushing his hair out of his eyes and glaring at her. 'Why wouldn't you talk to me at breakfast?'

Jane felt the now-familiar sensation of irritation mingled with attraction that rose in her whenever she spoke to Philip. He looked like a cross little boy – petulant, hurt and very handsome.

'Look,' she said, trying to defuse the situation. 'Sit down a moment, will you? I'm sorry I was rude this morning at breakfast. I was a bit confused.'

Philip sat on the bed where Ben had sat a few moments ago, but where Ben had been all sprawling limbs, Philip was languid grace. 'What's confusing you?' he asked softly.

'Well, I just got out of a relationship that messed me up a little. And you have this reputation . . .'

'That's my reputation, Jane,' Philip said, his expression inscrutable. 'That's what people write about me, not what I'm actually like. You of all people should know the difference.'

'Are you saying it's not true?' said Jane, and then went on quickly, before he could reply, 'Look, don't answer that. It doesn't matter.'

'Would you believe me if I said it wasn't?' he asked.

There was a long silence, while they looked at each other, and then Jane said, uncomfortably, 'I'm not sure. No offence.'

He stood. 'None taken, I assure you,' he said. 'I'll see you in the morning, Jane.'

He turned and stalked out of the room, and Jane dropped her head into her hands, unsure whether to laugh or cry. So much for behaving badly. She'd managed to drive away her only romantic prospect on this trip.

9

The day of the tree-cutting ceremony dawned as hazily grey as every other day so far.

After her early night, Jane was ready before the rest of the group and found herself alone in the lobby. She spent the time drinking a coffee and reading the framed articles on the walls. Articles about how the area had been affected during the war. She hadn't realised they were so close to one of the German wartime submarine bases – less than half an hour away, on a local island.

She stopped in front of one of the framed clippings about a local war hero called Lukas Gulbrandson. He had an arresting face, with a determined expression, thick brows and dark hair. Jane read the brief piece.

Lukas Gulbrandson lived on the nearby island of Otteroy during the war. A key member of the Norwegian resistance movement, he was one of the six Norwegian commandos parachuted in to bring supplies and aid to the Allies at Telemark. He was shot by the Gestapo in 1944. He was survived by his wife and child.

Gradually, the others started to filter in, looking sleepy-eyed. Thomas, in his greatcoat and muffler, sat down nearby with a little groan. He opened the paper and began reading. Freddie, wearing a thick, fluffy orange sweater that enveloped her like a very stylish rug, sat down and took out a book.

Lucy, clutching an enormous mug of herbal tea, sank

into an armchair nearby, continuing what sounded like a whispered argument on her phone.

'No, you can call *me* when you've got something nice to say,' she snapped at last. 'Until then, don't bother. I'll see you in a few weeks.' She hung up abruptly and tossed down the phone.

'Harry's being a dickhead, as usual,' she muttered to Freddie. Her eyes were slightly reddened, but she looked defiant, and beautiful as ever.

'What's the fight about this time?' Freddie asked, and from her dutiful tone Jane had the impression it was a question she asked a lot.

Lucy shook her head, thick hair tumbling about her shoulders. 'He's cross that I'm not coming home straight after this. Keeps saying he hasn't seen me in months. It's not my fault that the Edinburgh job crashed in.'

'That's rubbish,' Freddie said sympathetically. She laid down her book. 'Do you think he's jealous, though? He never sees you. Not that it excuses him being grumpy, but he might be sad about it.'

'I think he's being an arse,' said Lucy tightly. 'He's cross that I'm missing his band's gig.'

'Hey. He's a good guy,' said Freddie, stretching out her foot and lightly kicking Lucy's shin.

'All we do is fight,' said Lucy sulkily. 'He wants to talk about the relationship all the time. What's the point? I should just break up with him and save us both the trouble.'

Jane put down her cup, stung on the unknown Harry's behalf. 'Fighting isn't necessarily a bad sign,' she said. '*Not* fighting is worse. At least he wants to make things better. At least he's *trying*. Someone pretending that everything is fine and they're supportive of your career and then just, I don't know, *walking out* one day and breaking up with you by email is worse. For instance.'

There was a silence. Jane could feel Ben's eyes on her and flushed.

'Not that I should be giving relationship advice,' she added.

Lucy leaned forward. 'So, wait. You think it's a *good* sign that we're fighting?'

'I think,' said Jane, 'that you're both busy with your respective careers and you have to work out a balance.'

'Huh,' said Lucy thoughtfully.

Lena appeared. 'Which hat will photograph better?' she asked seriously, holding out one in soft baby-blue wool and another in red. 'I left the green one upstairs because it clashes with your coat.'

'Blue against the snow,' said Freddie. 'With red lipstick.'

'Obviously,' said Lena, tugging the hat on over her glossy dark hair. 'I can't wait to see the huskies. Do you think we can take photographs with them?'

'I imagine that's why they've been drafted in, yeah,' said Freddie, picking up her book again.

Thomas, meanwhile, had wandered over to the clippings on the wall and was staring at one of them, seemingly lost in thought.

Natasha appeared in the doorway. She was wearing a chunky cream knit jumper dress that just skimmed her knees, thick wool tights flecked with silver and knee-high tan boots. Her blonde hair hung about her face in artful waves. Jane was sure that both Philip and Ben's eyes flickered briefly in her direction.

'Are we ready?' Natasha said, her gaze raking across them. 'All present and accounted for and full of beans and raring to go?' She applied lip balm in the mirror and in its reflection gave Jane a sour look. 'Glad to see you've joined us this morning, Jane. Sorry that the four-course Michelin-starred dinner we laid on last night couldn't entice you.'

'Yeah, I didn't know dinner was optional,' said Nick grumpily.

'It's not,' snapped Natasha. '*None* of this is optional.'

'Sorry to have missed it,' said Jane cheerfully. 'But today I am here to see absolutely everything, I promise.'

There was the sound of a car horn outside and they began to file out. Ben was, Jane noticed with no surprise at all, well kitted out for the snow in proper gear.

He nodded at the cars. 'Excited? This is the main event.'

'We're going into the forest to watch a tree being cut down,' she said, shivering as they stepped outside. 'I'm not going to get my hopes up.'

'You might be surprised,' he said. They watched as Thomas was helped into one of the cars and a warm rug was spread over his knees. 'After all, it's not just any tree.'

The huskies stood waiting for them, each pair drawing a light, pretty little sled.

'Are we not too heavy for them?' Jane wondered aloud.

Ben shook his head.

'They're Viking dogs,' he said. 'They're super hardy.'

They set off, led by an outrider on a pony, the dogs moving with astonishing speed across the snow. The sleds tore round the bends and Jane found herself yelping along with the others, partly from nerves and partly from excitement. All around them was immaculate snow, with no other sign of human life as far as the eye could see.

When they entered the forest, a reverent hush descended as the trees closed about them. The huskies swept daringly between the tree trunks with unerring grace, until they entered a clearing and slowed.

Ahead, a delegation of people was waiting: a group of five forest rangers, the tree-choosing committee, a cluster of angelic-looking schoolchildren, a short, stocky woman with sandy hair, who was introduced as the mayor of Oslo, and a tall, thin man who was the mayor of Westminster. He was less well equipped for the snow than the others, and the tip of his nose was bright pink. Thomas was quickly welcomed by the foresters, and they were soon chatting and laughing. There was also a battered little dark green van serving drinks, and Jane caught the smell of cinnamon and coffee.

The mayor clapped her hands.

'Please, quiet all,' she said in English. 'After much conversation about size and girth, we have decided on our final candidate. I hope it meets with the committee's approval.'

'Girth, eh?' murmured Philip into Jane's ear, and she bit back a laugh. It seemed that his frostiness of last night had thawed.

'And here she is – our Queen of the Forest!'

The mayor indicated a tall pine set apart from the others, tall and majestic in the forest glade. Jane watched, fascinated, as the rangers presented the chosen tree to the committee, who all examined it gravely. As part of the selection, a sample was drilled from the trunk and they carefully counted the growth rings, pronouncing it old and venerable enough. Ben hovered, taking pictures.

'Now,' called one of the foresters, 'the mayor must make a phone call for permission to select this tree.'

Jane could see Philip clenching his jaw to stifle a yawn. The mayor spoke on her phone and then nodded, saying something in Norwegian that was whisked away by the wind. Everyone started laughing and clapping, so Jane gathered that permission had been given.

The mayor called for silence once more. 'Before we begin to cut down this chosen beauty, I have a few thank-yous to make.' She gestured at the group to her left. 'I would like to begin by thanking the committee of woodsmen and -women, the custodians of these great trees. Fifteen years ago, they selected four candidates, one of which would be crowned queen. They nurtured these trees so that they might bask in solitary splendour and unobstructed light. One stood out above the rest. You have chosen wisely, and our queen does you proud.'

There was a smattering of applause.

'They know this is a tree, right?' Philip whispered. 'Not an actual queen?'

'Hush,' Jane whispered back. 'We're getting to the good bit.'

The mayor continued. 'Thank you next to the representative from London, the Lord Mayor of Westminster, who will accompany the queen on her voyage across the sea. And of course, thank you all, dignitaries and journalists, for coming to witness this great tradition.' She paused. 'And now I would like to introduce my old friend, Thomas Erikson.'

Thomas stepped forward, tall and upright, and the mayor laid a hand on his arm.

'Many of you will already know this man's name,' she said. 'He is famous in this part of Norway for a particular act of bravery – when he helped our king escape the Nazis in 1940.' She turned to Thomas. 'My friend, I and my country owe you a great debt. It is an honour to ask you to take part in this ceremony.'

Jane looked at Thomas with increased interest. There was hearty applause from the small crowd and Thomas held up his hands for silence, beaming.

'My old friend,' he said, his voice warm as he addressed the mayor, 'you have given many thanks, but I must add one more. I like this tradition of giving an old friend a gift, and Britain is an old friend to us. She gave us sanctuary when we needed it.'

The Westminster mayor smiled politely, and Thomas went on.

'This tradition of ours, it is sentimental perhaps.' His eyes met Jane's fleetingly. 'It looks backwards, all traditions do. One cannot be sentimental about the past. In fact, one must *not* be so. I have lived a long time and I know that is a dangerous road. And yet I think that traditions give us something valuable. They remind us of who we are, deep down. Thank you, then, to our British friends. May we always offer sanctuary to those who need it. May we always look outwards instead of inwards.'

There was more applause. At last the crowd fell quiet and waited expectantly for Thomas's next words.

'And I would like to say thank you also to the brave men and women who worked alongside me during the war,' he said. 'I did not act alone that day in Nybergsund. They too should be honoured.' He hesitated, a shadow crossing his face. 'That is all of my little speech.'

The Oslo mayor was handed a saw by one of the foresters. 'Thomas, will you cut the tree with me?' she asked, holding it out.

Thomas flexed his gloved hands jokingly. 'It has been a long time since I cut down a tree, but I will certainly make the attempt.' An impish smile broke out on his face. 'For the photograph, at least.'

The Oslo mayor and Thomas took a few ceremonial strokes, all documented by Ben. Then they stepped back, relinquishing the saw, and the foresters took up the work in earnest.

The mayor nodded to the group of children and they

began to sing, their thin voices carrying on the still air. Jane did not understand the words, but there was something about their childish voices and the lilting melody that made her feel sober, as though she was in church. She glanced briefly at the rest of the group and saw that they too had fallen silent, their eyes fixed on the tree.

Afterwards, the others clustered round the drinks van, stamping their feet and chatting, but Jane found herself unable to look away from the tree, which was being removed from the ground with such dignity and care. She had half expected to find the ceremony ridiculous, but instead it had been surprisingly moving.

Ben came over with a steaming paper cup and something wrapped in a napkin. She took the cup and sniffed gingerly.

'Thanks. What is it?' she asked.

'Apple wine,' he said, handing her the bulky napkin. 'And *pølser*. Sausage with pancake and mustard.'

He bit into his and Jane copied.

'Here.' Ben reached out with a napkin and dabbed the tip of her nose. 'Mustard. It's an occupational hazard of eating *pølser*.'

Jane looked out over the gathered crowd. Thomas stood apart and she was startled to see a grave expression on his face as he gazed at the tree. He looked his age now – old and tired and, she thought, worried. As though he was not just remembering the past but seeing it clearly, as one sees a reflection in a mirror – and did not much like what he saw there.

10

They drove back in sleepy silence, Freddie's head nodding until it rested gently on Jane's shoulder, and she snored lightly. They reached the hotel in time to rest and change before dinner.

'Which you will *all* be attending this time,' said Natasha, fixing Jane with a gimlet eye.

Jane nodded meekly.

Keen not to doze off again, Jane spent her precious hour of freedom listening to more of her book in the sitting room, curled up in front of the roaring fire with a glass of tea at her elbow. Freddie wandered in after a while and started working on a laptop, nodding her head along to music from her headphones. Ben joined them too, also bent over a laptop, sleeves rolled up and expression concentrated.

They settled into a cosy, companionable silence. Jane was more gripped by the audio story of the king's escape now she'd discovered the role that Thomas had played. She skipped to the section about Nybergsund.

The king was left with a terrible choice: accept Quisling as prime minister and capitulate to German demands or put his country in terrible danger.

At Nybergsund, the cabinet met with Hitler's emissary, Bräuer, who urged him to capitulate. Speaking to his cabinet, King Haakon told them that he would sooner abdicate.

The cabinet stood with their king. The response was swift and brutal. German bombs rained down on Nybergsund, and the king and his cabinet took shelter in the nearby woods.

At this point, we must turn to the true hero of that night – a soldier, barely past his nineteenth birthday and with less than a year's experience in the army, who, against almost unsurmountable odds, managed to get the king out of the woods and to the safety of the border.

'Amazing,' Jane murmured, resting her cheek on her hand. 'I have a million questions for him about this.' She was quiet for a moment, watching the fire leap in the grate. 'I could work it into the article. I could—'

Natasha appeared in the doorway, wearing a cream, woollen dress. 'Dining room in ten,' she said shortly. 'That is, if you're still gracing us with your presence tonight, Jane?'

'Oh, absolutely,' Jane reassured her, then glanced guiltily down at her thermal leggings and thick socks. 'I'll just go change.'

Ben shrugged. 'Don't bother,' he said, staring fixedly at his laptop again. 'You look great.'

Jane looked over at him. He was wearing his usual jeans and an enormous baggy jumper and his glasses were slightly askew.

'Don't you ever worry about what anyone else thinks?' she asked. 'Don't you ever worry about fitting in?'

He burst out laughing. 'All the time!' he said.

She narrowed her eyes at him. 'Give me one example,' she said, 'when you, Ben Andersen, have ever felt uncomfortable and insecure in a situation.'

'Well . . .' He thought for a bit. 'When I was a teenager—'

'I knew it!' she said triumphantly. 'Teenage insecurity doesn't count. The only people who aren't insecure as teenagers are psychopaths.'

He smiled. 'I was *really* anxious around girls. Never knew the right thing to say.'

'Until you met the right one?' Jane said, unashamedly probing. She wasn't sure what girlfriend would put up with Ben's lengthy absences and irrepressible good cheer, but she was willing to bet he'd found one, as sunny and functional as he was. To her surprise, Ben shook his head.

'It's been a weird few years,' he said. He nodded over her head as the others began to file past the door. 'Anyway, I think it's time for dinner.'

'Hurry up,' Natasha said. 'The hotel is laying on a traditional Norwegian' – she consulted her itinerary – '*Julebord*, or Christmas party.'

'A little early, isn't it?' Jane said, and then caught Ben's eye. 'Sorry, I mean, how delightful.'

He held out his hand and dragged her out of her armchair. 'It's never too early for Christmas, Scrooge.'

They were led into the large dining room to find a roaring fire, sending shadows high up to the cavernous ceiling, and a vast table laid with platters of smoked meat, boards stacked with roast pork belly, enormous jugs of gravy and bowls of creamy mashed potato. Jaunty, old-fashioned music played on a record player. Jane accepted a glass of treacly, dark beer and sipped it cautiously.

Natasha ran her fingers through her hair and then made a beeline for Philip, who was sitting on a sofa alone, nursing a whisky, wearing blue jeans and a white shirt with the sleeves rolled up.

Soon the pair of them were laughing. Natasha leaned closer to Philip, her waterfall of golden waves obscuring her face, one long, tanned leg draped over the other. Jane gritted her teeth. It looked like she had missed the boat when it came to snagging the famous lothario. Which was *fine*, she thought. Who needed a holiday romance anyway.

Sandra, Nick, the bloggers and Ben were in the corner being shown a variety of beers by a hipster-looking bearded barman wearing braces. Jane noticed Thomas sitting apart on a sofa and went over to him.

'May I join you?' she asked quietly, hovering in front of him. He seemed to be looking through her rather than at her.

He blinked and smiled. 'Of course, my dear. Forgive me. I was a million miles away.'

'You haven't got a plate. Shall I fetch you some food?' she asked, but he shook his head.

'No, thank you.' He glanced at the laden table. 'A bit too much for me, all this. I will go to my room soon, I think.'

She sat down next to him, tucking her legs under her. 'It was a busy day,' she said. She had many questions she wanted to ask him, but something about his abstracted manner made her unsure how to begin.

'I had no idea you did so much during the war,' she said finally, deciding to just go for it. 'The mayor mentioned it in her speech – that you were instrumental in getting the king out. I've been learning all about it. Without you, there might have been no allied Norwegian government during the war.' She hesitated, watching his face. 'You must be very proud.'

To her surprise, his expression clouded over. 'I *am* proud,' he said shortly. 'But as I said out there in the forest, I did not act alone.' He rubbed his forehead. The preoccupied look was back on his face. 'If only I knew the right thing to do,' he muttered, as though speaking to himself.

'Can I help?' Jane asked. She had spoken without really expecting an answer, but to her surprise, he turned and studied her for a long moment.

'I wonder,' he said at last. Then he nodded, seeming to make up his mind. 'I would like to ask a favour of you. Would you be able to come to my room after the party here, so that I can explain properly?'

'Of course,' Jane said. 'If there's something I can help with.'

'Thank you,' he said. 'I am going for a rest now. It has been, as you say, a long day.' He rose stiffly and Ben came over.

'Are you all right, Thomas?' he said. 'I'll give you a hand upstairs if you like?'

'No, no,' Thomas said. 'I will be quite fine. This young lady' – he nodded at Jane – 'has agreed to visit me after the supper party.' He looked around at the table decked with pine and laden with food. 'Christmas in November,' he said, shaking his head. 'Everything is moving very fast indeed.'

He left the room.

'Why are you going to see him tonight?' Ben said.

'He asked me to. I'm not sure why.' She gave him a sideways look. There was something here – she could feel her investigative radar prickling. 'Do *you* know? It's been a whole forty-eight hours, after all. He's probably adopted you as a surrogate grandchild by now.'

Ben laughed but shook his head. 'No,' he said. 'No idea.'

Jane leaned back against the couch and sipped her drink. Her mind went back to the tree-cutting ceremony and that odd expression she had seen on Thomas's face. He had seemed bothered by something then too.

'Can I get you a refill?' asked Ben, shaking her out of her thoughts. 'It *is* Christmas.'

'No, thanks,' Jane said. 'I want to be fresh for whatever excitement is on the itinerary tomorrow.'

'Chocolate-making,' said Ben promptly, and Jane shuddered. 'Why would I make it when I can buy it from a shop?'

'We'll get through it together,' said Ben. 'Promise.'

'All right, you're on,' said Jane.

Just then her phone buzzed in her pocket and she took it out. Margot, presumably wanting an update on her non-existent Norwegian romance. She gestured at it apologetically and Ben melted away back to the bar.

'Hi,' Jane answered. 'Are you in labour yet?'

'Fat chance.' Margot sounded tired. 'Actually, I'm just fat. How's the wild man of the woods? Has he taken you roughly in the sauna yet?'

Jane's gaze flickered, despite herself, to Philip. He was sitting on the edge of a corner sofa, surrounded by Lucy, Lena and Freddie now, as well as Natasha; they were all leaning forward, eyes wide, hanging off his every word. As though he knew Jane was watching, he looked up and, to her surprise, gave her a little wave. She hesitated and then gave him the smallest wave back.

'Well?' Margot demanded.

'No! No one has taken anyone anywhere. In fact, we had a bit of a row and now I'm not sure he likes me anymore.'

'Jane.' Margot's voice sounded muffled. 'He's a washed-up TV star with a dodgy reputation – you're a prize-winning journalist. He's probably just in awe of you. And arguments are good. Arguments can be a prelude to amazing sex. As far as I dimly recall, anyway.'

'Are you eating?' Jane asked. She was sure she could hear chewing noises on the line.

'Of course I'm eating. KFC bargain bucket. I'm eight months pregnant and food is my only joy. Listen,' Margot said, her voice becoming petulant, 'you'd better make this happen, because, let's face it, I probably won't have sex ever again. Give me *something*, for God's sake.'

'I'm just ignoring that,' said Jane. 'How are things back in London? No twinges?'

'Not a peep,' Margot groaned. 'This baby is going to be late, just like me. I know it. Oh, hang on.' She called out something, presumably to Kate, and then came back on the line. 'Listen, I have to go. So-called *architect* Kate isn't doing a brilliant job on building this crib and I need to supervise operations. How long can I keep up the demanding-pregnant-woman act once the baby is actually here?'

'Knowing you, for ever,' said Jane affectionately. 'Bye. Give my love to Kate.'

'Will do. Love you. And remember – tonight, in the sauna, and you take notes, OK?'

Jane hung up, laughing, and then realised Philip was standing over her. He looked, unbelievably, rather sheepish.

'Hi,' he said. He was staring at his expensive-looking suede shoes.

'Hi,' she said. After a moment, she moved her bag from beside her. 'You can sit down if you want.'

He dropped onto the seat next to her.

'Look,' he said, staring at his knees now, 'I want to apologise. I think maybe we got off on the wrong foot. I'm not usually this . . .'

'Pushy?' she suggested.

'*Insecure*, I think the word is.' He glanced at her. 'You make me nervous.'

She stared at him. Aristocratic ex-Etonian, handsome lothario and wealthy TV star – she made *him* nervous?

He smiled rather bitterly. 'I meant what I said last night. Don't believe everything you read about me. But you . . . you're smart and you have articles in the *Courier* that win awards and, well, what do I have?'

'Ratings,' she told him.

'Right, *ratings*. We all know how reliable they are.' He took a deep breath. 'Anyway, I have a proposal to make.'

'Interesting,' she murmured.

'I'd like to start again,' he said, with a grin. 'If you feel the same. Get to know you properly. There's more to me than you think, I promise.' He leaned forward and his knee brushed Jane's. Despite herself, she felt a treacherous prickle of desire creeping up her spine. 'Look, I'm sorry that some arsehole back in London broke your heart, but wouldn't it be a mistake to shut down whatever . . . *this* is, when you haven't even given it a chance?'

Jane hesitated.

'All I'm saying is, don't judge me yet,' he went on. 'Get to know me first. *Then* you can judge me.'

Jane laughed in spite of herself.

'Or you can tell me to get lost and I'll stop bothering you,' he said.

He sat back and watched her expectantly.

They were silent for a while. Jane sighed. She had Margot's instructions to obey, after all. 'Don't get lost,' she said, at last. 'Not yet, anyway.'

He grinned. 'I *knew* you found me irresistible.'

She punched his arm lightly, then glanced at the time. Nearly ten o'clock. If she didn't want it to get too late, she should go and see Thomas now.

'See you later,' she said. 'I'm off to bed.'

His face fell. 'Already? Can we have coffee in the morning, then? Before all the madness starts up again.'

She considered him. 'All right,' she said. 'I'd like that.'

'I'll come and pick you up in the morning. It's a date.' He grinned at her disconcerted expression. 'Sweet dreams, Jane.'

II

Thomas opened his door wearing old-fashioned striped pyjamas and a thick flannel dressing gown.

'Thank you for coming, my dear. Let me call room service for some tea,' he said, but Jane shook her head.

'I'm all right, thank you,' she said.

'Then please, sit,' he urged, and she took a chair opposite his. He sat slowly and unhurriedly poured more tea into a glass by his side.

'It was very kind of you to come and miss the rest of the party,' he said, with his charming smile.

'Oh, that's all right,' said Jane. 'I'd had enough Christmas cheer for one evening.'

He nodded, paused and then said, in a sudden rush, 'It is difficult to know what to do. Today, seeing the Christmas tree being cut down – a little ceremony, no more – and yet . . . and yet I have a sense that if I am going to do something about all this, then it has to be now.'

Jane stayed quiet, knowing that people always talk more if you let them. He drank some tea and glanced at her.

'And then I thought, Jane is a journalist. She tells stories for a living, and I have a story. She could give me some advice.'

'I will if I can,' she said cautiously.

'Don't worry,' he said. 'These are not the reminiscences of a sentimental old man.' He frowned suddenly. 'Or perhaps that is exactly what they are.'

'Why don't you tell me about it?' said Jane encouragingly.

He nodded, then set down his tea. 'I knew a woman during the war, a woman called Marit Elson. She wrote to me a few times when I was in London, and then her letters stopped. I should like to find her.'

She stared at him. 'That's it?'

'I have a particular reason for wanting to find her. Something that has been on my conscience for a long time.'

He leaned forward and pushed an old black-and-white photograph across the little side table towards her. 'That was her. Marit.'

Jane picked up the photograph and looked at it. The soft focus of pre-war photography couldn't diminish the woman's force of character – dark, springing hair, a high forehead, eyes that met yours squarely. A face that wasn't beautiful, precisely, but interesting. Yes, surely Marit Elson had been an interesting woman.

'Have you tried the usual ways of tracking her down?' she asked.

Thomas nodded. 'Absolutely. I have done the usual Google research and applied to the National Register. There were a few other Marit Elsons, but no one of the right age or description.'

'Do you have the letters she sent you?' Jane asked. 'That might be a good starting point.'

'I know where they are,' he said. 'It's not too far from here – a few hours' drive. And yes, I thought you might be the right person to find the letters.'

'You thought that *I* might . . .' She trailed off. 'You want *me* to find her?'

'That's right.'

'Oh,' said Jane, flustered. 'I'm sorry, but I'm not sure I can do that.'

'Why not?' He sounded curious, but not put out.

Jane marshalled her thoughts. 'Number one, I'm here to work on an article for the *Courier*. Number two, you need a detective, not a journalist. And number three, I'm going home in a few days.'

'That will be quite enough time,' he said confidently. 'Find the letters and you will find Marit. I know you are here to work, but this won't take long. And as for a private detective, no, no. Far too melodramatic.' He took another sip of his tea. 'You will do a better job.'

Jane stared at him. She should say no, she thought. She had work to do on this trip. And yet there was something about his manner that made her pause. Perhaps there was more to this than he was letting on.

'When did you last see her?' she asked, stalling for time. 'Perhaps if you could tell me a little more, then I would understand better . . .'

He smiled. 'I last saw Marit Elson in a snowstorm. In the woods, outside a small village called Nybergsund.'

Nybergsund, 11th April 1940

He doesn't like her very much, when he first meets her.

Her very presence seems peripheral to the whole exercise, an afterthought. They are soldiers, on a desperate mission. What did they need with some local girl, slowing them down?

'She will show you the route beforehand,' his officer explained, guiding the car over the rutted track. 'Marit Elson, her name is. She knows the area – she grew up here. She's giving us the best route out of the forest and into the mountains.' He glanced at Thomas. 'We can trust her,' he said.

He had imagined, then, a shy thing, dumpy in her thick skirts, with plaits down her back. Meek eyes and a stolid expression. Quiet around the men.

He is surprised when she appears, a tall woman with a level gaze and a cosmopolitan air despite her worn tweed suit. She isn't loud or talkative, but neither is she shy. She looks him full in the eye as they shake hands, and her grip is firm and businesslike. Her eyes are navy-coloured, fringed with curling lashes. Thick, dark, springing hair that she winds round her head in braids. She seems assured, worldly almost.

The hotel where they gather is large enough for the king and his cabinet. The days begin to blur. Endless phone calls, meetings behind locked doors, debating what to do. Thomas feels uneasy – he always assumed that his fate was guided by men wiser and smarter than him. And now, everyone seems as frightened as each other. Ridiculous that this weighty decision will be made so quickly, in a little hotel in Nybergsund. Bräuer, the intermediary between them and Hitler, has made his case. After so much anticipation, Thomas is surprised to see that he is just a short, dark man with a compassionate face. He does not seem evil. He seems like he just wants the best thing for them.

And what is that? Norway has, till now, been neutral. As far as Thomas is concerned, the best thing for him, probably, is war.

War is when his life will become exciting.

While the king and his cabinet talk and argue, they just hang around, he and the girl. He thinks that they might enjoy themselves while they wait – play some cards, talk – but she is disinterested. She is only five years older, he discovers, twenty-four to his nineteen, but she makes him feel like a schoolboy.

He finds her, on their second night, sitting on the steps, smoking, a thick overcoat slung over her shoulders against the bitter night air. He knows a little more about her now, a little more about what they will do.

He stands there for a moment, and at first, she doesn't acknowledge his presence, but then a few seconds later, she shifts along for him to sit down.

'Do you have a cigarette?' he asks. Now they are sitting next to each other, their thighs are touching.

She doesn't reply but reaches into her coat pocket for the pack and shakes one out for him. He takes it.

'A light?'

She sighs, her breath a cloud in the chill air. Then she takes out a box of matches and strikes one. He leans towards her and her gloved hand rests briefly against his as the cigarette catches. They sit there in silence, smoking, the cold seeping up from the steps and through his thick wool coat.

'Have you eaten?' he says at last. 'There's some food left.'

'I have, thanks,' she says, in a low, hoarse voice, and in English that sounds to him perfect. She registers his surprise and smiles. 'I've been practising,' she says. 'You should too.'

'All right,' he says obediently, also in English. Hers is better, he thinks.

They listen to the murmur of voices within that seem to rise and fall, and then he says, 'What do you think they're talking about, in there?'

'Who knows?' she says. 'We'll find out soon enough.'

'Are you sure you know the way?' He blows out smoke. 'For tomorrow. We cannot afford to get lost. And we need that truck.'

He says it partly to provoke her, but she doesn't rise to the bait. She nods, slowly, considering. 'I should do,' she says. 'When you're a child, you know every inch of your little world, don't you? Well, I know every inch of these woods.'

She smiles. 'Don't worry, soldier. I'll show you the route all right. There's a cottage where we can rest, and I'll plot the rest of the way. And the truck is in the barn. You just concentrate on getting hold of a map. You won't have me with you in the mountains.' She stubs out her cigarette and stands. 'Goodnight,' she says.

He raises a hand in salute, and the door closes behind her.

He smokes and listens to the voices inside, and a dreamy sort of exhaustion settles on him. Someone shouts and pushes back their chair – he can hear it scraping across the floor – and then there are soothing sounds.

What will the king do? They are up against the wall, pushed as far as they can be pushed, hiding out like animals in the frozen woods, cornered. But still, still the king has a choice.

And as for the ordinary soldiers, the men like Thomas, they are in limbo. Not yet at war, no longer at peace. At what point will that change? At what point will there be no going back?

Two days later, one of the officers has found him a map, and Thomas and Marit set off at dawn.

He is in charge of provisions, including their own dinner, and he packs a tin of sardines and some bread that is not too fresh. He purloins a bottle of wine. He feels foolish doing so, but after all, they might be dead tomorrow.

Marit walks a long way without complaining, picking her way through the undergrowth like a goat. She never once asks to consult the map. He memorises the route, and she points out small markers and signs he can use to follow it in the truck, even in the heavy snowstorm they predict for tomorrow.

'Here,' she says, stopping in a small clearing. She lays a gloved hand on the trunk of a twisted red fir. 'This is a good tree to remember. You should turn left here.'

'All right,' he says, looking up at the tree. 'You remember this from your childhood?'

She gives him a brief smile. 'Of course. It's the tree where the fairies live.'

When they reach the cottage, the dark has settled in, thick and heavy, and he is chilled to the bone. The barn is down a small, rutted track, and they force the doors open, tramping down bracken. He turns his torch beam on the dusty space and sees, to his relief, the truck.

'I told you,' she says, rubbing her hand over a dirty window.

He surveys it. 'Will it start?'

'Only one way to find out.'

The truck doesn't start, but he has brought tools and she holds the torch steady as he works, sleeves rolled up. He feels confident when it comes to machinery. This is just like taking his father's car engine apart, and he has done that many times.

'You know what you're doing when it comes to cars, soldier,' she says, watching him.

'I wanted to be a mechanic before I joined the army,' he says. 'My parents didn't like the idea.' She is quiet, and he talks into the silence. 'They're from old families in Oslo, very wealthy, very proper. They don't like the idea of me getting my hands dirty.'

He doesn't know why he is telling her this. He wonders whether he wants to impress her, but if so, it doesn't seem to be working.

At last the work is finished, and the next time he starts

the engine, it splutters into life. It doesn't look like much, he thinks. Not like it will get them across a field, let alone the border. They fill the trunk with the provisions they have brought, the food and water canisters, the first-aid kit. She wipes down the seats with a cloth.

'You don't want the king getting dust on his breeches,' she says.

Afterwards, they go to the cottage. He fetches some water from the well outside and fills the ewer and washes his hands. They sit at the little table and he takes his wares out of his bag – the bottle of wine, the sardines, the loaf of bread. He pours wine into tin cups. He feels, under her cool gaze, both embarrassed and defiant.

He raises his mug. 'To success,' he says. 'To tomorrow.'

'To success,' she repeats, knocking her mug against his. 'You're very serious, Thomas.'

'Aren't you?' he asks irritably.

'About this? Of course.' She drinks some of the rough wine and doesn't cough or splutter.

He cuts up the bread and puts oily fish onto a plate for her. They eat hungrily, in silence.

'Where will you go?' he asks, the darkness promoting a strange kind of intimacy. 'When tomorrow is over.'

She shakes her head. 'It has barely begun. Let's get the king out first.'

'He hasn't decided yet.' He looks at her. 'Maybe he'll capitulate.'

She shrugs. 'Maybe.'

'But afterwards,' he says persistently. 'Where will you spend the war?'

She gives him a wide-eyed stare that reveals nothing.

'Probably at home, back on the island. I'll look after the chickens while my brother fishes.'

He laughs and lights a cigarette. For all he knows, it could be true.

'We should get some rest,' he says. 'We leave at first light.'

'All right,' she says, yawning and standing. 'I'm going to wash my face.'

He can hear her splashing about in the corner, and when she emerges into the light, her face is scrubbed and pink, and her hair is damp around her forehead.

'There's a bed of sorts upstairs,' she says. 'It's that or the truck.'

'Let me come with you,' he says – ambiguously, he thinks – but she just walks out and allows him to follow. He takes the torch and guides her up the stairs with it.

There is a rough trestle bed. The rooms are cobwebby, damp, freezing. He should feel miserable, but he's happy, here with her. Suspended in this moment before the rest of their lives begin.

She sits on the bed and coughs at the dust.

'Bet there are spiders,' she says callously.

He lights one of the lamps and the room fills with a sickly yellow light.

'Any better?'

'It was better before.'

He stands watching her. He wonders now whether this has all been in his head, after all, when she gives him the briefest smile, just a slight quirk to her lips, and says quietly, 'Come here.'

He goes to her and she traces the lines of his face with her fingers.

'How did you get that scar?' she asks.

Afterwards, she lies against his chest, but he can tell she is elsewhere – remote again.

He lights a cigarette and she takes it from him. They smoke, handing the cigarette back and forth, silence all around them. He is reminded of boarding school, perhaps – talking with his friends in the dark. Smoking stolen cigarettes, playing at being grown up.

'You're beautiful,' he says suddenly.

She says, with a smile in her voice, 'I bet you say that to all the girls.'

'There aren't any other girls,' he says, and then thinks uncomfortably of the one he has promised to return to.

Marit smiles against his chest, as though she can read his mind.

'What about you?' he says and strokes her shoulder. He can't help himself. He wants to imprint every memory he has of her onto his brain.

She laughs.

She shifts away from him, leans back against the wall. Her bare shoulder now rests against his. He is silent, overwhelmed all at once by the great gulf between them even as they are – astonishingly, wonderfully – close. He can hardly believe she is here. That alabaster skin, the thick hair that his hands had tangled only half an hour before.

He feels panic rising in him, the sensation of impending loss. This is too much like a dream – a good dream, but a dream that will vanish in the cold light of day.

When he wakes in the grey dawn, she is gone from the bed. He can hear her moving around outside. He checks his watch. They are not late, but they will have to hurry. He dresses quickly and makes his way outside to the truck.

'Good morning,' he says, and she nods at him.

'Good morning.' Light as a bird's wing, her lips brush his cheek.

That afternoon he checks the truck a third time for oil. He loads their meagre belongings into the boot, takes out the map and traces his finger along the route they have agreed. He is ready.

It is then that they hear the bombs.

He leaves the engine running. The king and his men are waiting in the clearing, shaking as though from the aftermath of some great terror. Marit runs towards them and they part to let her in. He hangs back, close to the truck.

The king made his choice last night and the bombs fell this evening. None of them had expected such ruthless speed. They hurry towards him now. He finds himself looking over his shoulder, as if expecting to see German troops appearing through the trees. Suddenly their mission seems not just foolhardy but utterly impossible. Suicidal. Doomed. The stuff of spy stories and comic books.

And now that it is happening, Thomas finds that he doesn't want to go. The boy of yesterday, who longed for war, is gone. Marit has changed everything for him and he hasn't the time or the words to say so. He takes her hand in his, the briefest of handshakes. Her pulse beats fast in her wrist. Her cold cheek is pressed against his.

'Take care of yourself.'

'And you.'

'I will write.'

He nods, wrenches away, scrambles into the car, where the men sit in silence. Foot to the floor, ploughing through the snow, he watches through the rear-view window until she is gone, swallowed up by the endless white.

12

'And did she?' asked Jane eagerly. 'Did she write?'

'Yes,' Thomas said, his voice tired. 'The king and I made it over the border, eventually. It was a long, arduous journey. The king was elderly, and as we knew, he was no soldier. I went to London, where I worked for the War Office, and she wrote to me there. Then, towards the end of the war, the letters stopped.

'I was engaged to be married. A month before the wedding, after the war, I came back to Nybergsund carrying the letters with me. I thought I might find her. It was a fool's errand. No one knew a Marit Elson. All I had was a handful of old letters and a description of a local girl who had helped the king one day in Nybergsund.'

'What did you do with the letters?' Jane asked.

'I hid them,' he said. 'Inside the chimney breast of the old cottage where we spent that night together, in case she ever came back.' He shrugged. 'It seemed like the right thing to do at the time.'

'And why are you telling me all this?'

'Because I should like you to go to Nybergsund and get my letters back for me,' he said simply.

'How far is it?'

'Half a day's drive. A few hours, if you ignore the speed limit.'

'But why not . . .?' She trailed off.

'Go myself?' He shook his head. 'I can't manage a whole day of travelling in a car, and the roads are bad . . . I'll give you precise instructions. I want those letters, Jane. And I want you to find Marit. Or her family, if she is no longer alive. It doesn't much matter which.'

Jane turned the photograph between her fingers.

One night of passion between two people poised on the brink of war.

She wanted, she realised, to know what happened next.

She thought of the itinerary for the next day. She could spend tomorrow visiting a local chocolatier. Or she could solve Thomas's mystery, find these letters from Marit, whose spirit still called to him after all these decades.

'All right,' she said at last. 'I'll go.'

His eyes met hers. 'Thank you,' he said.

She let out a snort. 'But what on earth am I going to tell Natasha?'

'Tell her,' he said with a smile, 'that you are going on a very important errand for a sentimental old man. And that it'll keep you out past lunchtime.'

13

The next morning dawned grey as always. Jane awoke early and lay there for some moments, listening to the silence. She imagined Thomas and Marit back in 1940, lying in another little bed, in another room in the snow, all those years ago. That silence before the sound of bombs to come.

She rang for room service and a yawning waiter brought hot coffee, warm rolls wrapped in a tea towel and cherry jam in a little earthenware pot.

Jane showered and dressed quickly in a white shirt, grey jumper and jeans. A quick search of Google Maps had shown she was indeed a mere half-day from Nybergsund. She planned to drive there and back herself in a car she would hire in the nearest town, if she could get a taxi there. She laced up her snow boots and took her heavy ski jacket.

She glanced at her watch – it was still not yet seven thirty. She would be able to order a taxi from reception and slip away before anyone noticed. She decided against letting anyone know – the sooner she got away, the sooner she would be back.

She stepped into the corridor and almost collided with Philip. His hair was damp from the shower, he was clean-shaven, and she was startled, as usual, by his handsomeness.

'Hello,' he said, looking pleased. 'Thought you might be a fellow early riser. Ready?'

She stared at him blankly. 'Ready?'

'We were going to have coffee,' he reminded her, his smile fading slightly. 'Our date, remember?'

'Oh, sorry – I forgot,' Jane said, feeling guilty. 'I just had breakfast in my room.'

'Coffee, then?'

'Had coffee too, I'm afraid. Buckets of it.'

'A walk? Before the youngsters drag themselves out of bed and we embark on today's itinerary?' She shook her head again and he looked at her suspiciously. 'What are you up to, Jane? You have a very furtive expression for this early in the morning.'

She hesitated. She was becoming, she recognised, focused on the story and excluding everything else – exactly what Simon had always hated. Thomas hadn't asked her not to tell anyone what she was doing, and she could use the help. After all, Philip did have his own car.

'Jane?' he asked again, looking at her with his head on one side. 'Are you planning to do a runner and avoid the ice bar? Because if you are, I'm telling Natasha.'

She laughed, making her mind up. 'I'm not doing a runner, but I do need a lift into town. Fancy a drive?'

'Let me get this straight,' Philip said, as they wound their way down through the mountains. 'You're driving half a day to a village to look for some old letters that may or may not still be there? All because that old man asked you to last night?'

'Yes. No. I mean, yes, sort of. They're love letters, hidden in the cottage where he and this woman . . .'

'Shagged?' Philip saw her expression and laughed. 'Apologies. I mean "consummated their wartime romance"?'

'Better. They never saw each other again. And now he wants to find her.' She watched Philip's profile as he drove. 'Don't you think that's romantic?'

'I think he's off his rocker,' he said, his eyes on the road. 'There probably never *were* any letters.'

'He's not. He's sharp. And he doesn't seem like the sentimental type,' Jane said, feeling a surge of protectiveness towards Thomas. 'I think there might be something here.'

'Your journalistic antennae are twitching?' said Philip.

'Maybe.' She glanced at him again. 'You think it's ridiculous?'

He didn't answer. They had left the mountain road behind and were driving through empty streets now. A solitary dog wandered into the road.

'Here we are,' he said. 'The nearest town.'

'The car-hire place should be outside the station,' said Jane, consulting her phone. 'Thanks for the lift. Can you please tell Natasha I've gone for a walk or something?'

He turned to her and his eyes were dancing. 'Oh, you're not getting out of this that easily, Jane. I'm going to drive you to Nybergsund to find these letters myself.'

It was oddly liberating driving along the motorway. Philip drove fast, his sleeves rolled up, window rolled down a crack, heater on full blast, whistling tunelessly. He seemed happier and more relaxed than Jane had yet seen him.

She fumbled with the radio until she found a station playing cheesy hits – Toto's 'Africa', Rod Stewart's 'Baby Jane' – interspersed with Norwegian pop songs. Philip sang along with gusto, getting most of the words wrong, improvising with the odd filthy lyric, and Jane found herself laughing and joining in.

They stopped at a service station and drank bad coffee and ate sweet biscuits, stamping their feet in the cold.

'What do you know about Nybergsund, then?' Philip asked.

She consulted the map. 'It's on the eastern banks of the

Trysil River, and it's near the border with Sweden.' She glanced up. 'Which must be why the king and cabinet hid out there – because it was close to the border.'

She traced her finger along the map.

'Thomas picked them up in the forest and drove them to Molde.' She shook her head. 'Not that long ago really – 1940.'

'Well, extraordinary times and all that. It's not too far now,' Philip said cheerfully. 'Ready for the final push?'

They drove in silence for a while, and then Jane said abruptly, 'That time you were in Norway last, to see the Northern Lights. Were you here with Donna?'

'I was,' he said, his voice light.

'What happened with her?' asked Jane, and then, when he said nothing, said, 'Sorry. You can tell me it's none of my business.'

He was silent again for a moment, then shrugged. 'No, not to worry. It's ancient history now. We got together on the show and that's all you need to know really. Any relationship that you start when filming is bound to end in disaster.' He rubbed his nose reflectively. 'Lots of highs. And then lots of rows.'

'And she went back to her husband?' asked Jane. 'After one of those rows?'

'Yeah, she said . . .' Philip stared ahead, his blue eyes clouded. 'She said it had been bad for her image, leaving him for me. That she needed to do some "damage control".' He winced slightly. 'She's presenting a new series now. I think it's doing well.'

'Oh,' Jane said, feeling rather nonplussed. The tabloids had cast Philip in the role of heartless seducer, but it seemed he was the one who had been left scarred.

He turned to her and smiled, the serious expression vanishing as though wiped from his face by a sponge. 'What about you, anyway? That chap who did a number on you, back in London.'

Jane sighed and stared out of the window.

'I should have seen it coming,' she said at last. 'He never liked me working so hard – and in the end that drove us apart. Things are always clearer with hindsight, aren't they?'

He laughed. 'Tell me about it. TV stars get together on set, break up marriage and – shocker – it doesn't last.'

Jane smiled. 'If only someone could have warned us.'

'If only.' He smiled again, his blue eyes warm. 'Still. I'm not completely sorry we both had our hearts broken. Not if it meant us ending up here.' Jane could feel her pulse quickening as their eyes locked and held for the briefest of moments. Then Philip turned back to the road. 'Not even a little bit,' he added.

When they reached Nybergsund, Jane followed the directions Thomas had given her, which took them through the village and out the other side. They drove along a winding road into a forested area, the smell of mulch and damp earth rising up around them.

Jane peered out of the window, half wondering whether she would see a twisted red pine, and then, to her amazement, it appeared on a little plot of land in between a forked path. She cried out in glee and the car skidded to a halt.

'What?' Philip said.

'Turn left here,' she said.

They drove down a rutted track, and there ahead of them was the cottage.

'This is it,' she said, trying to sound calm when inside she was fizzing with excitement. It didn't, she had to admit, look like it had ever been the scene of a night of passion. It was a small, demure, whitewashed wooden building, with stone steps leading up to a little porch.

Philip looked up at it. 'I do hope we find a nice fat stash of Nazi gold.'

'Unlikely,' said Jane. She peered through the window, noting the neat lace curtains and fresh flowers. She took a deep breath, climbed the steps and knocked on the door, feeling suddenly awkward.

The door was answered by a woman with a pleasant face and grey hair cut into a neat bob. '*Kan jeg hjelpe deg?*' she asked, and Jane hesitated.

Philip took over. 'I do apologise for interrupting you like this,' he said, his voice warm and charming. 'Do you speak English?'

'A little,' the woman replied, looking between them.

'Wonderful,' said Philip smoothly. 'May I introduce myself? I'm Philip Donnelly.' The little pause he gave after saying his name, as though expecting it to be recognised, and the blank look on the woman's face, made Jane bite back a smile. 'And this is Jane Brook.'

The woman shook their hands. 'I am Sofie Larsen,' she said.

'We're journalists,' Philip went on, rather grandly, 'and we were wondering whether you might be able to help us. We've had a rather odd request from a friend that has brought us here.'

Jane found her voice then and launched into the story of the night that Thomas Erikson and Marit Elson had spent in this little cottage on the eve of the king's escape.

'And Thomas said he came back just after the war and left some letters here, in the chimney breast. They may be long gone, but . . .'

'But you would like to check, just in case? It might be worth looking,' Sofie said. 'Most of the cottages around here have been kept as they were in the war.'

She gestured for them to enter. Inside, the cottage was all light and wooden walls, with black-and-white rugs on the floor and house plants everywhere.

'This is so cosy,' Jane said, looking around the calm and peaceful room.

Sofie smiled, her face creasing into wrinkles. 'It is very small, but enough for one.' A cat wound itself between her ankles. 'Or two,' she said with a grin.

Sofie led them through into the sitting room and nodded at the fireplace. 'There you go,' she said. 'I've had it cleaned and they never found anything, but there are recesses in old chimneys. Unless you knew to look, you could easily miss something small.' She gestured. 'Please, feel free to look. I'll bring you both some tea.'

They approached the fireplace, and Jane moved aside the fireguard and crouched down. It looked dark and sooty up there.

'All yours,' Jane told Philip. 'This is real hard-man stuff.' She smiled sweetly at him. 'Thomas is tall, after all. It's no good *me* poking around up there.'

He shot her a dirty look before stepping into the fireplace. His long body disappeared up into the chimney and she heard him fumbling around. A scatter of soot and some swearing followed.

'Perhaps I need to get a chimney sweep in more often,' Sofie said gravely, returning with a tray of tea.

'Perhaps,' Jane agreed, watching as more soot scattered onto the clean floorboards. She sat beside the woman on the sofa. 'It's very kind of you to let us barge in like this.'

Sofie waved her hand. 'I am intrigued. I have heard the name Thomas Erikson before, I think. A soldier?'

'He's something of a local celebrity,' said Jane. 'Have you lived here long?'

'My whole life,' Sofie said, and laughed at the surprised expression on Jane's face. 'This was my aunt's cottage and I would spend summers here. When she died, it came to me. No other family, you see.' She poured Jane some tea. 'It is perfect for me.'

Jane looked around her, at the pristine room, full of lovingly tended objects.

'I can understand that,' she said softly. 'Finding where you want to be and staying there.'

Philip let out a sudden yelp and they looked over.

'Any luck?' Jane called.

'A dead bird,' he called down. 'This is like *Indiana Jones*, only with extra vermin.'

Jane snorted. 'Thomas would have put it quite far back, to avoid the fire,' she called.

'Thanks for that, Einstein.' There was some more shuffling, another shower of soot, and then Philip said, in a different voice, 'Ah. Hang on. Got something.'

He emerged, black smudges on his face and hair dishevelled, clutching a brown oilcloth packet. Jane hastily moved one of the rugs out of the way, but he scattered yet more soot over the floorboards.

'Sorry,' she said.

Sofie looked at the dusty little package in Philip's hand and her eyebrows rose. 'So they were up there after all. Well, well. You must take them to Thomas.'

Jane hesitated. 'I feel we should leave you some sort of proof of identity,' she said. 'These letters are on your property.'

But Sofie shook her head. 'They belong to your friend,' she said firmly. 'I am glad to help a war hero. But I should be very grateful if he would write to me one day and tell me what they said.'

14

'Well,' said Philip. They were sitting in the car and Jane was staring at the packet in her lap in stunned disbelief. She had never quite, she realised, believed she would find them. 'Success, right?' He swiped suddenly at his face. 'Ugh. I feel like I've got spiders crawling all over me.'

Jane laughed. 'You were heroic.'

'I know.' He glanced at her and then reached out his hand and, very gently, brushed his fingers across her cheek.

Electricity prickled up Jane's spine.

'You've got soot on your face,' he said quietly.

'Really?' said Jane. 'Because as I recall, you were the one up the chimney.'

'Yes, just a little here – and here . . .'

He leaned across, cupped her chin in his hand and kissed her.

He pulled away slightly, still holding her face in his hand, still very close to her. 'Sorry about that,' he said, grinning. 'I couldn't resist.' He nodded at the letters in her lap. 'Aren't you tempted to open them? Go on. Have a quick look – the old man won't know.'

'No.' She shook her head, her heart still beating fast. 'They're his.'

'You're much too honest, but if you're sure, let's get back to the hotel, shall we? I've a feeling we're going to be in a lot of trouble with Natasha.'

* * *

They did not play the radio this time, and Philip drove fast and in silence, which Jane was glad of. She wanted to think.

Philip was right – she *was* tempted to open the letters. She was sure there was more to this than met the eye. But that would breach Thomas's trust. She would just have to wait until he was ready to tell her about it himself, if he ever was.

'Shit,' muttered Philip, glancing at the dashboard and nudging Jane out of her reverie. 'Shit.'

'What?' she asked.

He gave her a somewhat embarrassed smile. 'You won't believe this, but we're out of petrol.'

'You're kidding.' She leaned over to look at the gauge, on which a red light was frantically blinking. 'Is this some ploy to get me into one of those motorway hotels?'

'Actually, that's not a bad idea at all, but no.' As he spoke, an ominous beeping sound started up.

'How could you let us run out of petrol?' she cried.

'I don't know!' he said. 'I assumed they'd filled the tank.'

'Oh, *they*,' Jane said, glaring at him. 'Who's *they*?'

He shrugged. 'The people who work at the hotel.'

Jane scowled at the TV brattishness of it. Did he never have to think for himself? And how did a survival expert manage to run out of petrol, of all things?

'Well,' she said coldly, 'given that *they* haven't refilled the tank, I guess we're about to break down in the freezing cold, miles from anywhere.'

As if on cue, the car made a grinding noise and the engine cut out. Philip guided it gently onto a verge, where it rolled to a stop.

'Damn,' he said forcefully.

'That pretty much sums it up,' she said.

'We'd better call the AA,' Philip said. 'Or whatever the equivalent is in Norway. I assume they have something like it.'

'I've got no signal,' Jane said, looking at her phone. She glanced back at the main road. 'Can you not fix it with a lighter and a hairband?'

Philip shook his head ruefully. 'Sorry. Fancy a walk to the nearest garage? Because it looks like that's our only option. That or hitchhiking.' He eyed the road ahead. 'We're actually not too far from the hotel. I wonder whether the easiest thing might be to walk it, try and hitch a lift . . .'

'When you say "not too far", what do you mean?'

He unfolded the map and squinted at it. 'Maybe a three-hour walk?'

'Three *hours*?'

He smiled sheepishly. 'Think of it as a pleasant hike. Uphill.'

She glared at him, then looked out of the window at the rapidly descending fog. It was cold and bleak out there and it would be dark soon. But it was cold in the car too and she didn't think they had much choice. 'OK, then,' she agreed. 'I want it on record I'm not happy about this. And your *Survival of the Fittest* credentials are revoked.'

He walked round, opened the door for her and held out his hand. 'I'll buy you a drink at the hotel,' he said.

'The drinks on this trip are free,' she muttered, taking his hand and stepping outside.

The walk was not pleasant. The fog made it hard to see more than a few feet ahead. Walking along the road itself was dangerous, so they stuck to the verge. Jane tightened her scarf about her neck, but the cold seeped into her bones. She tried to distract herself by thinking about Thomas and Marit, and their long, arduous journey through the woods that day in Nybergsund – a journey made in altogether more noble circumstances.

Ahead of her, Philip stopped. 'How are you holding up?' he asked.

'I've been better,' she told him, her teeth chattering.

He pointed a little way ahead. 'There's something there – a bus shelter, I think. We can rest a minute.'

Under the flimsy shelter, Jane shivered, looking out at the road, her hands deep in her pockets.

'Try rubbing your wrists,' said Philip. 'That's where the circulation is. Here.' He took her hand and began massaging her wrist gently. 'This is great, isn't it?' he said cheerfully. 'We're really experiencing the country in the raw.'

'Yes, really great,' said Jane. 'Just how I wanted to spend the day.'

'There's no need to glare at me,' he said. 'You dragged me along on this wild goose chase, after all.'

'I didn't drag you, and it wasn't a wild goose chase,' Jane said. 'We found the letters.'

'So we did,' he said soothingly. 'You're not considering using them in whatever piece you're writing for the *Courier*, are you?'

She was silent, thinking. 'Maybe,' she said eventually. 'If Thomas lets me. I'm not sure why, exactly. I just think there's something here worth exploring.'

'Well, you've clearly got good instincts,' Philip said.

'Not always,' she said, giving him a small smile. 'I've been known to misjudge people.'

His warm fingers closed about her wrist. 'But you always give them a chance to redeem themselves, right?'

Just then, headlights appeared in the gloom and Jane shot out of the shelter. 'Help me flag them down,' she called. She began waving and the car driving towards them slowed and pulled over. The window rolled down, revealing a pair of cold blue eyes and an irritated expression.

It was Natasha. And beside her, in the driver's seat, with the tightest expression Jane had ever seen him wear, was Ben.

Philip and Jane sat in the back of the car like naughty children. The fog cleared slightly as they drove up the mountain, and Jane watched the scenery fly past. The only difference between this journey and the one out was that Ben was sticking rigidly to the speed limit.

'Do be careful, Andersen,' drawled Philip. 'You wouldn't want to hit a stray goat.'

'I still don't understand what you're doing out here,' Natasha said irritably to Jane, for the fourth time, swinging round to interrogate her.

'We just fancied a drive,' Jane said. She glanced at Philip, who was looking out of the window and whistling lightly under his breath, clearly leaving this one to her. 'But I'm sorry if you were worried.'

'*I* wasn't,' Natasha declared, turning to look out front again. 'Ben was the one who suggested we drive around and look for you both when the fog came down. He said that as of last night, you were a hundred per cent committed to the chocolate-making class.' She flipped down the mirror and fluffed her heavy fringe. 'Well, you missed it, and thanks to you, we've had to cancel the artisanal candle-making workshop. Not to mention that someone, and I bet it isn't going to be you, Philip, has to call the insurance company so they can come and deal with the car.'

They lapsed into an uncomfortable silence until they saw the hotel looming out of the snow. Ben pulled the car to a careful stop.

'There we go,' he said.

'Fabulous,' said Philip. 'Thank you for driving us back so, ah, conscientiously, Andersen. We might have been quicker on foot, but at least we were warm.'

Natasha got out and slammed the car door, stomping up the steps to the hotel without looking back. Philip moved to get out also, but Jane hesitated.

'Aren't you coming?' he said to her.

'Just a minute,' she said. She needed a moment to clear her head. It had been a long and intense day.

'Sure,' he said, and slid out, giving her the faintest wink as he did so. 'See you inside.'

Ben turned around and looked at her. 'All right back there?' he asked. He seemed to have relaxed now Philip was gone.

'Yes,' she said, looking at Philip's retreating back as he walked up the steps into the hotel. 'I just need five minutes.'

'Well, if I've got you captive for five minutes, I can make you look at my latest works of photographic genius. I think you might find them interesting.'

He held a folder out to her and she opened it on her lap. Inside were the photographs of the tree-cutting ceremony. Jane turned them over. The cherubic carol singers, eyes wide with wonder. Lucy, Lena and Freddie, faces glowing under their bobble hats. The mayor of Oslo, laughing with Thomas as they managed the saw between them. The foresters as they began work in earnest. The committee counting the growth rings of the tree, their faces intent.

'These are lovely,' she said, meaning it. He managed to capture everything exactly as it was but then force you to look at it properly.

And then she turned over another and her breath caught.

Ben had photographed Thomas, standing among the trees in his greatcoat and scarf, snowflakes mantling his shoulders and hair. His lined, handsome face was caught in that moment of abstraction Jane had noticed yesterday, dark eyes focused on something, or someone, in the distance that only he could see. A curious, unreadable expression on his face that was not quite fear and not quite anger but something in between.

'This is amazing,' she said to Ben, holding it out so that he could see. 'I was watching him yesterday and wondering what on earth he was thinking about to make him look like that. And now you've captured it on camera.'

'Interesting, isn't it?' Ben said. 'I'd wager his mind is on something other than that Christmas tree.'

Jane chewed her nail. 'I think he looks haunted.'

Ben nodded slowly. 'Maybe. I think it looks more like . . . like he's trying to figure something out. Like he's worrying about something.' He took back the photo and slid it into the folder. 'Are you going to tell me about your mystery jaunt, then?'

Jane reached into her bag and pulled out the little packet of letters. 'You know Thomas asked to see me last night? Well, he told me a story about his wartime romance with a woman called Marit Elson. She sent him letters throughout the war apparently, which he put in a chimney breast in a cottage outside Nybergsund. He asked me to get them today.'

'He asked you and Donnelly to go?' Ben asked. His voice was neutral, but Jane found herself flushing slightly.

'Philip just came along for the ride,' she said. 'Anyway, we found them, just where Thomas said they would be.'

'And those are the letters?'

'They are.'

'Have you read them?' he asked curiously.

'Of course not,' Jane said, stung. 'What sort of conniving journalist do you think I am? Plus, they'll be in Norwegian. And they belong to Thomas. I'm going to take them to him right now.'

Ben looked at the packet, blackened by time and soot. 'I'm a bit worried about him, that's all. He seems vulnerable to me, for all that he's so sharp. If these are letters from his past, and he's been dreaming about them all these years, getting them now might be a shock.'

Jane thought that he might be right – she would have to tread carefully. Offer to stay with Thomas perhaps, while he read them. And in all honesty, she was desperate to know what the letters said. She said, at last, 'I think there's a story here.'

Ben laughed. 'So you *are* a conniving journalist. I thought this was about an old man's nostalgic journey into the past.'

'It is! A decade of journalism hasn't completely debased me. I'll be careful. But once he's had some time, I'd like to interview Thomas properly. Find out exactly what he did in the war. And I want to find out what happened to this woman, Marit – why she stopped writing to him . . .'

'I suppose you'll have to read the letters, then,' said Ben. 'If he lets you.'

'Mmm,' said Jane thoughtfully. 'About that – fancy coming to his room with me? I think he likes you. You might help soften the blow.'

'All right,' Ben said, after a moment. His eyes met hers. 'I have the feeling I'm being dragged into a scheme, though.'

'Just go with it,' Jane said. 'Why don't I go up and give them to him now, and then you could just sort of pop in after a few minutes?'

'No problem.' He yawned. 'Let me get a coffee first.'

'OK, thanks.' She laid her hand on the door handle, then stopped. 'And thanks for finding me today, Ben. Only someone as pathologically nice as you would have bothered to wonder where I was.'

'I couldn't leave the *Courier*'s best journalist out there in the snow, could I? Nadine would have killed me.' Then he added, 'Wait, you think I'm *pathologically* nice?'

'I think you have a bit of a problem there, yes,' she said, fighting to keep a smile out of her voice.

He rubbed his hand across his forehead. 'Great,' he muttered. 'Pathological. Just great.'

'It's not a bad thing,' Jane protested. 'I was really glad to see you.'

'I bet you were,' said Ben, unbuckling his seat belt and clambering out. 'I mean, what kind of idiot forgets to put petrol in the car?'

15

Jane and Ben found the others gathered in the lounge. They were surrounded by scraps of felt, cotton wool and spools of thread, and were in the middle of making what looked small, red-capped gnomes. A fire roared in the grate. They glared at her when she walked in. Philip was already sitting in an armchair, flicking through a magazine.

'Where have you been?' Lena demanded. 'Philip is being annoyingly mysterious.'

'I didn't realise we were allowed to just *leave*,' muttered Nick.

'What *are* you making?' Jane asked, eyeing the little figures.

'This is *nisse tomte*, the not-at-all creepy Norwegian Christmas elf,' said Freddie. She held out a misshapen figure to show Jane, then mouthed, 'Save yourself.'

Natasha appeared in the doorway. She had taken off her warm ski jacket and Jane saw that she was wearing yet another immaculate cream jumper, this time of some sort of fluffy material. Her hair was up in a loose knot, tendrils framing her angelic face.

'I suggest you three ring housekeeping if you want anything to eat,' she said. 'I'm certainly going to. I didn't get any dinner. I was off rescuing idiots who can't be bothered to check whether or not the fuel tank was full before buggering off on an unscheduled drive.'

'Let me get you a drink,' said Philip, laying down his magazine and turning a dazzling smile on her. 'I'm eternally grateful to you, really – and mortified I didn't check we had enough fuel. My *Survival of the Fittest* credentials are in tatters. Here, sit down.' He guided Natasha to a sofa, while Jane backed out of the room and ran upstairs to Thomas's room.

Jane tapped on the door. He called for her to come in, and when she did, she saw that he was hanging up the phone and smiling.

'Hello,' he said. 'Come in and sit down by the fire. I've been Skyping the grandchildren. We try and read a story together once a week. Today it was "Why the Sea Is Salt".' He sat down in his armchair, groaning slightly, and his gaze landed on the slim packet in Jane's hands. 'Ah,' he said. There was a brief pause. 'You found the letters?'

'I did.' She held the packet out to Thomas, but he did not take it. 'In the chimney breast of the cottage, exactly where you left them all those years ago. The owner couldn't believe it.'

'I must make sure to thank them. Well, well,' he said, his eyes fixed on the bundle. 'I am surprised, I have to say. I thought they would have been removed long ago.' He reached out and squeezed Jane's hand. 'Thank you, my dear, for going all that way. It means a lot to me.'

'I hope they give you some answers.' She laid the packet down on the table beside him. He said nothing, and she rose, rather regretfully. 'Well, I'll leave you to read them in peace.'

She was halfway to the door when his voice stopped her.

'Jane?' Thomas said. 'I wonder if I might ask another favour.'

She turned.

'The memories might be easier to bear with someone else here,' he went on. 'Would you be so kind as to sit with me while I read?'

Jane smiled and walked back towards her seat.

'Of course,' she said. 'I was starting to worry you wouldn't ask.'

They sat like that for a few minutes, and then Thomas, very carefully, opened up the packet. He shook the letters out into his lap and ran his forefinger across them gently.

'The envelopes are missing,' Jane said, looking down at them.

He nodded. 'So they are. Perhaps someone did find them after all – worth money, stamps. You can peel them off with steam from a kettle. I did it myself as a boy.'

He unfolded one of the letters and began to read. Jane found herself watching his face intently for a change in expression and was surprised to see a faint smile tugging at the corner of his mouth. He glanced up at her.

'Marit,' he said, 'would be laughing at me now, I think. An old man still stubbornly living in the romance of the past. Who can barely even read the words on the page without bifocals.'

There was a knock at the door and Ben stuck his head into the room.

'Hello,' he said. 'The, ah, gnome-making workshop is over, so I thought I'd see if either of you needed anything before I head to bed.'

'Ben, my boy,' said Thomas, stretching out a hand. 'Come in and sit with us. We are taking a little journey back through time.'

Ben came and dropped into the armchair beside Jane, stretching out his long legs. 'These are your letters? Jane told me she found them in Nybergsund.'

'That's right. In fact,' Thomas said, glancing between the two of them, 'if you have the time, Ben, then I wonder whether you might translate them for me now. My eyes are tired, and I should like Jane here to understand them also.'

There was a pause. Jane could feel her heart thumping excitedly in her chest. She widened her eyes at Ben meaningfully, signalling to him to agree.

'All right,' said Ben, after a moment, taking the letters from Thomas. 'If you're sure.'

'I am,' said Thomas, leaning back and closing his eyes. 'I should like you both here for this.'

Ben unfolded the first letter and looked down at it for a moment, his lips shaping the words. 'I'm probably a bit rusty,' he said apologetically. 'But I'll do my best.'

Jane reached out and took Thomas's hand in hers as Ben scanned the faded words before him. And then, haltingly at first but growing in confidence, he began to read.

Dear Thomas,

I hardly know what I am writing or why. I do not know if you will even read this letter. Who knows what will have happened in the time since we said goodbye?

I know that you have a girl back home. You did not say so, but I know. But I'm allowed to think of you still. And hope for good things for you. I hope that you are safe in London.

I think of that night all the time. When I'm washing up, feeding the hens, braiding my hair, washing my face in the cold water. I remember how you walked towards me in the darkness and kissed me. Do you remember that? I felt nothing except panic.

Panic, not because I didn't want you to kiss me but because I did.

We had a terrific storm last night, on the island. The rain came down so hard that it sounded like gunfire on the tin roof. The sea was boiling, like in the old story. And in the morning, all the fish were lying on the beach. It was the strangest thing. As though nature itself was saying, 'Enough.'

I think of you while I look out across these wild beaches. How strange it is that we ever came together at all. You in London, drinking tea, and me here, with Lukas, bird-watching – how on earth did those worlds collide?

Thomas, I hope you get this letter. Perhaps you might save the stamp. I know you collect them. You are such a boy still.

I know why I write, after all. I write because I must talk to someone or go mad.

Your Marit

Dear Thomas,

I went for a long walk today, the length of the whole island. Dawn to dusk. Like a mad eccentric, with my mackintosh flapping in the wind and my great scarf wound about my neck. I took sandwiches and an apple from the orchard, and ate my lunch looking out at the fjord. If I squint and the day is clear, I can just about see the mainland. I could row across to it in – what, half an hour? Less? I'm bored, bored, bored – but not at all frightened, still, so there is that.

We have settled into a routine on the island, Lukas and I. He fishes in the morning, and I watch the birds through my glasses. We cook and eat supper together in the little kitchen. Every morning, every night, exactly the same.

I think of that dinner we ate in the cottage. The cigarettes smoked in the dark. Your voice rumbling in your chest against my ear when you spoke.

I said that I am not scared, and that is true, but I do want it all over. And when it is, I'm not going to spend any longer on an island full of old men and goats, that's for sure.

I shall go to New York and get work – as a secretary maybe, or a waitress. I don't mind what, so long as I get to eat in diners, wear nice clothes and travel the subway. And then Paris, maybe? London?

No, perhaps not London. I might run into a man with dark eyes and a scar, and that would be embarrassing for both of us.

What about you? Will you marry that childhood sweetheart? Take up the family business? I think that you will. You seem like a man who will do exactly what is expected of him, in the end.

Or you might find me, Thomas.

Your Marit

Dear Thomas,

It rained today, like it does most days. I did my chores and then some cooking – a great vat of mushroom soup, with dried herbs and stock cubes and powdered milk in place of anything good, like cream or butter. One of the farmer's children is sick and I thought I might take it to them. A dutiful neighbour. And then I sat indoors, smoking and drinking black tea, watching the raindrops chase themselves down the window. The rain was too heavy to see the fjord.

This dull old business of living a life. Pot of tea for one. One slice of bread. Brushing my teeth, putting up my hair. Washing out my stockings at night and hanging them up to dry. It feels so stupid. I miss Lukas, probably. He's gone to work on the fishboats for the next few weeks.

I'll tell you something that I do when I fall asleep: I try very hard to remember you that night. I think about your mouth on mine. Your eyes and your distinguished nose. The way your hair fell forward. Your short laugh, and the way you bit your knuckle because you were nervous. I think that I know you at once awfully well and not at all.

I've become very romantic since you last saw me. I think it's the boredom.

You're rich, aren't you, Thomas? You told me you were. Showing off a bit, weren't you?

Well, I still want to travel the world, so let's do that. Hotels with the softest beds, steak and champagne every night. I am awfully sick of potatoes, apple sauce and soup. I have to say that from where I'm sitting, that life doesn't sound bad at all.

Yes, you might find me, Thomas, when this is all over.

Your Marit

The final letter was, unlike the others, still in its envelope, stamped and addressed to Thomas Erikson, Maida Vale, London, England. Jane turned the envelope over in her fingers, tracing the faded ink.

The letter was briefer than the others and dated years later, 1945. *The end of the war,* Jane thought.

Dear Thomas,

This will be the last letter that I write.

I thought at first that I should not mind, but after all it is hard, writing and getting no reply. What goes through your mind when you get one of my letters? Does your heart leap?

You know it's over – I don't need to tell you so. But I am writing one last time because I think I should like someone to know how clever I have been. I managed, didn't I? So I thought you might like to have this memento. 'Well done, Marit,' I should like you to say.

You are the keeper of my secret and perhaps you might see it told.

Do that for me. And maybe one other thing. Come back one day. Come back to where we spent that last night, before our lives completely changed. Afterwards, you can go off and live a nice respectable life with your nice respectable girl. But come back to me, just once.

Your Marit

Ben's voice sounded softly in the quiet room as he spoke the last words. A lump of coal fell from the grate into the hearth and Jane jumped, disorientated by her return to the present.

The atmosphere those letters had cast over the room was not easily shaken off. The words were old, but Marit Elson – bold, sharp-tongued, trapped on an island but with dreams of travelling the world – seemed to have been sitting among them.

Jane looked at Thomas, sitting there, his face cast into shadow, eyes closed. It wasn't such a stretch to imagine him as a young man. Why had he never written back to her? And why now, after all these years, did he want to find her again? The romance that had leaped off the pages had cast its spell over her. She longed to discover the ending to Marit's story.

Ben cleared his throat and laid down the letter. Jane met his eyes, which, she noticed for the first time, were very clear and grey. His cheeks were slightly flushed from the fire. He folded the letters quickly, then rose abruptly, tripping over the rug.

They both looked at Thomas, who was lying back in his armchair, his eyes still half shut. Jane hesitated, unsure whether he was asleep or awake, when he spoke.

'Thank you,' he murmured. 'Thank you both very much.'

'Why did you never write back to her?' asked Jane, leaning forward. Her own voice was no more than a whisper.

Thomas didn't seem to have heard.

'Come on,' said Ben. 'He needs some rest.'

She half rose, but Thomas laid a hand on her wrist. His touch was as light as a feather.

'Would you stay, Jane?' he asked. 'I have one more thing to ask of you.'

'Of course,' said Jane, and Ben went quietly from the room.

There was a long, peaceful silence then, broken only by the soothing crackle of the low fire.

'Would you look for Marit?' Thomas said at last, his voice hopeful.

Slowly, Jane nodded. He smiled.

'I think that you will find her on an island still. An island near here, I think.' He closed his eyes. 'Take the letters with you, will you, while you find her? Ask Ben to translate them for you. Look after them for me.'

His breathing became gentle and even. Jane drew the plaid blanket more closely about him and then settled back into her own chair, her body leaden with fatigue. She felt her eyes drifting shut. The last thing she saw before she fell asleep was the fire flickering and dying in the grate, and the letters drifting from her fingers onto the floor.

16

When Jane awoke, it was dawn. She sat up in the armchair, easing her stiff neck. Thomas was still sleeping, his face peaceful, his breathing even. Jane rose, stretched and then kneeled and gathered up the letters, putting them carefully into their packet and stowing that in her bag. Then she crept quietly from the room.

The whole hotel was silent. She hesitated outside her room; her gaze was drawn to the trees outside, wreathed in mist. Her head felt thick and heavy, her body restless. She wanted to walk outside, among those trees. She pulled on her warm navy jumper, wound her scarf about her neck and walked downstairs. The hotel lobby clock told her that it was 4.30 a.m.

She wandered out into the thick mist, her ankles quickly becoming damp in the dew-sodden grass. Branches caught at her hair. She could hardly see more than a few feet in front of her. She stumbled, caught at a branch and laughed, torn between fear and exhilaration.

She felt drunk with exhaustion, drunk on the smell of pine, on the words she had heard last night. If Marit had laid herself open to love, if she had written to a man she hardly knew for years, then couldn't Jane also take a chance? Maybe Margot was right.

As she walked on, she thought she heard footsteps, treading carefully. Her heart began to pound. Was there someone else out here, or was it her mind, playing tricks on her?

And then, just like in a fairy tale, the mist parted. She was in a clearing, lit by a shaft of weak moonlight, and standing there, with his back to her, was a figure.

Philip.

Her chest tightened painfully. The rush of desire she had felt yesterday in the car came flooding back, heightened by the romance of Marit's letters. Her breath came quickly.

Jane took a step towards him, the memory of his lips on hers coming sharp and clear.

Another step.

'I thought I heard someone crashing about.'

The mist cleared and she saw clearly.

Not Philip.

Ben.

'What are you doing up so early?' he asked.

Jane laughed, rather shakily. 'I wanted a walk, but I had no idea where I was going.' She pushed her damp hair back from her forehead. 'You gave me a fright.'

She peered more closely at him. He was, she noticed, carrying a rod and a canvas bag. 'Are you going *fishing*? It's four thirty a.m.'

'I'm part-Norwegian,' he said, with his slow smile. 'Fishing is our thing. My parents' friends have a lake house just through the forest here – I told the husband I'd meet him at dawn for a boat trip. I won't catch anything: I never do. I think that's part of the reason Sven enjoys it so much.'

'Ben and Sven?' Jane said, laughing. 'Really?'

'What?' asked Ben.

'It's just . . . your names . . . rhyme,' said Jane, trailing off rather lamely.

'Oh, right,' he said, sounding confused. 'I don't suppose you'd like to come too? Sven would love to take a real tourist fishing.'

She shook her head automatically, and then, surprising herself, she said, 'Actually, you know what? I would love that. The full Norwegian experience.'

He smiled. 'Excellent. This way.'

She picked her way behind him through the trees, twigs crackling underfoot.

'So, last night was pretty intense,' she said. 'Listening to you read those letters.'

'It was intense for me reading them,' he agreed, pushing ahead. 'It must have been hard for Thomas too.'

'He seemed exhausted,' Jane said. 'He was asleep when I left.'

'I don't think he's as strong as he looks,' said Ben. 'And he's being dragged around on all these press activities.' He caught her elbow as the ground sloped beneath them. 'Still think there's a story there?'

'Maybe,' she said. She stumbled over a tree root. 'Where *are* we going?'

'There's an inlet down here where Sven keeps the boat.'

'I've already had one unscheduled hike through inhospitable terrain and I didn't like it,' said Jane with feeling. 'I don't want to get lost.'

'I might not be a famous survival expert,' said Ben, holding a branch back so that she could squeeze through, 'but I promise I won't get you lost.' He glanced at her. 'Have you thought about asking Thomas if you can use his letters for the *Courier* piece?'

'It's *all* I can think about,' she admitted. 'I was going to ask you to write me a translation so that I could read them over.'

'Sure,' he said. 'If Thomas is all right with it.'

'He suggested it. Here.' She handed him the packet and he put it carefully into his inside coat pocket. Jane chewed her lip. 'Don't you think it's weird she wrote to him for all those years without getting a reply? The woman Thomas describes sounds so . . . independent.'

'I don't know,' he replied. 'She may have been very much in love with him. Or maybe she was just lonely.' Ben suddenly pointed through the trees. 'Look, I told you I'd get us here in one piece. There's the fjord.'

As if by magic, they had descended into a little hollow, which opened up into a rocky harbour and, ahead of them, a great expanse of water, silver in the moonlight. There was a fishing boat waiting, and a stocky, kindly-looking man with a short, white beard gave them a wave.

'Benjamin!' he called, and Ben waved back.

They skidded down the shale path towards the fjord, the heady smell of the sea, salt, damp earth and the diesel from the boat engine all tangled up together.

'Sven,' said Ben warmly, and the men hugged.

'It's been too long. Who's this?'

Ben rested his hand briefly on Jane's arm. 'I hope you don't mind – I've brought a friend. This is Jane. She's a journalist on this Christmas-tree press shindig.'

Sven held out his hand for her to shake. It was warm, dry and calloused. 'Nice to meet you, Jane. Is there much to say about a tree being cut down?'

'You'd be surprised,' Jane smiled. 'It's good to meet you too.'

'Anyway,' said Ben, rumpling his hair, 'Jane's never been fishing before, so I asked her if she'd like to come along.'

'It isn't fishing if you don't catch anything, Ben,' Sven said, grinning. 'We should leave now. Fishing is best done before dawn.'

He climbed into the boat first, leaping nimbly and lightly onto the boards. Ben followed, holding out a hand to help Jane, who scrambled ungracefully after him. They settled themselves, Sven and Ben at either end and Jane perched on the seat in the middle. She offered to row, but Ben shook his head.

'You can row on the way back,' said Ben. 'When I'm tired out. In the meantime, have this.' He handed Jane an enormous yellow raincoat and she struggled into it. 'Very fetching,' he laughed, rolling up his sleeves to row.

They slipped through the water as silently as a darting fish. The fjord glistened in the moonlight like something out of a medieval tale. It started to rain lightly, no more than a faint, not unpleasant, spray. Ben rowed easily, and in her exhausted state, Jane found herself transfixed by his forearms, tensing and flexing as he rowed. She turned away quickly, looking out at the fjord.

'See that island?' Ben called, and she turned back. There were drops of rain on his cheeks. She followed his gaze to a dark hummock, in the mist no more than a blurred outline of rocks and trees. 'That's Otteroy. There are only a few local people living there – farmers, mostly. My little sister, Cathrin, and I were obsessed with the place. We'd swim across the fjord in the summer, with food in waterproof bags on our shoulders. We'd build a big fire and stay there till it was dark. Cook sausages and drink stolen wine, then swim back when it was too dark to see.'

'Didn't your parents worry?' Jane eyed the wide expanse of water and tried to imagine swimming across it even now, let alone as a child. Norwegian children must be fearless.

'No.' He shook his head. 'Well, I mean, they must have done, but they let us go anyway.' He grinned. 'Does that sound right, Sven?'

Sven laughed. 'Mine do what they please. I have no control. They're grown up now,' he explained to Jane. 'But I'll be worrying about them all their lives.'

Jane thought of her mother, Aileen, sending her off into the unknown, to London and university. Her first nights of terrible, gnawing homesickness, waking every morning with swollen red eyes. She had rung her mother every night for a week, curled up on her single bed, telling her what a mistake it was to have come at all.

'Please can I come home?' she had begged.

'No.' Her mother had tutted down the phone.

'But I don't have any friends, Mum.'

Aileen's voice had been firm, no-nonsense.

'Listen to me, Jane. You're going to get up off your bed, you're going to knock on the door of the room next to yours, and you're going to talk to whoever is in there. Do that and I bet that by the end of the week, you'll never want to come home again.'

Jane, ever obedient, had hung up the phone and walked into the hall, thick with smoke and the smell of stale beer, and knocked hesitantly on the door next to hers. Margot had been inside – Margot, wearing a Beta Band T-shirt and a splash of red lipstick, smoking a cigarette.

She glanced over at Ben, rowing in silence. He was, she thought, a very peaceful person, which was surprising given his job. They moved through the water with remarkable speed.

'Are you secretly sporty, Ben?' she asked, and he laughed.

'Do I not look it?' he said.

'Maybe you do,' she said. 'I must have been distracted by your mild-mannered persona.'

Ben responded to this by gently flicking water at her. 'I could surprise you yet.'

For a while it seemed as though there was no sound at all except their breathing, the lap of the waves and the soft splash of the oars. And then, with a little cold wind, the rain picked up and dashed across the lake as though sprinkled by an impatient, unseen hand. Jane caught Ben's eye and laughed, exhilarated.

'It's amazing,' she said. 'You were so lucky to grow up here.'

'I was,' he said. 'A dream childhood.'

Sven dropped his oars.

'We can fish here,' he said. 'But first, breakfast.' He reached for a tin pail at his feet and drew out greaseproof paper containing slices of black rye bread and herring.

'I never thought I'd eat herring for breakfast,' Jane said, eyeing it suspiciously. But to her surprise, out there in the fresh air, it tasted delicious. When she had finished, Sven handed her a little flask and she took a large swallow, expecting it to be coffee. She came up spluttering and gasping.

Ben laughed. 'Fishing breakfast always includes cognac.'

She took another mouthful, feeling the warmth sink into her chest. 'Really?'

'It helps with the cold.' He gave Sven a sly grin. 'And the boredom.'

But as the hours went by, Jane found that she wasn't bored. The rain eased off, leaving the air soft and the motion of the boat lulling. The night had left her exhausted, but pleasantly so. She dreamily watched the pale light move across the water and thought of Marit, bored, trapped for years on an island with only her brother, Lukas, for company.

Lukas . . . where had she heard that name before?

The press cuttings framed in the lobby! That was it. A local war hero, Lukas Gulbrandson, living on the island of Otteroy during the war, with only a few goat farmers on it.

She lifted her eyes to the mass of land before them and regarded it thoughtfully.

Marit had mentioned rowing across the loch to reach the mainland in her letters. If Lukas Gulbrandson, war hero, had been the brother Lukas of her letters, then this island would have been where Marit had spent the war. She might still be there. Or if not, then there might be family.

Ben's voice broke into her trance, making her start. 'It's nearly eight o'clock – we should go back,' he said. 'I don't want to mess Natasha around.'

Jane looked down. At her feet, there was a pile of silver fish.

'Not if we value our lives,' she said. 'Here, it's my turn to row. And your turn with this very attractive raincoat.'

Her hands ached almost immediately, but she soon found a rhythm that matched Sven's. As they were docking and Ben was busy tying up the boat, Jane squinted at the island again. It was worth a shot, she thought.

'The island over there.' She pointed it out to Sven. 'Otteroy, Ben said? People lived there, right, during the war?'

'They did,' Sven said. 'Not many, though. It was near a German naval base and I think people cleared out during the war, except for the most stubborn.'

'But people still live there now?'

'Oh yes. Holiday homes and farmers. Cottages stay in the family for generations in Norway. There's a ferry from the mainland – it's only a ten-minute crossing, if that.'

Jane stared out at the dark mass of land, biting her lip. Part of her wanted to ask Ben if he thought it could have been Marit's home during the war. But he thought she should back off for now, give Thomas some time. Something told her to keep quiet about her idea.

'Come on,' Ben called. 'Let's go and have some breakfast that isn't herring.'

They walked along the beach, Sven and Ben slightly ahead and Jane following. She was considering her options. If she left for the island now, she would make it back to the hotel in time for lunch. It would be her last chance before they headed to the ski resort later that day, and she longed to see the look on Thomas's face if she managed to locate his precious Marit.

Ben stooped suddenly and picked something up from the beach.

'What is it?' Jane asked, stopping beside him.

'Just a stone.' He was smiling to himself, looking down at a flat, grey pebble in his hand. 'Cathrin and I used to have competitions to find the best skimming stone.'

Sven stopped too, smiling. 'You two and your stones,' he said fondly. 'I always think of you both lining them all up to be judged.'

'Cathrin was the worst,' Ben said. 'I don't have a competitive bone in my body, but she was always a fighter.' There was something odd in his voice, Jane thought. He held the stone out and she took it.

She stared at the pebble, lying in her palm. Grey, even, light when she hefted it, the edges sanded smooth by the ocean. The daintiest of dark grey freckles, like a plover's egg. Perfect. Ben closed her fingers about it.

'For you,' he said. 'A souvenir of Norway.'

'Thank you,' said Jane. She slipped the stone into her pocket and held it loosely the rest of the way back, solid and warm in her fingers.

17

As she and Ben neared the hotel, Jane thought about what to do next. She needed someone to help her get to the island – someone who wouldn't ask too many questions or have any concerns about ditching the day's activities. She looked at Ben's profile thoughtfully as they walked, but decided against asking him. She needed someone unscrupulous, who took pleasure in doing the opposite of what anyone told him to do.

So, after telling Ben she was going to shower, Jane ran upstairs and rapped briskly on Philip's door. He let out an irritable, sleepy noise.

'Rise and shine,' she called.

When there was no reply beyond a low groan, she tried again.

'It's Jane. I need a favour.'

'I'm busy,' Philip called out. 'Sleeping.'

'You owe me after yesterday's debacle,' she said. 'Get dressed. I want you to drive me somewhere and we only have a few hours.'

Silence.

'I'll buy you a coffee at the ferry terminal,' she added persuasively.

'The *ferry* terminal?'

'I'll see you downstairs.'

She hurried to her room and put the photograph of Marit into her bag, along with her wallet. She had promised Philip a coffee, after all.

Downstairs, she checked his car was now out front and had just returned to the lobby when Philip emerged, rubbing his stubbled face and grimacing.

'Tell me this isn't to do with those bloody letters.'

'It's to do with those bloody letters,' she admitted. 'But the good news is, I think we have a lead.' She took him over to the framed cutting on the lobby wall. 'Look. Lukas Gulbrandson, local war hero, lived on the island of Otteroy, just across the fjord here. Marit mentions a Lukas in her letters.'

'You read them?' he said, raising his eyebrows. 'I thought that was against your moral code.'

'Thomas let me,' she said. 'Anyway, it would add up geographically. I know it's a bit of a punt, but I think it's worth checking out. There's an address for the cottage Lukas lived in during the war. No one knows Marit Elson, but someone might know Lukas Gulbrandson, war hero. Marit might have used a fake name if she was helping the king escape and the Nazis were about to invade.'

Philip stared at her for a moment, rubbing his jaw.

'She won't even be alive anymore,' he said. 'She'd be over a hundred.'

'I think he just wants to find her family. But if you don't want to come with me,' Jane said, 'I understand.' Then she added innocently, 'I know that this morning's activity is making Christmas wreaths.'

Philip shuddered. 'In that case,' he said, 'you're on.'

18

Thanks to some ferocious driving on Philip's part, they made the first ferry with time to grab a coffee from the van outside. The crossing was brief and Jane stood on deck, watching the island draw closer in the faint, grey daylight.

It was fanciful, but she found herself imagining Marit making this same journey back in 1940, in only a little fishing boat, having had the adventure of a lifetime. Why had Marit come here, to the island of Otteroy? Why had the woman who had dreamed of Paris, New York and London chosen to hide herself away on a little island, with only goats for company?

'Do you know where we're going once we arrive?' Philip asked, rubbing his eyes sleepily. He was staring down at the deep water.

'I think so,' said Jane, peering at the map on her phone, which was sketchy at best. 'This was Lukas Gulbrandson's cottage. And it would make sense with her letters. But it's probably nothing. Who knows if Lukas Gulbrandson even had a sister.'

Philip nudged her. 'Hey,' he said. 'Don't knock your journalistic instincts.'

She nodded. 'Let's just see,' was all she said.

They drove off the ferry and wound their way up the track road that the map said would take them to the Gulbrandson cottage. Jane found herself staring out of the window, looking for clues. They drove through an orchard and she realised they were apple trees – the orchard that Marit had talked about in her letters, she thought excitedly. Hens and goats clustered by the sides of the road. It seemed as though nothing much had changed in all those decades.

They parked outside a crimson cottage. It looked demure, with bright curtains in the windows. Through the silvery light of the morning, Jane could make out a gravel path leading down to the beach – it would be lovely in summer. Jane flipped down the mirror and smoothed her fringe. Her hair was tangled and windswept from the boat trip across the loch. She caught Philip looking and pulled a face at him.

'Might as well at least try and look professional. Didn't get much sleep last night.'

'Neither did I,' he said, his eyes teasing. 'Something was keeping me up.'

'Indigestion?' she said, snapping up the mirror.

'Ha. Nope.'

He reached out a hand and stroked the nape of her neck, a gentle touch that made the hairs on the back of her arms stand on end.

'I was thinking about kissing you in the car yesterday and how nice that was.' He smiled at her. 'You look beautiful this morning. All pale and bedraggled like some sort of nymph from the fjord.'

She shook her head at him, feeling a flush creep into her cheeks.

'You're mixing your mythologies.' She tore her gaze away, then scanned her phone one more time. 'This *must* be it. Ready?'

He nodded, withdrawing his hand from her neck. The distracting flutter in her chest subsided. Jane scooped up her bag, and they stepped out of the car.

It was raining heavily now, and they were soaked by the time they reached the porch. At the cottage door, Jane raised a hand to knock, only for two children to come tumbling out, both with fat brown curls and pink cheeks, dressed in impressive-looking wet-weather gear. They stopped abruptly, startled, and stared at Philip and Jane with wide eyes.

Two people appeared behind them, an attractive woman in her late thirties and a handsome man with blue eyes and a clipped black beard flecked with grey. They were also wearing raincoats, and a dog frolicked on a lead. They were clearly about to go out for the day and the whole family looked like some sort of advert for healthy Norwegian living.

They looked at Jane and Philip curiously. The man said something in Norwegian and Jane said apologetically, 'Sorry – only English, I'm afraid.'

'Can we help you?' the woman asked.

'My name is Jane Brook,' said Jane, extending her hand. 'I'm a journalist,' she added. She drew out her card and gave it to them. 'I was asked by a friend to try and find someone for him, someone he knew at the very start of the war. This woman,' she said, holding out the photograph Thomas had given her. 'I think she lived in this cottage during the war with her brother, Lukas Gulbrandson, who was a war hero.'

The man nodded. 'Lukas Gulbrandson was our grandfather. He did have a sister.' He held out his hand. 'I am Iacob Gulbrandson, and this is my sister, Susan Hansen.' Jane and Philip shook their hands.

'My friend knew her as Marit Elson,' Jane went on. 'Anything you can tell me would be helpful.'

Susan took her arm. 'Let's get inside out of this rain.'

They huddled in the hallway and the children began tugging off their rain gear with delighted shrieks. Iacob stared at the photograph for a long moment and then handed it to his sister.

'Is it . . .?' he asked, in English, and she nodded, frowning.

'I think so,' she said.

He turned to Jane and Philip. 'Yes, I think we know her – although not as Marit Elson. Please, come in.'

Jane and Philip followed them through to a light, airy kitchen, and Iacob bustled around them all making coffee, while the children rolled around on the rug, laughing hysterically.

'Sorry for interrupting your day,' Jane said.

'Oh, not to worry,' said Susan. 'We're on holiday, no real plans. The kids are delighted to get out of a walk, in this weather. But I have to give them a run each day – they're like dogs. My husband will be joining us later, so he can deal with the fallout.' She smiled. 'If you'd come a day earlier, we'd have all been in Oslo and the cottage would have been shut up.'

Iacob set down a little cafetière and a plate of pale yellow biscuits, a dab of jam on each one. 'Wait one moment,' he said. 'Let me get the photograph of Great-Aunt Margaret and then we can be sure.'

When he returned a moment later, he laid another photograph next to Jane's on the table.

'It's her,' he said.

His sister nodded. 'Dear woman.'

'Margaret Elton,' he said. 'She died about ten years ago, in a hospital in Vienna. She is buried in Austria, where she was living at the time.'

So Marit was dead.

And not Marit Elson but Margaret Elton. Jane looked down at the two photographs, side by side, undoubtedly of the same woman, although changed by the years. The one that Thomas had given her showed a formidable young woman, wearing a sensible tweed suit. And the other showed an older woman, glamorous, with waved hair under a dashing little hat and furs drawn about her shoulders. Still that strong jaw, though, and the gaze that looked you dead in the eye.

'She was Norwegian, though,' Jane said, and the man nodded.

'My great-aunt was born in Norway, not far from here. But she went to Europe at the end of the war. This is our holiday cottage now, the same one that she lived in with her brother during the war.' He smiled. 'We come and spend weekends here, but you hardly ever get tourists in the winter. That's why we were so surprised to see you.'

'She must have changed her name after the war, then,' said Jane. 'Do you know why?'

'To suit her English life, she always said. She lived in London for a time and then she hopped around all over, went where the work was. She was a photographer, a good one. She worked as a . . .' He gestured with his hand and turned to Susan. 'I don't know the English word.'

'Photojournalist,' Susan said. 'Photos for the papers.'

'That's it.' He looked at Jane. 'This is for a friend of yours who knew Auntie during the war?'

'Sort of.' Jane stared at the photos, tapping her pen against her teeth. Philip remained quiet beside her, his expression thoughtful. 'I met an old man called Thomas Erikson recently – we're on a press trip together over on the mainland. He's something of a local celebrity . . .'

Susan nodded. 'I know the name. A hero like my grandfather. What did he have to do with Auntie?'

'Marit was there when the village of Nybergsund was bombed by the Luftwaffe. She helped the king on the road to safety.'

Iacob stared at her. 'Auntie *Margaret*?'

'She never told you?'

Iacob shook his head, looking dazed. 'No. We always understood she lived quietly here on the island during the war. Are you sure?'

Jane nodded. 'She helped them plot a route into the mountains and get the king out. Thomas – well, he spent a night with her in a little cottage outside of Nybergsund. He never forgot her. She wrote to him for years. She sounds like an amazing woman.'

Iacob was still shaking his head. Susan laughed suddenly.

'Well, it doesn't surprise *me*, Iacob,' she said. 'Auntie Margaret was always vague about her past, but she was very cool under pressure. You could put her in any city and she could find her way without a map. She used to say that all she needed to get by was her brains and her camera. I can absolutely imagine her doing something like that.'

Iacob smiled fondly. 'It is true. She used to flit in and out of our lives growing up. We'd hear nothing for months and then suddenly she would appear in our flat in Oslo having just flown in from Paris with macaroons, or we'd get a postcard from St Peter's Basilica in Rome.' He looked down at the photographs on the table. 'Always very chic, very smartly dressed. Never staying anywhere for very long. "Wild", our granny used to call her.'

Susan laughed again. 'Perhaps she was jealous.'

'Probably. She adored us children. And we loved her.'

Exactly what Marit had said she wanted, then, Jane thought. She had travelled the world, just as she had longed to do.

Jane said, 'Thomas wanted me to find Marit or her family. Now that I have, would it be all right if I put you in touch? Perhaps the two of you can piece together a picture of Marit *and* Margaret.'

'I should like that.' Iacob grinned, shaking his head again in disbelief. 'Who would have thought that Auntie had it in her?'

Susan laid a hand over his.

'I think we always knew she would surprise us till the end, didn't we? That was the sort of woman she was.' She smiled at Jane. 'Tell your friend to get in touch with us when he's ready. I should like very much to find out about his Marit.'

19

On the ferry back, Jane could feel a familiar excitement rising in her, the feeling she had when a story started to take shape. It would be different to her usual work, but the emotions of this story rooted in the past had captured her imagination. *Marit* had captivated her. She still had so many questions. And she wanted to find the answers.

She shook herself, staring out across the fjord as the mainland neared. It wasn't *her* story, not yet at least. It was Thomas's.

Philip glanced at her, his expression amused. 'What are you thinking about?' he asked. 'I can practically hear the cogs whirring.'

'Oh, just that Thomas will be pleased,' said Jane. 'I found out who Marit is. There are family members for him to contact now, if he wants to know more about her.'

'You've done a good deed,' said Philip. 'And you were very sexy in journalist mode. I would have told you anything.' He held her gaze just a shade too long, and then they both looked away, laughing.

All this romance was catching, Jane thought to herself.

Back at the hotel, Jane packed hastily, arriving in the lobby at speed, to find it empty except for Natasha, looking immaculate in another Scandinavian-inspired jumper, jeans and snowboots, flicking through a magazine. She looked up at Jane with barely concealed dislike.

'If you don't want to do *anything* we've organised,' she snapped, flicking a page viciously, 'then why did you come? You missed the Christmas-wreath weaving session and the biscuit decorating.'

'I'm sorry,' Jane said. 'I didn't sleep well last night. Had to catch up.'

'Really,' said Natasha coldly. 'Because when I knocked on your door, I got housekeeping.'

Freddie, Lena and Lucy arrived then, lugging their suitcases, with Sandra and Nick following after and Ben bringing up the rear.

'Convenient that you *and* Philip were missing,' continued Natasha loudly, turning another page of the magazine with venomous force. 'Again.'

Jane saw Thomas come in and hurried over to him.

'Could I speak to you for a moment?' she asked quietly. 'Alone, perhaps?'

He followed her into a little side room off the main reception and sat down in an armchair.

'You look as though you have news, my dear,' he said.

'I do.'

She sank to her knees beside the chair and took a deep breath, remembering Ben's words of caution. Thomas might not be as strong as he seemed.

'I found Marit's family,' she said softly, considering the impact of the news she had to bear. 'I was out on the fjord this morning and it just occurred to me that the island near here, Otteroy, might have been where she spent the war. I went over to have a look and I found her cottage.'

There was a silence and Jane laid her hand on Thomas's.

'She died about ten years ago, I'm afraid. But she had an extraordinary life. She went to England after the war and became Margaret Elton.' He nodded slowly, his expression unreadable. 'She was a photographer, travelled the world. Her relations have the cottage now.'

Thomas nodded again. He looked, thought Jane, not distressed but distracted.

'And you have the name of these relations?' he said.

'I do. And they gave me this.' She handed him the later photograph of Margaret Elton. Thomas looked closely at it, an odd smile lifting his lips. Jane watched, wondering what was going through his mind.

'They're called Susan Hansen and Iacob Gulbrandson,' Jane said. 'They'd like to hear from you. They couldn't believe it when I told them Marit had played a part in the king's escape.'

Thomas looked up at her, a frown on his face. 'They had no idea of what she did that night in Nybergsund?' he said.

'None at all,' Jane said. 'They were amazed.'

'I shall be in touch with them,' Thomas said. 'Thank you, my dear.' There was finality in his tone.

Jane hesitated before she spoke again.

'Thomas, I'd love to talk to you about doing a story,' she began.

Thomas was still looking down at the photograph.

'That's certainly something I would consider,' he said, his voice distant. 'But there are one or two things I need to weigh up first.'

The note of dismissal in his voice was more pronounced and Jane immediately felt guilty. She'd got carried away.

'I'm sorry if this came as a shock—' she started, but Thomas was turning towards the door.

'I think I hear the cars arriving,' he said. 'It is time to say goodbye to the forest.'

20

The journey to the ski resort was broken at a pretty little village with an organic deli and several expensive clothing boutiques that seemed at odds with its rustic charm.

'You get one hour,' called Natasha as they left the coach. Thomas stayed behind on the coach – resting, he said.

They wandered through pretty cobbled streets, the bloggers stopping to take photos. Nick, Natasha and Philip walked ahead, with Ben and Jane falling behind.

'Do you think Thomas is OK?' Jane asked Ben.

'Why wouldn't he be?' he said, and Jane ducked her head guiltily. 'Jane?' he asked. 'What did you do?'

'I found Marit's family,' she said. 'On the island in the fjord. That's where I was this morning.'

'You got the ferry?' he asked, surprised.

'Yes – Philip drove me.' Ben was silent and Jane found herself carrying on rather hastily. 'And I met Marit's family. She's dead, but it sounds like she had an amazing life. Maybe I could have told him a bit more sensitively . . .' She shook her head. 'He can't have expected her to be alive after all this time.'

There was another silence. 'He's probably just absorbing it,' Ben said at last. 'While I remember – here.' He handed her the little oilskin packet. 'I put a rough translation of the letters in there for you. It's not very flowery, I'm afraid. I'm not good at that stuff.'

Jane squeezed his arm. 'Thanks,' she said. 'Now I just have to hope he lets me use them for the story.'

'What are you two talking about?' Philip turned around. He was watching them closely and Jane found herself quickly dropping Ben's arm.

'Ben translated Thomas's letters for me,' she said.

'How helpful of you, Ben,' said Philip. 'You're always turning up, being helpful, aren't you? It's like your special power.'

'At least I'm not running out of petrol on deserted country roads,' said Ben.

'We're stopping here,' called Natasha, halting abruptly in front of them outside a picturesque café. She eyed them thoughtfully. 'I think we all need to take a break.'

In the café, they sat chatting over hot chocolate. Natasha clinked a spoon against her cup for attention and everyone stopped talking.

'As you'll know from the itinerary, which I assume you have committed to memory, skiing is on the agenda for tomorrow,' she said. 'Is there anyone who wouldn't like to? There's a beginners' slope, and there will be a refresher lesson in the morning with our instructor' – she glanced at the sheet – 'Daniel, and his assistant.'

'Not for me,' said Sandra, draining her cup. 'I haven't been up a ski slope in over thirty years, and I hated it then. I'm assuming there's a spa – that's where I'll be.'

'Me neither, I'm afraid,' said Nick. 'My old bones aren't up to it. I had a knee op last year.'

'Fine,' said Natasha, her nostrils flaring slightly. 'The rest of you?'

Lucy, Lena and Freddie signed up enthusiastically. Jane could just imagine them whizzing down the slopes, making it look easy.

'Do you fancy it?' Ben asked Jane. '*Can* you ski?'

Jane hesitated. Last winter, with one of his grand, impulsive gestures, Simon had taken her away on a skiing trip. She'd had a week's worth of intensive ski lessons, been told she was a natural and had been cheerfully skiing down the red runs by the time she had left. She'd loved every minute of it – the open air, the mountains, the keen hunger after a day on the slopes and the cosy dinners afterwards. But that had been a year ago. She wouldn't have a clue how to do it now.

'I don't know,' she said. 'I think I'll probably sit this one out.'

'There's a surprise,' muttered Natasha irritably. 'Look, at least have the lesson. It's Norway. It's virtually flat.'

'Come on,' said Philip, sitting to Jane's left. 'You'll love it.'

He dropped his voice, so that only she could hear, and murmured directly into her ear, 'I promise I'll catch you if you fall.'

Jane felt a delicious shiver run up her spine. The thought of being on the slopes with Philip made up her mind. If anything was going to tip their flirtation over into full-on romance, then it would be this.

'All right,' she said. 'I'll do it.'

'So glad we could convince you,' said Natasha, and made an ostentatious tick next to her name. Just then, Jane's phone began to ring. Nadine, calling from the office.

'I've got to take this,' she said, and ducked outside.

'Jane, hello,' said Nadine, her voice crisp and businesslike as always. 'How are things in the land of the midnight sun?'

'Good,' said Jane. 'Everything you promised and more. And tonight we're going to a ski lodge with a hot tub.'

'Wonderful,' said Nadine drily. 'You certainly sound chipper.'

'I've had a bit of an adventure, actually,' said Jane. 'I met an old man out here called Thomas Erikson who used to be in the Norwegian Army. One of the soldiers who helped King Haakon escape to Britain. Anyway, the night before the king escaped, Thomas had a fling with a local girl. She wrote to him for years without reply and he hid her letters in a chimney breast at the end of the war. He's thinking of her now, at the end of his life, and he sent me off to find her letters.'

'Which you did?' asked Nadine.

'Of course,' said Jane proudly. 'And not only that, I traced the woman too. Marit Elson. She lived in Norway during the war, but afterwards she changed her name to Margaret Elton, moved to Europe and spent the rest of her life travelling as a photographer. "Wild", her sister-in-law called her.'

'While her soldier lover had a quiet life in Norway?'

'Yes. Bit of a role reversal, wasn't it?'

'Hmm,' said Nadine. Jane could practically hear her brain whirring. 'Do you think there's a story here?'

'Yes,' Jane said. 'And I think I could tie it in with the Christmas tree. Watching it get cut down was very moving, in a way.'

Nadine cackled. 'Don't tell me that it melted your Grinch-like heart?'

'Let's not get carried away.' Jane screwed up her eyes, thinking about the story. 'I could begin the piece by setting out on the trip, the bloggers, the amazing perks . . .'

'And then,' continued Nadine, 'this tale of shallow commercialism takes an unexpected turn as we discover a heart-warming love story, decades old . . . Faded letters, telling the story of wartime courage. Can you quote the letters, do you think?'

'I can't do *any* of this yet,' said Jane regretfully. 'I haven't got Thomas Erikson's permission.'

'But do you think you could get it?' asked Nadine.

'I don't know,' said Jane. 'He didn't say no, exactly. I think he just needs a bit of time to digest it all. He seems a bit stunned.'

'Hang on.' Jane could hear Nadine's muffled voice barking instructions, and then she said, 'Jane, we're setting aside a feature for this in the Christmas edition. If Thomas Erikson is amenable, you can get cracking with my blessing. Go to town on it. I want my heart strings thoroughly tugged.'

'Got it,' Jane said gleefully.

She hung up as the others began filing out of the café and onto the coach.

'Come on, Jane,' called Natasha, all but tapping her foot.

When they reached the ski resort at Trysil, Jane felt obscurely disappointed. The resort was heaving with life, full of shrieking groups of skiers drinking beer and hot chocolate. After the magical isolation of the forest, Jane now felt very much part of the modern world.

She was getting spoiled, she told herself.

'Was that Nadine on the phone earlier?' said Ben, as the coach wound its way through the streets.

'It was,' said Jane.

He frowned. 'She's given you the go-ahead, then? What's the angle?'

'Not sure yet,' said Jane. She could sense that Ben wouldn't approve of her and Nadine's plotting. 'I'll try and come up with something. I don't want it to be too cheesy.'

'I hope it's properly heart-warming,' Ben said. 'Make sure you mention the husky dogs. I got some great pictures.'

'I'll see what I can do,' Jane said.

'If you can't lay on the cheese at Christmas, when can you? Although, that might damage your tough-as-nails reputation.' He turned to Nick, who was staring out of the window, looking anxious. 'What about you, Nick? Are you inspired?'

'I *want* to write about how we should mirror our government's hospitality to the Norwegians by extending our hospitality to refugees,' said Nick gloomily. 'It would almost definitely get me sacked.'

Ben laughed. 'It'd be worth it. And Sandra? A searing dissection of the cured meats?'

She gave him one of her rare smiles. 'A "stay warm the Norwegian way" recipe special.'

'Staying warm has been the theme of this trip,' chimed in Lucy. 'Look how many likes that fireplace in the hotel got on my 'Gram.'

She held out her phone, scrolling past posts of the last few days, and Jane watched as a curated vision of their trip so far sped past her eyes. The girls drinking hot chocolate outside a market stall, sipping cocktails on the rooftop bar, petting the husky dogs, their eyes bright and smiles wide under their woolly hats. And other moments too, less glamorous ones – a picture of Lena next to a fishing boat with a caption about how Greenpeace was bringing pressure on the Norwegian government to agree fishing quotas. Lucy had told a story too, as edited as Jane's article would be, only with pictures instead of words.

Jane remembered the article she'd begun for Nadine at the start of the trip, with its nasty bit about shallow fashion bloggers, and felt glad that they would never see it.

The ski lodge itself was impressive: a vast wooden building, divided into three separate houses, with pointed roofs. Behind it, a hot tub could be glimpsed, steaming amid the snow. Dusk was falling and the lodge glowed brightly in the twilight. Inside were tall ceilings, wooden floors, comfortable sofas and roaring fires. It was all expensive and luxurious, but Jane couldn't shake the sense of unease that had started when they left the forest. She was conscious that the trip was nearing its end – and real life would begin again.

'Downstairs in two hours for canapés and cocktails,' called Natasha as they headed up to their rooms. 'And then it's a club night.'

There was a resigned chorus of assent.

'And that means *all* of you.' Her brow furrowed as she consulted her phone. 'Some big-name DJ is playing, apparently.' She smiled maliciously. 'Sounds exactly your sort of thing, Jane.'

'Absolutely,' Jane said meekly.

No wriggling out of this one, she told herself.

Inside the comfortable but rather bland suite, Jane laid out her clothes. She pulled on her swimming costume, in case there was no getting out of the hot tub either, then threw on jeans and a jumper over the top. She set up her laptop and opened the document for her *Courier* article. She had yet to secure Thomas's permission for the story, true, but there was no reason she shouldn't draft it and copy out the letters. He could only say no.

She read back over what she'd written that first day and shook her head. After all that had happened, it seemed mean-spirited and bitchy. If you couldn't be decent and sentimental at Christmas, then when could you be?

She laid the letters out in front of her along with Ben's translation and began typing them out, the age-old words filling the page. Certain words and phrases jumped out at her.

I felt nothing except panic.

Panic, not because I didn't want you to kiss me but because I did.

Had Jane in her life ever felt that way about another person? Simon, for instance? With some distance, it seemed as though Thomas and Marit had known each other better after one night than she and Simon had after a year.

The weak light had faded to that eerie bluish dark by the time Jane had finished. She rubbed her eyes, which felt gritty. She felt keyed up, nervous. Perhaps it was the thought of the evening ahead.

Or perhaps it was the simmering flirtation with Philip Donnelly that was unsettling her. Whatever was going on between them seemed to be reaching a head. Something was about to happen that would tip their tentative relationship over into . . . something else. All her promises to Margot that she would seize the day were about to be tested, and she wasn't sure she was ready for it. She sighed. She'd misjudged Philip that first evening, she thought. He was more than just suave charm and rugged good looks. He'd jumped into this adventure with her feet-first and teased and flirted with her every step of the way.

The problem wasn't that Jane didn't want something to happen – it was that she was no longer sure she wanted the casual fling Margot had in mind.

Margot. Jane could just imagine her disapproving face.

There was a knock on her door. Jane found Natasha standing outside. She was wearing another of her chunky sweater dresses that stopped mid-thigh. How many had she packed? Jane wondered.

'I said I was coming,' said Jane, half outraged and half amused. 'You didn't need to come and escort me.'

Natasha smirked.

'Experience would suggest otherwise, so I decided to pull rank.' She gave Jane a curious look. 'Besides, I want to know what you and Philip have been up to. Ferry trips, secret excursions – why?' She watched as Jane picked up her key card.

'I have no idea what you're talking about,' said Jane, ushering her outside. She could already hear the distant, pounding beats of the music and repressed a shudder. 'Shall we go? I'd hate to miss a minute of this.'

Downstairs was a raucous scene, and Jane thought longingly of the forest and its serene, solitary calm. Loud music was coming from some decks in the corner, presided over by a DJ who looked about fifteen. Waiters carried trays of multicoloured drinks, and there was a large crowd of hearty-looking skiing types, all downing shots and dancing enthusiastically, if not well.

'Jane,' said Freddie, appearing at Jane's side. 'Are you having fun yet?'

'Erm,' said Jane, looking in alarm as someone in the corner of the hall began to juggle fire. She was offered a shot from one of the trays, and after a moment's hesitation, she downed it. She needed something to get through this. 'Not my thing,' she confessed, as the alcohol hit her bloodstream.

'You don't say,' said Freddie, her eyes dancing at Jane over her glass. 'You definitely seem like someone who would enjoy clubbing. The impulsive type.'

'Ha, ha,' said Jane. 'As it so happens, on this trip I am being *extremely* impulsive. My best friend gave me strict instructions to behave badly in Norway.'

'And how's that working out for you?' said Freddie.

'I'm not entirely sure,' Jane said honestly, accepting another lurid drink from a waiter wearing flashing antlers.

Lucy appeared, looking adorably fresh in a delicate wrap dress covered with sprigged holly.

'Can we go to bed yet?' she said, as a waiter walked past wearing only a bow tie and hot pants. She held her hand to her eyes. 'I feel like I'm on some weird hen-do. This is *not* going on my Instagram. How long do you think we have to stay?'

The waiter started pouring shots from a bottle at his belt.

'And do you think they've slightly misjudged their audience? I mean, what exactly are they going for here? Nordic by way of Ibiza?'

Natasha came over, grabbed two shot glasses and drained both within seconds.

'This is awful,' she said, putting the empty glasses down. 'I admit it. But it's all OK – I have a plan.' She gestured to a waiter who was trailing behind her carrying a massive ice bucket containing a bottle of champagne and one of schnapps. 'Come on,' said Natasha. 'And we'll need glasses. Right, you three – outside, now. The deck is heated, and at least,' she said, eyeing the waiter unfavourably, 'everyone will be fully dressed.'

Outside, it was all a lot more civilised, although Jane's ears were still ringing from the pounding music. There were benches and cushions on the wooden deck, flickering braziers and music playing low.

Sandra and Nick were sitting on a bench, bundled up warmly and drinking steaming hot toddies. They were deep in conversation with Ben. He was wearing his navy pea coat and a grey scarf, the light from the brazier casting shadows along his cheekbones. He had a nice face, Jane suddenly realised. A face that grew on you.

'Before you say anything,' Sandra said warningly to Natasha as they approached, 'I tried it in there. I gave it a good shot, but I could *not* stay another moment. Someone tried to squirt alcohol into my mouth from a water pistol.'

Natasha waved a hand breezily and dumped down the

bucket. 'I don't blame you for leaving,' she said. 'I endorse the decision. We're escaping too.'

'Well,' said Sandra, mollified. 'In that case, please do join us.' She eyed the schnapps. 'That will warm us all up nicely.'

Natasha poured the schnapps into shot glasses. 'And sparkling water for Freddie,' she murmured.

'You don't drink?' said Sandra, turning to the girl. 'I think I'm ninety per cent wine at this point in my life.'

'Never have, never will, I don't think,' Freddie said. 'Don't like the taste. Don't really fancy it either. I've seen too many people behaving like idiots after a few drinks.'

'So young, so wise,' said Natasha, handing out the shot glasses. 'But it makes you look cool, right? Now, everyone, down in one.'

'Honestly,' said Nick, looking put out. 'This is really good schnapps. We can't just down it.'

'Oh, I think we can,' said Natasha, fixing him with a firm look. 'Come on. One . . . two . . . three!'

They all drank, spluttered and then burst out laughing, their eyes streaming. Jane had dribbled some schnapps down her chin. Freddie, sipping her mineral water, looked at them with amusement.

'You're right,' she said. 'I get it now. Hand me some schnapps. Drinking *does* make you look cool.'

'I wish I had your willpower,' sighed Sandra, wiping her eyes. 'Mind you, I think I only really started drinking properly when I had children. Before that, I could take it or leave it. But the children – they pushed me over the edge. By the time Reg got home after work and the kids were asleep, I would be slumped on the sofa eating something very un-gourmet, like Dairylea triangles and crisps, with half a bottle of wine already gone and the entire flat covered in toys and old food.'

'Did he mind?' asked Freddie, and Sandra laughed.

'Mind? He'd sit right next to me and rub my feet.' Her eyes went misty. 'He was a man in a thousand.' She shook her head. 'Children are great, particularly mine, but I miss my partner in crime.'

'What happened to him?' Ben asked.

'Cancer,' Sandra said briefly. 'It's a real bastard.'

'It really is,' Ben agreed, with feeling in his voice.

'You're lucky, though,' said Lucy. 'At least you had someone.' Her voice was sad.

Freddie nudged her. '*You* have someone, Luce,' she said. 'You have Harry, who adores you and is also adorable.'

'Yeah, he is,' said Lucy, chewing her lip, her eyes troubled. 'He really is.' She shook her head. 'Hey, I thought we were doing shots?'

'We sure are,' crowed Natasha, pouring them all another round. 'Everyone, drink. I'm in charge here.'

They obeyed her more quickly this time, and Jane found that she was getting used to the burning sensation in her chest. She felt suddenly immensely cheerful and fond of everyone around her. Even Natasha.

'What about you?' Jane asked Natasha. 'Do you have a . . . person?'

Natasha smiled at her benignly. 'A person? How politically correct of you. But the answer is, no, I don't have a person. Zero people in my life. Or let me rephrase that . . .' She smiled. 'There are actually quite a *lot* of people. In fact, too many to be specific.'

Freddie giggled. 'That's the attitude. Plenty of time to settle down.'

'Who says I even want to settle down?' said Natasha, frowning as she poured more schnapps, lining up the glasses with owlish concentration. 'They call it "settle" for a reason.

A mug's game, if you ask me, commitment.' She jerked her head at Jane. 'It is obvious, for instance, that Jane here is in recovery.'

'From what?' said Jane.

'Heartbreak,' said Natasha thoughtfully. 'I originally thought it happened in the last three months, but now I'm putting it closer – within the last month.'

Jane tested herself for the reflexive shock of pain she felt whenever she thought about Simon, but Natasha's words didn't sting as they once might have. The heartache of Simon was still there, but it was buried under layers of schnapps and the memory of Philip's mouth on hers. 'Five weeks ago exactly,' she said, counting them on her fingers. 'Spot on.'

'God. Still raw, then,' said Freddie sympathetically. 'No wonder you seem so . . . well . . .'

'So *what*?' asked Jane indignantly.

'Nothing, nothing,' said Freddie soothingly. 'You seem fine. What happened?'

'Well, he was someone I worked with,' said Jane. She wasn't sure why she was telling them all about it, but the schnapps had loosened her tongue. 'Ben knows him,' she added.

'Slightly,' said Ben. He was looking at his hands. 'Enough to get a strong whiff of pompous condescension.'

'Hey!' said Jane defensively. 'Simon isn't pompous. He's really smart.'

'He called me Sam for six months,' Ben said.

'He's really smart, but sometimes he's bad with names,' Jane explained to the others.

'So, an office romance?' asked Lena.

'Yeah. Which is a terrible idea in the first place,' said Jane.

'What on earth were you thinking, Jane?' said Nick. 'Journalists love a gossip. Unless you're above all that over at the lofty *Courier*.'

Jane shook her head. 'No, everyone gossiped about us all right. But I didn't mind too much. I was so carried away. He made a real fuss of me at the start. And he was so . . . perfect.'

Ben snorted. 'Simon Layton? Perfect? Really?'

She waved her hand at him. 'Oh, he *was*. Smart and good-looking. But he had an ex' – Lena groaned knowingly – 'and she was *also* really . . . perfect. You know? They just matched. Pretty and smiley and sort of . . . glossy.'

They all nodded, watching her sympathetically. 'Anyway,' said Jane. 'I was working on a big story, the immigration scandal, and it all took off and, well, he found that hard.'

There was a silence and then Sandra cleared her throat. 'Just to clarify. *He* found it hard that *you* were working on a big story?'

Jane nodded. 'Yeah. I was never around, always missing dates. He said he felt . . .' She swallowed, as the memory of that dreadful day she had received Simon's email came back to her. 'He said he felt "invisible".'

'That was the story of the year,' Ben said softly. 'It was worth a few cancelled dates.'

'Abso-bloody-lutely,' hooted Sandra. 'Good riddance if you ask me. It sounds like this Simon chap has what I think we'd call a fragile ego.'

Jane sighed. 'Maybe. It must have been hard for him. Anyway, we broke up and then he went back to his ex, and I've just been . . . drifting ever since.' She finished her drink and noticed with interest that the earnest faces in front of her were rotating slightly. 'I don't know why it upset me so much,' she said. 'I really don't. It just knocked me sideways.'

'Some break-ups do that to you,' said Sandra kindly, patting her back. She topped up Jane's glass. 'It's not about the person. It's about what they represent.'

'That's true,' said Freddie. 'It's nothing to do with them and everything to do with you. Or what they represented to you.'

'Really?' said Jane. 'What did Simon represent to me?'

Natasha pointed an elegant finger at her, which wavered only slightly. 'I can answer that. Commitment,' she said firmly. 'Security. That sort of rubbish. You wanted all that stuff and so you projected it onto this Simon fellow, whether he could give it to you or not.'

Jane stared. 'I'm not sure that's true,' she said. 'We never even talked about the future.'

Had she wanted all that? If she was honest, the answer was a big 'yes'. Only it didn't seem so appealing anymore.

Natasha shrugged and downed the rest of her drink. 'Doesn't mean you didn't want it,' she said. 'Doesn't mean that if this basic-sounding Simon guy hadn't gone down on one knee with some basic ring that he bought at some basic jeweller's where all his basic mates got their rings, you wouldn't have said "yes". Am I right?'

'Maybe,' Jane said. Everything was muddled by the haze of schnapps. She could barely remember Simon's face, she realised. Maybe all that heartache *had* been for a dream, not a person. She thought of Marit, striking out for Europe and a life of adventure. She wouldn't have settled for the conventional life.

'See?' said Freddie smugly. 'Simon was neither here nor there. It was all about you. I was right.'

'Right about what?' came a languorous voice, and Jane felt a flush creeping up her cheeks as Philip joined them. He slipped into the seat next to Jane and she felt the warmth of his arm against hers. 'What are you all talking about?'

'Oh, nothing,' said Natasha, after a pause, and Jane felt a wave of gratitude towards her. 'We were just comparing war stories. Broken hearts and bastard men and all that.' She gave him a level look. 'Not something you'd know much about, I'm sure.'

'God, no,' said Philip. 'Not a thing.'

'Look at all this snow,' said Sandra, beaming around. She bent down and scooped some up into her mittened hands and absently patted it into a sizeable, neatly rounded ball. 'It's almost enough for a snowball fight.' With a swift movement, she drew back her arm and unleashed the snowball, and the next thing Philip was spluttering and wiping snow from his eyes.

'What did you do that for?' he gasped.

'Oh, I don't know,' said Sandra, smiling. 'I just felt like it.'

'In that case . . .' Philip ducked down, picked up a handful of snow and caught Sandra squarely in the face. She let out a decorous shriek. Then Natasha defended her, and Freddie and Lena joined her.

Ben and Lucy took up positions behind the bench, pelting the others. Jane found herself with a faceful of snow from Nick, and she pursued him round the table, firing shots at his back while he yelped. The peaceful scene quickly deteriorated into chaos as they ran, shrieking, here and there, scooping up snow. The waiters watched from the sidelines, their expressions bemused. Jane tripped and fell in the snow, taking down Ben, who landed beside her in a tangle of limbs.

'Get off,' she gasped, weak from laughing. 'You big lump.' He rubbed snow into her face and tears of laughter ran down her cheeks. Ben scrambled off her, and just then, Philip launched himself at his back, bringing them both crashing to the ground.

'Jesus,' said Ben, pushing him off. 'Calm down. We're not in the jungle now.'

'So sorry, Andersen,' said Philip, smiling brightly. 'I didn't mean to hurt you. Sensitive, aren't you?'

'We can't all be TV hard men,' said Ben, standing. 'Although, I've always wondered – do you really do your own stunts?' His voice was pleasant, but something about his tone made Jane, who was sitting up now and wiping snow from her face, look at him.

'Of course,' said Philip, dragging himself upright and visibly bristling.

'All of them? Even that one when you abseiled into an active volcano?'

'Even that one,' snarled Philip. 'I know it's not a war zone—'

'You,' said Ben, tapping him on the chest just a little too hard, 'are absolutely one hundred per cent right. It isn't a war zone.'

'It's called a job, Andersen,' said Philip, shoving Ben back so hard that he staggered. 'I wouldn't be so superior about it if I were you. I can't help it if I found a more lucrative career. I went to journalism school. I could have—'

'Of course you did,' said Ben. 'Shame you didn't get a decent job out of it. Thank goodness someone pulled some strings and got you a TV gig, hey?'

'All right,' said Jane, jumping up and standing between them. Philip's eyes were glittering in a nasty way, and she had never in all her years of working with him seen Ben look so angry. Or indeed, ever seen him angry at all. 'I think we can all agree that you are *both* doing very important work.' She looked between them. 'All right?'

There was a tense pause. Then Ben said, 'Sure.'

Jane relaxed. 'Good,' she said. 'Now—'

'If you think that telling celebrities to eat bugs is important work,' Ben said quietly, 'then Donnelly here is definitely doing it.'

Philip let out a roar of rage. 'I'm sick of you all! You think you're *so* superior,' he went on. He caught sight of Nick and his fury seemed to escalate. 'You, with your nasty little newspaper column, and you' – he pointed at the bloggers, who were staring at him open-mouthed – 'with your *likes* and *reach*, and especially *you*,' he said, turning again to Ben and jabbing his chest, 'with your *worthy* war photos. Well, I'll have you know I made more last month than any of you make in a year, and at least . . .' He looked at Ben spitefully. 'At least I don't drive like an old person,' he spat.

He turned on his heel and stalked off. They all stared after him, and there was a long, astonished silence. At last, Jane turned to Ben. 'What on earth,' she said, 'was *that* about?'

He scowled and looked at the floor. 'He just winds me up,' he said eventually. 'He thinks he's so great, but he's just a pair of sunglasses and a leather jacket.'

'Well, well,' said Natasha, grinning. 'It's always the quiet ones.'

Just then, there was a loud shriek, and the sky lit up with a flare of pink. They all jumped.

'It's the fireworks,' said Natasha. 'How apt. Now this *will* be Instagrammable. Come on, Ben,' she said, firmly taking his arm. 'And you too, Jane.'

'I'm just going to see what was up with Philip,' Jane said. 'I'll be there in a minute.'

Natasha grimaced. 'I think you'll find it's a severe case of wounded ego,' she said. 'But best to make sure.'

The others followed Natasha round the side of the terrace.

Jane took a deep breath and squared her shoulders, then traced Philip's angry footsteps through the snow and round the corner.

Lit only by little, glowing tea lights, the hot tub steamed gently in the darkness, and in it, scowling and looking very dishevelled – and almost painfully handsome – was Philip.

Jane walked over and perched on the side. 'That was fast,' she said. 'I should have known if there was a hot tub, you'd be in it.'

'Ha,' he said mirthlessly.

There was a pause.

'Would you like to tell me what all that was about, back there?' Jane asked.

He gave her a defiant look. 'I've had enough of everyone thinking they're better than me,' he said. 'Especially your mate. He's a superior, lanky—'

'Hey,' she said, standing up. 'If you're going to be horrible about my friend, then I'm leaving.'

'OK, OK,' he said, stretching out a hand. He entwined his fingers through hers. 'Don't leave. I take it all back. I love all of them, even that hack from the *Post* who ruined my life.' A wicked smile began to spread across his face. 'Now, as your keen investigative skills have deduced, you, Jane, are standing next to a hot tub.'

She found herself smiling in return. 'Looks like it,' she said.

'And since you're here, I think there's only one thing for you to do.'

'What's that?'

'You should get in with me,' he said.

21

'Wait,' Philip said, 'don't tell me.' He ducked his head under the water and came up grinning. 'Jane Brook doesn't do hot tubs, does she?'

She slipped off her shoes and sat, dangling her bare feet in the water. Bubbles rushed between her toes like a shoal of nibbling fish. 'I don't *think* she does,' she said.

'Right.' He smiled lazily at her. 'Just like she doesn't almost kiss men she's only known a day.'

'Exactly,' she said. She watched him, leaning back, arms resting against the sides of the tub. Arrogant, confident, sure of himself. His cheeks were flushed from the warmth of the water, his blue eyes fierce. Irresistibly handsome.

Margot's words drummed in her ears. *Behave badly. Exorcise Simon for ever. Do the wrong thing for once.* Suddenly, on impulse, she pulled her jumper over her head and unbuttoned her jeans. She was aware of Philip's eyes on her, but he didn't say a word, just watched as she stripped down to her swimming costume. She stepped in.

The water was gloriously hot, in heady contrast to the icy air. She waded through the bubbles to where Philip was standing.

'Jane,' he murmured. 'What *are* you doing?'

'Shut up,' she whispered. She walked closer, and he hooked his arms around her waist, held her there, suspended.

She bent her head closer and felt his breath catch, and then she kissed him.

Her mind went blank of thought and she felt only delicious sensation. If anything at all filtered into her brain, past the rush of desire and the fog of champagne, then it was disbelief. Here she was, she thought wildly, kissing an incredibly attractive man in a hot tub in Norway.

And then, hot on the heels of that thought, another permeated the haze of champagne and lust. *Am I really going to kiss Philip Donnelly in a hot tub at midnight, when anyone could walk past?*

No, she was not. There were plenty of other places that she and Philip could kiss – private, secluded places. Places like her bedroom.

She pulled away. Their lips were still close, and she could feel the heat of his chest against hers, and his strong arms holding her tight.

'Why don't we take this upstairs?' she said.

'That,' he said huskily, 'sounds like an amazing idea.'

22

Once they reached her room, however, Jane felt suddenly shy. To hide it, she politely asked, 'Why don't you have a seat?'

Philip sat on her bed, wearing nothing more than his towel and looking perfectly relaxed. He patted the bed next to him and she went over.

'This *is* better,' he said quietly. 'Now, where were we?' He bent and kissed her neck just below her ear. Jane closed her eyes, and then opened them again.

'What was going on down there really?' she said. 'Between you and Ben?'

'No idea,' Philip murmured against her neck. 'I think he's just jealous.'

'Of what?' asked Jane. 'Of you? Because I don't think he really wants to abseil into a volcano.'

'Of *you*, you idiot,' said Philip, laughing. 'He knows he can't compete with a man of my expertise for your attentions.' He began dropping kisses across her collarbone and Jane closed her eyes again. But confusion had overtaken desire. She needed some time to think.

'Hang on,' she said. She pushed him away. 'I'm going to have a shower.'

He groaned, falling back on the bed. 'Alone?'

'Alone.' She nodded at the minibar. 'If you felt like it, you could make me a vodka and tonic while you're waiting. Lots of ice and lemon, please.'

He gave her a little mock salute. 'Done.'

She hurried into the bathroom and shut the door behind her, leaning against it for a moment. Then she slipped off her towelling robe, turning the temperature to cool and the pressure up to high before stepping into the shower. She wasn't sure why she was suddenly so keen to buy some time, but she definitely needed to sober up a bit. She stood under the beating water and tried to let the events of the evening settle.

The snowball fight, Ben and Philip yelling at each other – it was all so confusing.

Ben was jealous over her? She shook her head. No. He was protective, that was all.

Only one thing was certain: Philip Donnelly was waiting outside, sitting on her bed, wearing no more than a towel. In a few minutes, she would go out to him – and then what?

What did she want to happen?

Did she *want* a one-night stand, or did she want something else? Something akin to the passion that had led Thomas to seek out his wartime lover again after all these years, even if it could only be through faded ink and worn paper.

She was doing what Margot had specifically told her not to – getting emotionally involved. 'There's not much I can do about it now,' she muttered to herself.

When she stepped out of the bathroom, swaddled in another of the thick white robes, hair wrapped in a towel, Philip was sitting on the bed, still in his towel, two glass tumblers full of ice and lemon in front of him.

'I hope you'll find this satisfactory,' he said, holding one out to her. She went and sat next to him and took a large swallow of her drink, even though the room was still swooping alarmingly from all the schnapps.

'You look lovely,' he told her. 'All scrubbed and innocent.' He kissed her bare shoulder.

'Philip,' she said, piecing together her words with drunken care. 'Look. There's something I want to talk to you about.'

He kissed her shoulder again. 'Talking,' he said, 'wasn't entirely what I had in mind.'

She put down her drink and turned to face him. 'I don't think I'm ready for this,' she said. He was silent, and she carried on, talking quickly, 'I don't mean I'm not *ever* going to be ready for this – whatever this is. I'm just not ready for it to happen right *now*. As in, tonight.'

She risked a look at him, and to her relief, his eyes were crinkled in a fond smile. 'OK,' he said. 'I understand.'

'You do?' she said, surprised.

'Yeah. I admit I'm disappointed not to have my wicked way with you, but I do understand.'

She breathed a sigh of relief. 'It's just, if we picked this up again in London, only without . . .'

'Without the posse of journalists and bloggers downstairs?'

'*Yes*,' she said, laughing. 'Exactly.' She shook her head. 'I don't know what it is about this country, but nothing has felt real since I got here. It's like I'm on a holiday from normal life. If this happens – whatever *this* is – then I want it to feel . . . real.'

He was looking at her intently and then, very slowly, he lifted her hand and brushed it with his lips. 'Me too,' he said quietly. He stood, his fingers laced through hers. 'I still get to take you skiing in the morning, though, right?'

'Absolutely,' she said. 'Can't think of anything better.'

She followed him to the door, where he stopped and pulled her against him in a surprisingly forceful kiss. When he moved away, she found that they were both breathing quickly.

'I'll go, then,' he said. 'See you in the morning, bright and early. Wear your sexiest ski thermals.'

She nodded, unable to speak, still catching her breath. If he had kissed her like that when she had first stepped out of the shower, she wasn't sure she would have had the resolve to send him away.

'I'll be there,' she said.

'Goodnight, Jane,' Philip said. He kissed her once more, on the cheek. 'Sweet dreams,' he said, and shut the door behind him.

Jane walked to the bed and fell back onto it. She lay there, a mass of conflicting emotions. Part of her wanted to bask in the aftermath of being kissed by such an expert. And that part of her wished she had cast aside her scruples and succumbed to a night of passion.

She recalled the tenderness in his eyes when she had suggested deferring the romance until they were back home. Did that mean he saw a future with her? And how did she feel about that? Could she, in a million years, see it working with Philip Donnelly off the telly?

Jane shook her head. The room was swimming from the schnapps and the night had raised too many questions. She groaned and flicked off the light. She was meant to be letting her hair down, living for the moment. Tomorrow – and reality – could take care of itself.

23

The next morning, Jane woke with a pounding head, a heaving stomach and every nerve ending throbbing. She'd suffered through several hangovers this trip, but this was surely the worst. The worst, maybe, of her entire life.

Perhaps, she thought as she fumbled with the zips on Margot's cumbersome ski suit, her fuzzy state would help rather than hinder her today on the slopes. Exhaustion might aid coordination.

Everyone assembled after breakfast in reception, also kitted out in their ski gear, except for Nick and Sandra, who were excitedly talking through a relaxing programme of spa treatments and a three-course lunch, and of course Thomas. Jane noticed he was ensconced in a large armchair, reading the paper and drinking a cup of coffee. She hesitated, unsure whether to approach him, but to her surprise, he waved her over cheerfully.

'Jane, my dear,' he said, setting down his cup. 'Are you off out on the slopes with the others? Cross-country skiing, I hear.'

'Well, I'm giving it a go,' Jane muttered, eyeing the mountains uneasily. The sky looked a bit cloudy and grey to her.

'I'm sure you'll be excellent,' said Thomas. 'Have confidence.' He lowered his voice. 'Listen, I've had a chance to think over what you suggested about the article for the *Courier*, and if you are willing to delay just one more week, then I would be happy to give you an interview about Marit and me. You can use the letters. Anything you need, in fact.'

'Oh, that's great!' said Jane, beaming and clapping her hands. 'That would mean we could make the Christmas issue. I'll do it really well, I promise. It wouldn't be cheesy.' She grinned, remembering Ben's words. 'Well, maybe a bit of cheese. It is nearly Christmas after all.'

'Exactly,' Thomas said. 'Why don't we discuss after dinner tonight?'

'That sounds good,' she said. 'I'll speak to Ben too. We could get some nice pictures of you against the pines, perhaps.'

He inclined his head. 'Whatever you think best, my dear. I'm in your hands.'

'Come on, everyone,' called Natasha. 'Chop, chop. Our instructors are waiting.'

Jane stood. 'I'd better go,' she said. 'But I'll see you tonight. And thank you for agreeing to this. I won't let you or Marit down. You can trust the *Courier* to do a good job on the story – and you can trust me too.'

'I always trusted you,' he said, his voice unexpectedly serious. 'I just wanted to get a few things straight in my mind first.' He smiled. 'I'll explain it all later. Go, ski.'

She hurried to join the others, who were gathering out in front of the hotel. They were joined by a tall, hearty-looking man with broad shoulders and blond hair tied back in a ponytail.

'This is Daniel,' Natasha was explaining. She laid a hand on his muscular arm. 'He's going to be taking us out on the slopes today. And this is his nephew and assistant, Anders.' She nodded to a grumpy-looking teenager with lank hair and a surly expression, who appeared at Daniel's side. He'll be helping the beginners.' She nodded at Jane. 'I think that's just you,' she said. 'We'll meet at a restaurant called Vivendel for lunch at two if you decide you're up to it. Anders will know it.'

Jane smiled. Trust Natasha to swan off with the hunk while she was stuck with his moody nephew and the hangover from hell.

Philip turned to her. He looked like something out of a James Bond film in sleek, black ski gear. 'Get back in the swing of things this morning,' he said to her, 'and then I'll take you out this afternoon,' he said. 'See you at lunch?'

'If I get my ski legs,' she said, rather nervously.

They all zipped off, their laughter carrying on the air, and she turned to Anders, who was looking at her with mild disfavour. It was clear he also felt he had drawn the short straw.

'Hi,' she said rather weakly. 'Er, so I've been skiing once.'

'Once?' he said, sighing. 'OK. Let's go. We can start small.'

'Excellent,' said Jane. 'And one other small thing to mention is that I'm not feeling so good this morning.' She mimed drinking from a glass. 'A *lot* of schnapps last night.'

He gave her a look that said he had seen it all before. 'Well, let's make a start,' he said.

Jane gave a small, mental groan. This was going to be a long day.

As it turned out, though, Anders proved a good, if monosyllabic, teacher, and Jane's hangover seemed to lend her a dogged sort of focus. Soon she was buzzing with delight at her aptitude; she had surpassed her own expectations and, she suspected, Anders's.

'I can't believe it's all come back to me so easily,' she told Anders, for the hundredth time, trying to ignore the nausea in the pit of her stomach that refused to subside. 'And with a hangover as well!'

'Yes, you're clearly a natural,' he said rather wearily, checking his watch. 'Shall we meet the others for lunch? It's a longer cross-country trail, but I think you're up to it.' He eyed her uncertainly. 'If you think eating is a good idea. You look a little green.'

She hesitated. Philip was at the top of the trail and – determined to channel some of Marit's spirit of adventure – she had her heart set on a romantic ski through the trees. 'I'm fine,' she said firmly.

They set off, stopping occasionally to look at the breathtaking views and allow Jane's waves of nausea to subside. The rather ominous, grey atmosphere of the morning had lifted slightly and the clouds had parted to reveal a glimmer of weak winter sunshine. Soon they had arrived at an idyllic little restaurant set halfway up the mountain, with wooden trestle tables and low-slung beams, where the others were gathered.

There was a relaxed, slightly tipsy air to the rest of the group. Natasha was virtually sitting in Daniel's lap, and Lucy, Lena and Freddie were giggling in the corner with Ben, who seemed his usual relaxed self again. His cheeks were flushed from the exercise, and his eyes were bright – he was definitely happy and at ease on the slopes or in a boat, Jane thought. Philip, further down the bench, broke into one of his charming smiles when he saw Jane and moved over so that she could sit by him.

They were all eating thick, meaty stew from hollowed-out loaves of bread, and Jane tried a few cautious mouthfuls before laying the spoon aside. She was feeling marginally better, but she wasn't sure she was feeling beef stew levels of better.

Daniel glanced out of the window.

'I hate to break up the party,' he said, 'but I don't like the look of that sky. We should think about moving on if we want to take the scenic route back. It really is stunning.' His hand slipped briefly onto Natasha's thigh and squeezed. 'Jane, you stay close to Anders. Storms can blow up quickly at this time of year.'

Jane nodded, only half listening and wishing she had thought to bring painkillers with her. Her head throbbed and she could feel the stew churning in her stomach. No more drinking after this, ever, she swore.

'Careful,' said Ben, as Jane strapped her skis back on. 'Make sure you stick close to Anders.' He hesitated, looking at the sky. 'Those clouds don't look good. I wonder whether you should just take the shortcut back.'

'It's Norway,' said Philip, his voice suspiciously pleasant. 'The route is practically horizontal. I think she'll be fine. I'll ski with you, Jane.' He winked at her. 'We can take things nice and slowly.'

Ben frowned. 'That won't be much use if a storm blows up.'

Philip smiled, showing his teeth. 'Are you lecturing *me* about mountain safety?'

Natasha rolled her eyes. 'Just stop posturing for long enough to pay attention to the route,' she said. 'Come on, everyone.'

They all sped off, zipping neatly through the snow.

Jane was still strapping on her skis, her fingers clumsy. 'You can catch them up,' said Philip to Anders.

Anders shook his head. 'I'll stay,' he said.

Philip tugged down his goggles. 'I'm a qualified ski instructor,' he said. 'Go on, make a start. I'll wait with Jane.'

Anders hesitated, but Philip radiated confidence. 'All right,' he said reluctantly. 'I'll be just ahead.'

'And we'll be close behind,' said Philip patiently. 'Ready, Jane?'

'I guess,' she said doubtfully. 'I'll probably fall on my face now and prove them all right.'

Philip kissed her forehead. 'You'll be fine. Just follow me.'

They set off. The others had long since disappeared, and soon even Anders was a blur in the distance. Jane found herself relaxing into the skiing. She couldn't believe how beautiful the landscape was, and how remote. It felt like she and Philip were alone out on the mountain. The only sound was that of the metal blades slicing through the icy snow, the whistling of the wind and their own breathing. Adrenaline and pride in her physical prowess coursed through her. She couldn't believe that this time last week, she had been sat hunched over a laptop in a hot, stuffy office and now she was out here, at what felt like the end of the world.

The snow stretched on for miles, punctuated only by the occasional pine; Jane had the oddest feeling, as though they were intruders in this pristine world.

As they skied on, though, her euphoria began to fade. The snow, which had been a few gentle flakes only moments earlier, seemed to be falling more thickly now, and Jane soon found it hard to see. The dull ache that had lurked behind her temples all day was building. A part of her wished she had insisted Anders take her the short way back to the ski lodge. She could be curled up right now on one of the cosy sofas, drinking hot chocolate and talking to Thomas.

Just ahead of her, Philip stopped and pulled up his goggles, his blue eyes blazing in his tanned face. His expression betrayed just the smallest flicker of annoyance.

'Doing great,' he assured her. 'Nearly there. Could we pick up the pace a bit, though?'

'I'm going as fast as I can,' she told him honestly.

'Oh, right,' he replied, frowning. 'I thought you could ski a bit better than this, actually. Well, let's go.' He peered more closely at her face. 'Are you all right?' he asked. 'You look pale.'

'I'm OK,' Jane said weakly. 'A bit of a headache. All that schnapps, I guess.'

'Right,' he said, turning away. 'Let's go. Not too far now.'

They skied on. The snow picked up, and within a few feet, the visibility had deteriorated so that Jane could hardly see. She skied doggedly after Philip. They *must* be nearly at the hotel, she thought. Surely it hadn't taken even half as long as this on the way up.

'Are we going the right way?' she called out.

He stopped to wait for her to catch up. 'Of course,' he said, scanning the route ahead in a rather unsettling way.

'Wait, we're not lost, are we?' she asked, trying not to sound scared.

'No,' he said coldly. 'We are *not* lost. Visibility is poor, that's all. But the hotel is just . . .' He gestured ahead. 'Just that way. If you didn't keep stopping,' he added, 'we'd be there by now.'

Jane bit her lip. 'All right,' she said. 'Let's keep going, then.' He was an orienteer, for goodness' sake. This must be child's play to him. She kept her eyes fixed ahead and skied determinedly after his shadowy figure. The whining sound of the wind filled her ears, and the endless white filled her vision. *Never again*, she thought grimly.

Just then, her ski went out from under her and her ankle crumpled. Searing pain shot up her leg, rendering her speechless, and she stumbled to her knees in a snowdrift.

'Philip,' she called out, into the swirling white. Her voice rose to a shriek. 'Philip!'

To her intense relief, she saw his figure staggering back through the snow, looking awkward and clumsy in contrast to his usual easy grace. He reached his hands under her armpits and dragged her upright.

'What's wrong *now*?' he asked testily. The impatience in his voice was barely disguised, but Jane was in too much pain to care.

'My ankle,' she said, gritting her teeth. 'I think I've sprained it.' At least, she hoped it was a sprain. She tried, tentatively, to stand and cried out. 'Maybe I didn't tighten my boots properly.'

'Oh, for God's sake,' he muttered. 'Can't you ski on it at all?'

She tried again, but the pain was too great. Hot tears spilled under her goggles and down her cheeks.

He stood next to her. 'Try leaning on me,' he said. She began limping after him, supported by his arm, but it was too difficult.

'I can't,' she said. 'It hurts too much.'

'Well, if you don't, then we're going to be stuck out here!' he snapped. 'Is that what you want? To be dug out of a snowdrift?'

She stared at him, aghast. 'We *are* lost,' she said. 'Aren't we?'

'We are not bloody lost!' he said. 'There is zero visibility. And it's *your* fault. We'd be back at the hotel by now if you hadn't slowed us down. It's not my fault you can't hold your booze and you can't bloody ski.'

'You told me it would be fine!' yelled Jane.

He squinted through the snow ahead. 'Look,' he said, relief in his voice. 'I know where we are now and we're not far. I think I should go on ahead, all right?'

'Go ahead?' Jane asked. 'And leave me here?'

He gave her a quick, impatient glance. 'It's protocol if someone is injured. Madness to try and drag you back to the hotel – it could take hours. I'll ski there far quicker on my own and then I can raise the alarm. Bring first aiders back with a skidoo.' He peered through the blizzard. 'There are some trees over there. Come on.'

He half-carried, half-dragged her towards a sprinkling of trees and began to pack the snow down. 'Here, shelter against this drift,' he said. 'You'll be perfectly all right for a bit. I won't be long.' He was pulling on his goggles as he spoke. 'Just stay awake till I get back, all right?'

'Please don't leave me,' Jane whispered, terror settling onto her chest. But he didn't seem to hear her and in a second, he was gone, vanished into the falling snow.

Jane sank back against the makeshift shelter. She was too frightened to cry. She tried to breathe calmly and steadily. How long, she wondered, did it take you to freeze to death in a snowstorm? What if Philip couldn't get help in time?

The wind howled, driving Jane further into the drift. She could feel a slow, seductive, creeping warmth setting in. A warning pierced her foggy brain. Surely it was when you started to think of the snow as warm and cosy that you were about to freeze to death? She clutched at one of the pine branches, and, with what felt like a superhuman effort, dragged herself to her feet, only to stumble back into the snow again. She was so tired.

That was it, she thought. She was going to freeze to death out here on a ski slope, on a ridiculous press trip. For some reason, she thought of Thomas and Marit. She imagined them huddled in their makeshift bed in the cottage, smoking in the dark, their voices mingling, laughter rising and falling, while a mile or so away, the king made his impossible choice.

And then, drowsily, the rest of the trip began to come back to her, splintered fragments blown on the wind. Philip leaning towards her, brushing soot off her cheek. His lips on hers. Ben's face turning to hers in the rowing boat, rain on his cheeks, his voice low in the quiet of Thomas's bedroom as he read aloud Marit's words and embers fell into the grate. On the terrace, laughing, his body landing hard against hers in the midst of the snowball fight. And she thought of Thomas, a remote figure in a cloud of steam, and the *Golden Express* drawing into the station as the train whistle blew . . .

A noise pierced the fog, close to her ear – the sharp, piercing sound of a whistle, blowing once, twice, three times. With what felt like an act of impossible strength, Jane hauled herself to her feet and waved frantically.

'I'm here!' she called.

And, amazingly, she heard a voice.

'Jane? Jane, can you hear me?'

She could feel gloved hands on her face and neck, gently clearing the snow from her mouth. Again, the whistle sounded and faintly, through the rushing sound in Jane's ears, she could hear an answering whistle. She closed her eyes.

'Thomas,' she mumbled. 'The letters. They're in the fireplace.'

'For God's sake.' The voice, clipped and autocratic, sounded heavenly in Jane's ears. 'I knew this would happen if you made your own way back with that tosser.'

Jane's eyes flew open in shock. '*Natasha?*' she murmured through numb lips. She found herself held upright in a firm, capable grip. 'Is it really you?'

'Yes, it's really me. Are you hurt?'

'Just my ankle,' said Jane. 'I think I've sprained it.'

'Help will be here any second. I alerted Mountain Rescue once we got to the hotel, then Ben, Daniel and I went back out again.'

'How did you know I needed help?' asked Jane.

'I had a sneaking suspicion. The visibility is terrible – even Daniel had a hard time getting us back and he knows the terrain. Can you stay awake? In fact, that's not a question. You need to stay awake, Jane, OK?'

'What about Philip?' Jane asked and Natasha snorted.

'He'll be fine,' she said. 'Stay awake.'

Jane nodded, but her eyes closed in spite of herself. It was so very warm with her eyes shut. She felt her head drifting against Natasha's shoulder.

'Jane.' Natasha's patrician voice sounded very loud and precise in her ear. 'Right now, I'm meant to be drinking cocktails by a blazing log fire, eating fondue and flirting with Danny the hot ski instructor, not standing in a snowdrift with an idiot who thinks she can ski back without a qualified instructor. Now, you stay awake, do you hear me? There is *zero* option here. Come on, Jane – you're tougher than this.'

That last phrase stung Jane into consciousness.

Suddenly there were torch beams. And now she heard another voice – Ben's, she thought, only she had never heard him sound like this, his voice ragged with worry.

'Jane,' he said roughly, 'you're fine, do you hear? The doctors are here.'

'Don't leave me,' she forced out.

'I won't. I promise.' He found her reaching hand and held it fast.

There were lights like pinpricks against her eyes, followed by a rush of activity, and she was gently lifted up. After that, she really was falling asleep, but she still clung to Ben's hand, and the last thing she remembered was his fingers closing firmly about hers.

24

When Jane awoke, it was to faint daylight, and all she knew was that everything hurt. Someone was holding her hand.

'I'm going to murder that prick Donnelly,' she heard Ben say. 'If he ever shows his face again.'

'Because that will help.' Natasha, her voice calm as always.

Jane let out a little moan, her eyes still closed. It was too much effort to open them.

'She's awake,' said Natasha.

'That's a relief,' muttered Ben.

'It means you don't have to murder anyone at least. Get the doctor back in – and tell Thomas. I can't bear him lurking outside like a guard dog.'

The hand on hers withdrew and there was the sound of a door closing. With difficulty, Jane forced her eyes open. The room swam blurrily into focus – her own room at the ski lodge, she realised. Her throat ached, and her whole body felt battered and bruised. She shut her eyes again.

When she opened them, a person she didn't know, a middle-aged woman wearing a white coat, her blonde hair in a neat plait, was sitting beside the bed.

'Jane?' the woman said. Her voice was reassuringly detached and professional. 'My name is Dr Erin Olsen. Can you hear me?'

Jane nodded her head slightly and winced. She cleared her throat, which felt as though it had been sandpapered. 'Yes.' Her voice sounded hoarse and strange.

'Good. Do you know where you are?'

'I'm in the ski lodge at Trysil,' Jane said. She cast her mind back. She remembered the blizzard and the sudden, agonising pain in her ankle, and then . . .

'Natasha?' she whispered.

'I'm here,' said Natasha, moving forward into Jane's line of vision. She was wearing cream leggings and a polo neck and looked, even in that moment, impossibly glamorous.

'What happened?' Jane asked.

'I thought you were a goner,' Natasha said, with more relish than the situation might call for. 'Turns out you had hypothermia and a sprained ankle.'

'Well,' said the doctor repressively, 'before we make a final diagnosis, let me examine our patient.'

Jane lay obediently still while the doctor carefully examined her. Then she nodded and said, 'Good. Your vital signs are normal. Your ankle is a sprain, but we'll monitor you for the next few days.'

Natasha smiled at Jane. 'Getting to be a habit, me rescuing you from the scrapes Philip gets you into.'

Philip. The last Jane had seen of him, he had been vanishing into the night and snow. She struggled to sit up and the doctor laid a restraining hand on her arm.

'You must rest, Jane, and stay warm. Recovery at this time is absolutely crucial.'

'You don't understand,' Jane said. 'There was someone else with me out there on the mountain.' She looked past the doctor to Natasha. 'Did you find Philip too? He'd gone to get help.'

There was an odd look on Natasha's face. 'Philip is fine,' she said. 'Mountain Rescue found him. He got a taxi to the airport early this morning, before most of us were awake. First flight to London.'

Jane stared at her.

The doctor stood. 'I want her to rest,' she said warningly to Natasha, before leaving.

'But I don't understand,' Jane said, bewildered. 'Philip went back to London? Why?'

Natasha hesitated, then tossed a newspaper onto Jane's lap. It was the *People's View*, the *Post*'s rival tabloid.

'This might have had something to do with it,' she said.

Jane lifted the paper and the first thing she saw was a black-and-white photo of Philip, glowering sexily out of the page.

FROM BLOGGER HELL TO SECRET WW2 ROMANCE
By Philip Donnelly
As my dawn flight touched down in trendy Oslo, the bloggers to my left took selfie after selfie. Filter. Caption. Got to get those likes, right?

I wasn't here for likes. I was here to see a famous Christmas tree. But as I trudged through the sleet on a November morning, I began to wonder whether it was worth it. Couldn't we all just go to IKEA?

Back at our cutting-edge hotel, the promised seasonal goodwill deteriorated faster than the guests could guzzle the free champagne. There was a tabloid hack. A faded celebrity food writer (lay off the three-course meals, darling).

And then the Insta-sham stars – empty-headed fashion bloggers living for the next click, constantly photographing the three-course meals they never eat. Conversation with these shallow beauties is like prodding a stagnant pool – nothing good floats to the surface. Topped off by a PA with a power complex.

And yet, in this cesspit that is modern PR, I found a ray of light.

A chance discovery in a nearby cottage. Letters written to a Norwegian soldier, during WW2.

Thomas Erikson was a soldier who helped the king of Norway flee Nazi occupation. Marit Elson was a local girl who helped him. They spent one night together – one night of passion. Thomas abandoned Marit to marry his childhood sweetheart, but all these years later, he sought out her letters.

Please find me Thomas, Marit begged. And in a way, perhaps he did. I reproduce extracts of the letters here. On yellowing paper, in faded ink, we can read her words – and believe in love again.

There followed extracts from the letters themselves, heavily edited.

Jane raised horrified eyes. 'Oh God,' she said, in agonised tones. 'Oh *God*.'

'You didn't know?' Natasha asked, her eyes on Jane's.

'Of course not!' Jane wailed. She stared at Natasha. 'Wait – is that what everyone thinks? That I was in on this?'

Natasha shrugged. 'We all know you've been buttering up the old man. We thought it might be to help Philip with this story.'

Jane scanned the article again. How had Philip got hold of the letters? Her eyes flew to the oilskin packet by the bed and she opened it. To her relief, the original letters were still inside, along with Ben's translations.

'That bastard,' she muttered. 'He must have taken pictures that night he was in my room.'

Natasha smiled faintly. 'In your room, was he?'

Jane shook her head wordlessly. 'A mistake,' she said. 'A huge mistake.'

Natasha tilted her head on one side, considering her. 'So *you* don't think I'm a PA with a power complex?'

'No!' cried Jane. She punched the newspaper with her closed fist, crumpling the byline, and Philip's handsome face. 'I can't believe he did this.' Her indignation ratcheted up a notch as Philip's full villainy came home to her. 'And I can't believe he left me in a snowdrift!'

'Barely half a mile from the hotel too, if he'd only realised it,' said Natasha drily. 'Not to rub it in.'

'Who organised the search party?' asked Jane.

'I did,' said Natasha. 'We got Mountain Rescue out. Ben and Daniel came with me. We're pretty strong skiers and they're prepared for idiots getting lost here. It turned out you were right by the hotel, shivering in a snowdrift, so I found you pretty much straight away and Daniel found Philip.' She patted a tendril of hair back into place. 'To be fair to Philip, visibility was nil.'

'And then he just . . . left?' asked Jane.

'I noticed him slinking into a taxi at about three a.m. Of course,' Natasha added, 'at that point we didn't know he'd decided to trash us all in the national press. We thought he was just embarrassed about getting lost. Until we saw the papers this morning.'

Jane groaned and covered her face with her hands. 'I might as well have helped him with the story,' she wailed. 'I laid it all out for him on a plate. How could I let him take me in like that?'

There was a pause. 'He's gorgeous,' Natasha said ruefully. 'We all thought so. The girls were so cross that he fancied you more than them. I was fuming myself.' She smirked. 'Until Danny showed up.'

Jane pressed her palms hard against her closed lids. She wished she could blot it all out. 'You're all welcome to him,' she said dully.

Natasha shook her head. 'No, thanks. I think everyone is well and truly over their Philip Donnelly crush. I don't know about you, but I like my heroes with a bit more common sense. If anything, this' – she tapped the paper – 'will put them off. Sandra is *murderous*.' Natasha stood and stretched, then gave an enormous yawn. 'Anyhow, I'm off to bed. Activities are suspended for today. I don't care what you all do.'

'I never even said thank you,' Jane said, suddenly realising. 'But thank you, Natasha.' She shook her head bitterly. 'I'd still be in a snowdrift if it was up to Philip *Survival of the Fittest* Donnelly.'

Natasha grinned at her, showing even white teeth. 'It was my pleasure. Got to live out my spy fantasies.' She gave Jane's arm a quick, friendly squeeze. 'And look – don't worry. Those girls downstairs have a sense of humour.'

'Thanks,' muttered Jane. 'But I need to apologise to Thomas.'

'When you're feeling better,' Natasha said gently.

Jane stared at the paper. They would all despise her now. Even – she realised this was maybe the worst of all – Ben.

'Natasha, wait,' Jane called. 'Was Ben here with me last night?'

Natasha raised an elegant eyebrow and nodded. 'He was,' she said. 'He sat with you all night, and at one point he was talking about airlifting you to hospital until the doctor told him to calm down.' She smiled at Jane's stunned expression. 'Sometimes, Jane, it's the quiet ones all along.'

The painkillers the doctor had given Jane made her thick-headed. Fragments from the last few days drifted through her mind like snowflakes.

Whichever way she lined those pieces up, though, the upshot was the same: Philip had stolen her story and hotfooted it back to London. Everyone who was on this trip thought that she had double-crossed them. Or that she was a gullible fool; she wasn't sure which was worse.

She was woken from a confused, uncomfortable sleep by a tap on the door. She pushed back her hair, blinking. 'Come in,' she called out, still barely awake.

It was Thomas, dapper as ever. He laid a slender bunch of red tulips, wrapped in brown paper, on the table between them.

'Tulips,' he said gently. 'A beloved Christmas flower in Norway. How are you, my dear?'

Two big, fat tears welled up in Jane's eyes. She blinked them away furiously.

'I'm all right,' she managed, in a small voice. 'Embarrassed.'

'You shouldn't be.' He sat in the chair by her bed. 'I'm more sorry than I can say about your accident. I have always hated skiing, which is sacrilege for a Norwegian to say. Pushing yourself up and down mountains with sticks. A silly sport.'

Jane laughed rather bitterly. 'After last night, I might have to agree.' She swallowed. 'Listen, Thomas – if you don't already know, Philip went to a paper, about you and Marit.' She risked a quick look at him, but he looked thoughtful rather than angry. 'It's partly my fault,' she confessed. 'I let him tag along with me. He met Marit's family. This should have been *your* story, not mine or his. Yours and Marit's.'

'I saw the paper,' Thomas said. He leaned forward and laid a gentle hand on hers. 'I don't mind. There is a lesson in our story, mine and Marit's. That when it comes to love, it is better to act. Not to bury love under a chimney breast for decades.' He tapped her shoulder lightly. 'Seize the day, Jane.'

She laughed rather shakily, blinking tears away again. 'Seizing the day is what got me into this mess,' she said.

'Ah, we are all allowed a mistake or two,' he said. 'The important thing is to move past them. Now, you get some rest, my dear. And I say again that I am not sorry about this.' He gestured to the paper. 'I am glad that the world knows Marit's story. Or at least, a version of it.' He shook his head. 'His writing, though, is execrable.'

Jane waited till the door had shut behind him, and then she wiped her eyes, pushed back her hair and reached for her phone on her bedside table. Nadine would have seen the *View* by now. She steeled herself, then turned it on.

Messages from the last forty-eight hours flashed up thick and fast. Messages from Natasha, ranging from polite yet frosty:

Can you tell me where you and Philip are, please, because I just got back to the hotel and there's no sign of you?

To testy:

Actual blizzard coming. Where are you?

To enraged:

We're about to send out a sodding search and rescue and if we don't find you in a ravine with a broken leg I'm going to push you in myself.

Jane grimaced, feeling mortification wash over her again. Her jaw set grimly. If her and Philip's paths ever crossed again, she would make sure he suffered.

There were texts from Margot too:

You've been quiet. Wild man, sauna – Y or N? Call me.

Then, a few hours later:

Not like you to go AWOL. Call me OK?

And a voicemail from Nadine, from the early hours of that morning, her voice icy:

'Jane. Why am I seeing that arse Philip Donnelly splashed all over the bloody *View* with a story you're meant to be writing for *me*? What the hell is going on over there? Call me now.' A pause and then, politely, 'Please.'

Jane sighed. Then, as the lesser of two evils, she rang Margot.

'Hello,' murmured Margot, her voice hoarse.

'I've messed up,' Jane said. 'I've done something really, really stupid. Wait – you're not in labour, are you?'

'Napping. Getting it in while I can, like everyone keeps telling me.' She gave a muffled groan and there was the sound of crinkling paper. 'OK, I've located the biscuits. Tell me everything.'

And Jane did, from Thomas's original plea for help, to the thrilling discovery of the letters and Marit's true identity. She told her about Ben reading the letters to her and Thomas, and then walking out into the night and rowing across the loch. Kissing Philip in the hot tub. The ill-fated ski trip and Philip's betrayal. Margot listened in silence except for an interested squeal when Jane mentioned the hot tub.

'It was a beautiful story,' Jane finished. 'And now Philip's gone and ruined it with his trashy article.'

There was silence on the other end of the phone, broken only by the sound of Margot chewing.

'Margot?' Jane whispered, alarmed. Margot was almost never quiet. 'How bad is this?'

'Darling, it's not that bad,' came the reply, a shade too hastily. 'Not that bad at *all*. I don't understand, though. You *knew* what Philip was like. You were meant to shag him, not fall for him and let him steal your story and dump you in a snowdrift.'

'You're the one who told me to seize the day,' said Jane, picking at the bedspread.

'But not lose your mind. Your problem, Jane,' said Margot, 'is that you've always taken things too seriously, and that goes for men too. Simon – utter wanker, yet totally delighted by himself – we could all see that. Philip – more of the same, with an extra side of ego.'

'You're probably right,' Jane said. 'I was an idiot, twice over. I've learned my lesson now. No more charming men.'

'Good,' said Margot. 'Because you're a good person, Jane, and you deserve someone lovely.'

'But what do I do now? Everyone here hates me.' Jane swallowed and said in a small voice, 'Even Ben, probably.'

There was a silence, and then Margot said in a speculative voice, 'Tell me more about Ben.'

'He's just from my work. He's a photographer.'

'A photographer. That's glamorous,' said Margot.

'He's not glamorous,' said Jane miserably. 'But he is nice.' She picked at the bedsheet some more, unravelling a whole thread. 'It doesn't matter anyway. I just have to get through the next few days and then I'm coming home and we're never going to mention Norway or Christmas again.'

'Listen,' said Margot, her crisp tones only slightly muffled by a thick layer of biscuit. 'I may have misjudged things a bit. I hold my hands up there. I told you to let your hair down and it went a bit too far. But I maintain that you *needed* to lose your head a bit, post-Simon. You've done that. Now it's time to come back to earth. There's nothing here that can't be fixed.'

'I don't see how,' said Jane. 'The story is ruined. And it's all Philip's fault.'

Margot was still chewing. 'Correct me if I'm wrong,' she said thoughtfully, 'but you *had* written a piece making fun of the bloggers? That wasn't all Philip's bright idea?'

'No,' Jane said. 'He pulled most of it off my laptop I guess. I suppose I did write it, or a version of it.' She sighed. 'And I did copy Thomas's letters without permission. OK, I see your point.'

Margot laughed. 'I think the *point* is, you were a bit quick off the mark with that story. Obviously, this is all Philip's fault, the scumbag, but—'

'But maybe,' said Jane, 'I owe them all a bit of an apology?'

As usual, she thought, Margot was right.

25

When Jane next woke, the light in the room was dim and it was dark outside. Hours must have passed. There was a different figure curled up in an armchair by the window, reading. It was Freddie, wearing enormous tortoiseshell glasses, a soft, grey hoodie, matching jogging bottoms, and fluffy pink socks. She saw that Jane had woken, put down her book and came over.

'Are you OK?' she asked. 'They asked for someone to sit with you and I volunteered.' Her expression was neutral – not quite friendly but not hostile either. Her exquisite face was bare of make-up except for the bright pop of lipstick she always wore.

'Freddie, I'm so sorry,' said Jane, dragging herself into a sitting position. Her ankle throbbed and her mouth was dry, but otherwise she felt more human than she had done earlier. 'I had no idea Philip was planning that horrible story! I swear to you, I would never have described you all as—'

'"Empty-headed fashion bloggers living for the next click"?' Freddie said, one eyebrow raised.

'See, I never said that!' Jane croaked indignantly. 'Philip wrote that.'

'Shut up and drink your water.'

Jane did, gulping thirstily. Her throat still felt sore.

'We don't hate you,' Freddie said. She sat down on the little chair next to the bed and cupped her face in her hands. 'We were taken in by Philip at first because, let's face it, he's outrageously handsome, but we know he's a grade-A tosser who would sell his grandmother for a comeback. And it's hardly the first time someone has described me as a shallow airhead travelling the world for a whiff of free champagne. Besides' – she grinned broadly and held out her phone to Jane, waggling it temptingly – 'I don't know if you've seen the papers today, but Natasha got busy. Looks like *someone* might need some good PR very quickly.'

Jane seized the phone, which was open on the *Post* website and scanned the page eagerly.

The byline was Nick's, and the main picture was an unflattering one of Philip, looking furtive, taken unawares through the taxi window at night-time. It must have been taken as he left the hotel. In the light of the flash, he looked sweaty and anxious, and Jane noticed for the first time how his eyes were set rather close together, giving him a shifty, ferrety look.

NORWEGIAN NIGHTMARE
'SURVIVAL' DONNELLY – NOT SUCH
A HERO AFTER ALL . . .

Survival of the Fittest love rat Philip Donnelly was left red-faced after a ski session with a fellow guest left them both lost in subzero temperatures – less than half a mile from their luxury hotel.

It seems that Donnelly – known for his hard-man antics on the TV show – is less tough off camera. He took an inexperienced skier on a gentle run, only to become disorientated and abandon her in a snow-drift. Eventually, both were found and given medical aid.

Donnelly wrote a scathing newspaper review of the press trip, but it turns out the dislike was mutual.

'We all thought he was pretty sad,' said Lucy Partridge, from the blog ThisModelLife.

'Chap seems unstable,' said renowned restaurant critic Sandra Riley.

Survival of the Fittest revealed today that they would not be renewing Donnelly's contract for the next series but declined to comment further.

'Goodness,' Jane said. She hadn't imagined Philip's downfall being executed so swiftly and efficiently.

'What do you think?' Natasha asked from the doorway. 'Some of my best work, though I say so myself.'

Jane looked at her in awe. 'I'd hate to have you for an enemy.'

'Good thing we're friends, then.' She grinned. 'Which I think we are now, aren't we?'

Jane found herself grinning back. 'I'd like to be,' she said. 'How did you manage it all so quickly?'

'A quick snap as he was leaving, then I pulled in the quotes from the others, who were gagging to take him down a peg, and Nick did the rest. Said he hasn't enjoyed a story this much in years.'

'That's amazing of Lucy to come my defence like that,' Jane said, feeling oddly touched.

'Oh, well . . .' Natasha exchanged a loaded glance with Freddie. 'Let's just say Lucy has an axe to grind where Philip is concerned.'

Jane looked between them, her heart sinking. It occurred to her for the first time that Philip might have been spreading his attentions rather thinly on the trip.

'He didn't . . .' she said.

'Oh, he did,' said Freddie bitterly. 'Made a move on her one night after she'd had a massive fight with her boyfriend. And then the next morning, he's all over you again, like it never happened.'

'Oh God,' said Jane. 'When was this?'

'The night we had the Christmas party in Oslomarka. You left early . . .'

Jane thought back to the *Julebord* feast. That had been the night that Jane had gone to see Thomas. Philip had pounced on Lucy and then shown up at Jane's room bright and early the next morning to fetch her for their coffee date.

'Well,' she said, shaking her head in disgust. 'Seeing him getting trashed in print is great, but I will never forgive myself for betraying Thomas. Not to mention that I have no story for my boss. This trip has been nothing but a disaster, professionally *and* personally.'

'It's not been so bad, has it?' said Freddie, nudging her. 'You met Thomas. And you met us.'

'That's right,' said Natasha. 'And it's not over yet. Don't forget the Christmas ball on Thursday.' They stared at her and she shrugged. 'Look, at this point, I'm not entirely sure *what* it will involve – I've been a little busy saving lives – but it will be major. You guys will love it.'

'Oh, I won't be coming,' said Jane. All she wanted was to keep her head down for the next few days and make it back home with the shreds of her dignity intact.

'Why on earth wouldn't you?' said Natasha.

'Yeah, why not?' came a voice from the doorway.

Jane jumped and looked to the doorway, where Ben was standing.

Her heart gave an almost painful leap. He looked so familiar and comforting, with his freckles and unruly mop of hair, in his shapeless jumper.

'Hi,' she managed.

'Hi,' he said, rather tersely.

Jane was vaguely aware of Natasha and Freddie hustling each other out of the room. She felt suddenly, acutely aware of her unwashed face, not to mention the unflattering baggy nightgown she had been given. She tried surreptitiously to smooth down her wild hair.

'How are you feeling?' asked Ben.

'All right,' she said. He looked grumpy, she thought. 'Hurt pride mostly.'

'It wasn't your fault. Philip should never have taken you out on his own. It was too dangerous.'

He had said that at the time, Jane remembered. A lump formed in her throat.

'I shouldn't have gone,' she said in a low voice.

'Well. Maybe not.'

They fell into an uncomfortable silence, unusual between them. Jane tried to think of something to say that would lighten the mood, but he was frowning in a rather discouraging way.

'Listen, Thomas asked me to check up on you again,' he said. 'He's been worried.'

'Oh,' said Jane. 'Well, in that case, you can tell *Thomas* that I'm fine. A few bruises, that's all.' She risked a look at him. 'Ben, I don't know what you're thinking about that ridiculous article, but—'

'You wrote it, didn't you?' he asked, staring at his feet.

'I wrote a *version* of it,' Jane explained. 'But I never meant for it to see the light of day, and I certainly didn't help Philip with it.' When he was silent, she said, 'Thomas understands.'

'Thomas is a very kind man,' Ben said. 'He's the last person to notice when someone is using him.'

'Is that what you think I did?' Jane said, her hurt turning to anger.

'You shared his story with Philip Donnelly, of all people! The man has "untrustworthy snake" all but printed on his forehead. You gave him the letters!'

'I didn't *give* them to him,' she snapped. 'He must have seen them while I was in the—' She broke off and there was another awkward silence. Ben had turned bright red.

They were quiet for a moment.

'I didn't come here to lay into you,' he said at last. 'Thomas asked me to see how you were, that's all.'

'You said that already,' she said, in a small voice. 'You can tell him that I'm fine.'

'I was—We were worried about you,' Ben said. 'When we found you the other night . . .' He shook his head.

'I'm fine now,' she said. 'Look, you're right about one thing. My judgement was certainly off where Philip was concerned. I don't often make mistakes, but when it comes to men, I really go for it.' She sighed. 'I should have seen through him.'

'Yes, you should have,' said Ben, the smallest flicker of a grin tugging up the corner of his mouth. He was clearly enjoying this. 'He's a prick.'

'Well, believe me,' said Jane, 'I've learned my lesson. I won't trust anyone who wears sunglasses indoors again.'

There was a short pause. 'That,' said Ben, 'sounds like a good plan.'

26

The next few days passed in a cosy sort of blur in which life and responsibilities seemed to be lifted from Jane's shoulders. She felt as though she were on a hiatus from normal life. Her sprained ankle subsided to a dull throb, and she was pleasantly drowsy from the painkillers.

Sandra came to visit, bringing soft-boiled eggs with buttered toast and strong tea. She also brought a stack of gory-looking 1950s murder mysteries. Most of the covers featured a face-down corpse with a dagger embedded in the back.

'Nothing as beneficial for recovery as a good murder,' she explained, plunging a soldier into her egg yolk. 'How are you feeling?'

'All right,' said Jane, biting into her own buttered toast. 'I'm sorry about Philip's article, by the way.' She felt like she was having to apologise an awful lot for him.

Sandra shook her head. 'Don't give him another thought – I shan't. You need a thick skin to be in the industry as long as I have, and I'm not going to let Philip make *me* feel inadequate. I was writing copy while he was in the cradle.'

Jane set down her toast. 'You were with your husband a long time, weren't you?' she asked.

'Oh, a lifetime. When Reg and I met, he was nineteen and I was twenty. We were children. Younger than those sweet bloggers, even. Imagine!'

'How did you both know, if you were so young?'

'Oh.' Sandra sipped her tea and considered. 'Well, he made me laugh – and you've no idea how refreshing that was. I was surrounded by all these pompous Oxbridge graduates who thought they were God's gift, and he was this smart wide boy with a sense of humour. But also . . .' She paused. 'I always knew we'd be a team. And we were, you know. Right up till the day he died.'

She shook her head. 'Eat your egg. You're still looking far too pale. I cooked these myself, because Michelin-starred or not, the kitchen simply could not get it right.'

She gave Jane a sideways glance. 'The problem with men like Philip, my dear, is that they're always going to put themselves first.'

Jane shrugged. 'I don't think he even really liked me,' she said. 'He just wanted the story.'

'Oh, he liked you,' said Sandra, patting her hand. 'Just not as much as he liked himself. Selfish.' She shook her head. '*Just* like his mother.'

Another day, Nick came and he and Jane played cards, drank more tea and had an enjoyable time gossiping about other journalists.

'I just wonder if there's more to life than the *Courier*,' said Jane, her gaze drifting to the view from the window. 'Maybe I should be more like Marit. Broaden my horizons.'

'At least you don't write for the devil's rag.' Nick took a gulp of his tea, his eyes wide behind his thick glasses.

'Have you ever thought about . . . *not* writing for them?' Jane asked cautiously. 'Not that it's any of my business,' she went on hastily, 'but you're far too nice for the *Post*.'

'All the time,' he said, with a lopsided grin. 'In fact – well, it's not been announced yet, but I handed in my notice yesterday. I'm going to tout for stories in *Rural Living* now they've ditched Philip, and Sandra thinks she can put in a good word for me at the *Gourmand*. Put all my wine knowledge to good use. Write about aquavit.'

'And I'll sing your praises too at the *Courier*!' said Jane. Her face fell. 'Assuming I still have a job that is,' she said gloomily.

'Oh, you'll have a job,' Nick said reassuringly. 'Don't worry about that. You're too good for them to let you get away.' His phone buzzed as a text came through. He opened it and smiled fondly. 'The kids chose a Christmas tree today.'

He showed her the screen – his partner, Robyn, with wildly curling hair, bundled up in a coat and scarf, and their two kids, standing alongside a giant, lopsided Christmas tree in an IKEA car park, all three of them beaming like maniacs. Jane looked at the photo and sighed.

'How did you know that you wanted to be with Robyn?' she said, asking him the same question as Sandra. Since she was turning over a new leaf, she may as well do a straw poll of all the functional relationships she knew about. 'For the rest of your life, I mean.'

'I just did,' Nick said absently, shuffling the cards, and she rolled her eyes at him.

'Stop being such a bloke. How did you *know*?'

He thought for a moment. 'It's a cliché, but I could be myself with her. I was going on all these internet dates, terrifying, but then she walked into the pub and – well, I just knew it would be all right. Comfortable. We . . . fit.' He smiled at her. 'I suppose that sounds pretty dull to you.'

'No,' said Jane. 'No, it doesn't sound dull at all.'

27

The penultimate day in the hotel dawned grey and overcast. Jane was able to move around comfortably, and the doctor came that morning to clear her for travel.

'I feel silly for making such a fuss now,' said Jane.

The doctor shook her head. 'Hypothermia is no joke,' she said. 'The mountains should be taken seriously.'

Jane nodded guiltily. Looking back, she couldn't believe that a heady cocktail of lust and hangover had made her so careless.

The others spent the afternoon getting ready for the farewell ball, but Jane busied herself packing for her flight the next day. She began with her snow gear, which she would have happily thrown in the bin without a second's thought had she not borrowed it from Margot.

Her gaze fell on the little packet of letters. She would return them to Thomas that night, she thought.

There was a knock on the door and she called out for whoever it was to come in. To her surprise, it was Natasha, followed by Lucy, Lena and Freddie, carrying a hairdryer, some straightening tongs and a make-up case. They looked suspiciously purposeful.

'What are you all doing here?' Jane asked.

'We heard you were wriggling out of the ball tonight,' Freddie explained.

'And that is not on,' said Lucy. She sounded cheerful. Philip leaving had clearly done her the world of good.

'Look,' said Jane, feeling alarmed. 'I'm sure the ball will be amazing, but I just want to keep my head down tonight.'

'We thought you might say that,' said Natasha, dropping onto Jane's bed. 'And we decided to make a case for you coming.'

'What do you need to enjoy a party?' said Lucy, ruffling her honey-blonde waves with her hand.

'Er. Um, I can't quite think . . .'

'*Friends*, number one,' said Lucy, holding up an elegant finger. 'That's us. We've bonded over our dislike of the *most* horrifying man. And *fun*. I mean, that's guaranteed. This party is going to be insane.'

'It really is,' said Natasha, with quiet satisfaction. 'One of the local interior designers has gone to town on the barn. We have an orchestra, canapés from one of Norway's best chefs, and Veuve are doing the champagne.' She allowed herself a small, pleased smile. 'It's going to be amazing.'

'I'm sure it will be,' said Jane, 'but—'

'So, *friends*, that's us,' Freddie jumped in. 'And *fun*, which it will be, obviously. And the third thing we need is . . .'

Natasha beamed. '*Fashion*, darling.'

'Fashion,' said Jane, staring at her blankly. 'You want me to dress up?'

'Bingo,' said Natasha. 'We're going through your closet.' She marched over. 'I am expecting a sea of navy jumpers.' She flipped expertly through the hangers. 'And I was correct. I see I'm going to have to find something of my own for you to wea— Oh, hang on a minute.' She drew out the cardboard bag Margot had sent. 'What's this I spy?' She peered more closely at the label. 'Well, well, well. Clearly you have someone in your life with terrific taste.' She drew out Margot's dress. 'This,' she said authoritatively, 'is perfect.'

Jane shook her head.

'I can't wear that,' she said decidedly. 'It's too . . .'

'Sexy?' said Lucy, slipping an arm around her waist. 'Gorgeous? Made for you?'

'That's the beauty of it,' said Natasha, rising and holding the dress against Jane. She turned her to face the full-length mirror. 'It's classy *and* sexy. Perfect for you.'

Jane shook her head. 'I'm flattered you think I'm either of those things, but it's *not* very me.'

'It really *is*,' said Natasha firmly. 'Just not the you that comes out very often.' She pushed the dress into Jane's hands and nodded towards the bathroom. 'Go on. Put it on, please, and then Freddie is on hair, and Lucy is on make-up, and we're going to order room service and drink some champagne – you can have ginger ale, Jane.'

Jane hesitated again, and Natasha gave her a steely look. 'We're not taking no for an answer. You have a whole life-time ahead of you to wear sensible jumpers. Tonight, you're wearing the dress.'

Natasha was true to her word.

Freddie tonged Jane's stubbornly straight, dark hair until it waved and then tied it back in a loose chignon with a few pieces arranged around her face. She secured the bun with a black velvet ribbon.

'Mum used to make me wear a ribbon like this in the eighties,' Jane scoffed, but Freddie nodded seriously.

'They're great – so retro.' She stepped back and ceded her place to Lucy.

'I warn you,' Natasha said, giggling. 'We're going full *Pretty Woman*.'

'I've never seen that,' said Lucy, laying out her make-up brushes with professional care. 'I don't watch old movies.'

'*Old?*' asked Jane, startled. 'I remember watching it. I had a massive crush on Richard Gere. It's not *old*.'

'It's old when it came out six years before you were born,' said Lucy, and Lena and Freddie nodded, smirking. Natasha and Jane stared at each other in horror.

Lucy's expression was intent as she worked away, brushing Jane's thick, dark brows, tapping concealer under her eyes, and then finally unscrewing a tube of scarlet lipstick.

'Oh no, not red,' Jane said hastily. 'I never wear red lipstick.'

'You do tonight,' Lucy said determinedly, bearing down on her with the tube. 'It's called Midnight Kiss, which feels optimistic, but hey. Don't worry – it'll suit you. Trust me.'

'Right,' said Jane uncertainly, and allowed Lucy to dab at her lips.

Natasha nodded approvingly from the bed. She had changed and was now wearing a black dress patterned with large, crimson flowers, with a flowing skirt and long, ruffled sleeves. She was painting her nails. 'It'll look cool, OK?' she said, taking a sip of her champagne. 'Lucy knows what she's doing.'

'Not always,' said Lucy, with a wry smile. 'Recent events have shown that.'

Jane squeezed her hand. 'I lost my head over Philip as well.'

Lucy sighed and stood back, looking at her handiwork. 'I haven't told Harry yet. He'll never trust me again. All these years of press trips, he was always suspicious of the sleazy guys and now this has proved him right. I think he'll dump me when I tell him.' Tears filled her green eyes and she brushed them away angrily.

'Then don't,' said Natasha. She shrugged. 'What he

doesn't know won't hurt him. You've learned your lesson.' She fixed Lucy with a stern eye. 'Haven't you?'

'Yes!' the girl stammered. 'God, yes, absolutely. It was an awful mistake and I love Harry loads. He's a hundred times the man Philip is, even if he does wear smelly old Converse and won't come with me to fashion parties.'

'Well, there you go, then,' said Natasha, sitting back and examining her glossy nails. 'Count yourself lucky you got out of this whole Philip debacle unscathed. Poor old Jane here' – she gave Jane a ghost of a wink – 'got hypothermia and a sprained ankle, not to mention the damage to her dignity and reputation.'

Jane gave her a dirty look. 'Natasha's right, though,' she said to Lucy. 'Why let Philip Donnelly ruin everything?'

'I agree,' said Freddie, emerging from the bathroom in a hot-pink trouser suit over a navy silk camisole. 'Jane,' she said, stopping, her eyes widening. 'You. Look. Amazing.'

'She's right,' said Lucy, turning Jane so that she could see herself in the mirror. 'You do.'

Jane stared at the woman looking back at her. A woman with glossy, radiant skin and dark hair drawn back into shining folds. Her large eyes with their thick lashes were subtly accentuated by Lucy's clever make-up. The red lipstick, soft and matte, seemed to make her whole face light up, and the red of the dress made her skin glow.

'I don't look anything like me,' she said uncertainly, and Natasha gave her a surprising hug.

'You look *exactly* like you,' she said. 'A really good version of you.'

They were driven in cars to the site of the ball, an enormous wooden barn, less than an hour from the resort. They entered down a staircase decorated with ivy, to the strains of a violin quartet. The air smelled deliciously of woodsmoke and pine, borne into the air from hundreds of flickering candles. A vast Christmas tree, bedecked with lights and heavy glass baubles, took up an entire wall, and waiters circulated, handing round canapés and topping up glasses of champagne. Above them, soaring arches sparkled with lights and delicate, glittering snowflakes were suspended by invisible wire, giving the effect of floating in the air.

As they descended the staircase, Freddie, Lena and Lucy walking ahead, and Natasha and Jane behind, there was a coincidental pause in the music and all heads turned to look at them. Jane saw Sandra, elegant in wine-coloured satin, and Nick, dapper in evening dress, cheerfully munching canapés with another guest in the corner; they waved cheerily at Jane. As she smiled at them, she saw the other guest turn and her eyes met Ben's, looking scruffily handsome in a suit. There was something in his expression – surprise, admiration and fondness – that made her flush and falter for a moment, before she regained her poise. He gave her an enthusiastic thumbs up and she rolled her eyes at him.

'It *is* magical,' Jane whispered to Natasha, as they reached the foot of the stairs. 'Thanks for making me come.'

Natasha nodded, already casting a swift professional eye around the room. 'They've done a good job,' she conceded. Her eyes narrowed. 'But I *specifically* told them to wait until the oyster puffs were gone before bringing out the beef tartare. Excuse me.'

She hurried off into the crowd and Jane wandered through the room, lost in its loveliness. She declined a glass of champagne and accepted instead a non-alcoholic cocktail that smelled of oranges. The other guests were all local Norwegian celebrities and dignitaries, and she spotted

Thomas deep in conversation with some of them, throwing back his head and laughing. In the soft candlelight, she could imagine him as the young man who had poured wine into a tin cup for Marit Elson, all those years ago.

She saw Freddie, Lena and Lucy taking a selfie in front of the Christmas tree, smiles stretched wide for Instagram. Lucy caught sight of Jane.

'Get over here!' she called, and Jane joined them. Lucy threw an arm around her and drew her into the group. 'Smile,' she instructed.

Jane beamed widely and Freddie groaned.

'Not like *that*,' she said. 'You have to put your head to one side and . . . Oh, don't worry. We'll fix it with a filter.' They all faced the camera phone. 'Everyone say "hot tub",' said Freddie, and Jane groaned, just as the flash went off.

As the night wore on, Jane found herself having fun. Her beautiful dress drew admiring glances and she glowed with pleasure at being someone everyone was looking at. She sipped sparkling water and drifted under a ceiling so strewn with lights, that she might have been walking under a starry sky. She remembered her first walk with Philip, also under the stars, and sighed. She had gone about this holiday romance all wrong, she thought.

'Oyster puff?' murmured a waiter, and Jane took one, letting the savoury, buttery pastry melt on her tongue. She sat down on one of the chairs, watching as the orchestra struck up a waltz and couples took to the floor.

'Excuse me,' said a voice, and Jane turned to see Thomas standing there, smiling. 'May I have this dance?'

'I can't waltz,' Jane said, laughing. 'Especially not with a dodgy ankle.'

'Then we won't waltz,' he assured her. 'We'll shuffle – but very elegantly.'

'Deal,' she said, accepting his hand. 'Isn't this amazing?' Jane said, looking around. 'I'll have to remember it when I'm on the seven-forty train on Monday.'

'Ah yes – back to the daily grind?' Thomas shook his head. 'Not something I have ever experienced. We had discipline in the army, but not the seven-forty train.'

'Well, it's time to get back to real life,' said Jane, not really wanting it to be true. 'And you?' she asked. 'You'll go back to Oslo?'

'Yes,' he said. 'I look forward to seeing my grandchildren. They will have grown even in the last week.'

'Will you speak to Marit's – Margaret's – family?' Jane asked.

'I have already done so,' he said. 'We are meeting tomorrow.' He smiled and Jane thought that he seemed lighter, happier, somehow, as though a great load had been lifted. 'I want to hear all about her life after the war.'

'I have your letters still,' said Jane. 'I need to give them back to you. Will you show them to Iacob and Susan?'

Thomas shook his head. 'No, no,' he said firmly. 'I should like you to have them,' he said. He tapped his temple. 'I have them all, anyway, up here. There might be more to Marit's story.'

She looked at him curiously.

'I don't know that there's anything else to say about her, Thomas,' she said gently. 'She wrote to you all those years and then she just – gave up. That's the end of it.'

To her surprise, Thomas gave her a mischievous smile. 'It's been good to meet you, Jane,' he said. 'And I am very grateful for your help. I have asked Ben to stay on with me for a few days – act as a translator. I'd like to write down a few of my old war stories.' He neatly guided Jane past a couple who were twirling energetically and then said, his voice deceptively casual, 'Are you and Ben friends at work?'

'Sort of,' she said. 'He's away a lot on assignments so we haven't spent that much time together.'

'I have become very fond of that boy. Keep an eye on him for me.'

'He's the one who's kept an eye on *me* this trip,' Jane said. 'Ben can take care of himself.'

'I don't know,' said Thomas. 'He seems very cheerful, doesn't he? But no one is that happy all the time. He's had his fair share of bad times too. He told me so.'

'Really?' asked Jane. It was hard to imagine Ben downcast.

'His little sister, Cathrin, has been very sick with cancer for years. In and out of hospitals since she was a teenager. It's why his family moved to Britain, so she could have treatment with a specialist doctor there.'

Cathrin, the little girl who had lined up pebbles on a beach and swum to an island in the dark with stolen wine on her back.

'I had no idea,' said Jane, shocked.

'People don't always show their pain,' said Thomas. 'He could use a friend, I think.' He twirled her gently under his arm. 'A good friend.'

Jane looked at him closely. 'Are you *matchmaking*?' she asked.

'No, no,' said Thomas. His face was innocent, but Jane saw that his eyes were twinkling.

'Because if you are,' Jane said, 'it's a waste of time.'

'That feels like a shame,' said Thomas. 'To let one bad experience put you off romance for ever.'

'*Two* bad experiences,' said Jane bitterly. 'One right after another. But I've learned my lesson. If there ever *is* a next time, I'm going for someone totally different.

Someone kind. Someone funny and generous and decent and straightforward and—'

'Ah, Ben,' said Thomas, glancing over her shoulder. 'We were just talking about you.'

Jane stumbled to a halt, flushing up to her hair. Ben was standing there, and yes, she thought, he really did look very handsome in his suit.

'Were you?' he said, looking between Jane and Thomas. Then he said, with a trace of awkwardness, 'I was actually going to ask if I might cut in.'

'Certainly,' said Thomas, releasing Jane. 'I need to sit down for a bit. Nothing too vigorous, though – Jane's ankle is still sore.'

'We'll go slowly, then,' said Ben. He held out his hand. 'I'm not much of a dancer anyway.'

Jane let him slip an arm around her waist, pretending that it felt totally normal to be in Ben's arms. That the way her stomach flipped meant nothing.

After a few moments of staring fixedly at Ben's shirt, she cleared her throat.

'You lied,' she said. 'You're a good dancer.'

'You're not so bad yourself,' he said softly, and Jane flushed again. She had definitely gone about this all wrong. Philip, with his fast moves and his arrogant good looks, had dazzled her, but what was it that Natasha had said about the quiet ones?

'All recovered from your accident?' Ben asked politely.

'Yes, thank you,' she replied, equally politely. She thought how easily she had always chatted to Ben, whether it was over a cup of tea in the office or in a fishing boat in the moonlight, and how awkward things were now.

'Where are you spending Christmas this year?' she asked at last. 'At home?'

'Yeah,' he said. 'At my parents' in Scotland. It'll be full on. Two of my sisters had twin girls a few years ago and nothing's been the samc since.' He grinned. 'Absolute mayhem.'

She could imagine what his family Christmas must be like – a big, shabby house, children running around shrieking with excitement, turkey in the oven, films on the telly. Games and long-standing family in-jokes. Warm, rowdy, cosy, chaotic.

Although, at the heart of the family, the sadness and worry about Cathrin.

No one had it that easy, she thought, not really.

'What about you?' he asked.

She summoned a smile. 'Mum died a few years ago. I usually go to my best mate Margot's, and she married an amazing cook, so that's good. But, well, they're about to have a baby, so . . .'

So that was that, Jane thought. She had been avoiding thinking about it, but she knew she needed to give Margot, Kate and the new baby time to themselves this year.

'So things might be different this year,' she finished.

'Kids have a way of shaking things up,' he said.

They danced in silence for a while. Something had shifted between them, Jane thought sadly, perhaps for ever.

Ben broke the silence first. 'I'm sorry,' he said. 'For how horrible I was to you, after your accident. I had no right to tell you off. I was just worried, but it came out angry.' He shrugged. 'I feel weird letting you leave without apologising.'

'It's OK,' said Jane. 'I understand. You were worried about Thomas.'

'Well,' he said quietly, 'I was mostly worried about *you*.'

'Oh,' she said, and they both fell silent again. His hand held her loosely in the small of her back and they moved easily together. Maybe they *were* both good dancers. Or maybe, Jane thought, it was just that they fit.

'Listen, Jane,' Ben said. 'I know things have been a bit weird between us, but I wanted to say . . .'

Just then, though, the music stopped, and a voice called for silence. The mayor of Oslo, whom they had last seen at the tree-cutting ceremony, was tapping a champagne glass with a spoon and calling for silence.

Everyone lapsed into silence and turned to face her. Jane could feel Ben's sleeve brushing against her bare arm. She felt an almost uncontrollable desire to reach out and take his hand.

'Thank you all for coming,' the mayor said. 'I won't say much – this party is too good for us to waste time talking. But I wanted to wish you all a very happy Christmas. I hope we have given you an idea of how we celebrate it here in Norway. About what tradition can mean.' She looked out over the crowd. 'Looking back, in the best way. Remembering the bravery of men and women, and the generosity of a country who gave us sanctuary. Christmas is not just about gifts and shopping and too much food, although that is nice, hey?' They all laughed. She raised her glass. 'To Christmas, to love, and to our Queen of the Forest.'

The applause rang out, and then suddenly Jane was surrounded by the rest of the gang, all hugging and kissing each other. They were splitting up. She, Nick and Sandra were flying out the next morning. Natasha was staying on for a few days to ski. Lucy, Lena and Freddie were on later flights because they were flying to Scotland for another press trip.

And Ben.

'You're going to stay and help Thomas?' Jane asked. She tried to keep her voice light.

'For a few days,' he said. 'I'll get in some skiing.'

Jane shuddered dramatically. 'I'll never ski again,' she said, and he laughed.

'And then after that,' he said slowly, 'I've got a job in Turkey.'

'Gosh,' she said. 'You're busy, aren't you?'

'Yeah,' he said. 'It's a bit of a problem.'

'Oh well,' Jane said. 'Good luck. I'll see you in the office in the next four to six months, I imagine.'

She held out her hand to Ben and he squeezed it.

'Goodbye, Jane,' he said, and then he was gone, swallowed up by the crowd.

Jane looked after him. So that was that, she thought. Anything there had been between them – and she wasn't even sure it *was* anything – had evaporated into the night air, along with the champagne bubbles.

'Goodbye, my dear,' said Thomas, enveloping Jane in a hug. She found herself clinging to him for a moment, burying her face in his shoulder.

He held her away from him, his dark eyes searching hers. 'Can I give you some advice, Jane, my dear?' he said suddenly. 'Because you have one of those faces, you know. It's hard to tell what you might be thinking.'

'I've been told that before,' Jane sniffed.

'There is nothing wrong with that. Good to keep your cards close to your chest. But occasionally people like you, who don't show much, can run up against people who are perhaps not too sure of themselves. When that happens, it is good to be honest.' He smiled the charming smile that had drawn Jane's attention that first night at dinner. 'Remember, I once let love slip through my fingers. I regret nothing of my life. I have been very happy. But my advice to you, Jane, is that if you find love, you should grab it with both hands, and not let go.'

Jane stared at him. 'I don't know what you're talking about,' she said.

'Perhaps not,' Thomas said. 'And then again, perhaps you know exactly.'

'I wish I could see you again,' said Jane. 'I don't suppose you'll ever visit London?'

He smiled. 'I would like to see the Queen of the Forest in her finery. You never know. Goodbye, Jane.' He turned and walked away, disappearing into the beautiful, shining crowd.

The lights were flickering on. The waiters were beginning to collect the dirty glasses and empty bottles. Jane could hear the cars arriving to take them home.

The trip was over.

28

London, 1st December

Reality hit Jane as soon as she stepped off the plane into lashing rain at Gatwick. The sky was grey, and the air was bitingly cold.

She trudged through passport control and customs with her suitcase alongside Nick and Sandra, hugged them goodbye, then set off home.

She got the train to Victoria and then waited for a taxi, rainwater trickling down her neck. Her overheated, stuffy cab sat in interminable traffic, taillights shining greasily through the rain-spattered windscreen, as drunken office parties spilled out of pubs. They drove through the familiar streets, back past the chicken shops and trendy bars to Stoke Newington and her flat.

Jane's key jammed in the lock of her front door like it always did when it had been raining and the wood was damp. She had to put her elbow to the door to force it open.

Inside, her flat seemed smaller and dingier than before. Two weeks of dust covered every surface, and the air was freezing cold. The delicate teacup Simon had given her was still half-full of tea, a skin of white mould now covering the top.

Jane flicked on a light, turned the heating up full blast,

then leaned her suitcase against the wall and dropped onto the sofa, still wearing her coat. She closed her eyes and let a whirlwind of images drift across her mind – elegant meals and beautiful hotels, her fingers closing about Thomas's wartime letters. A flame-coloured dress, gossamer-light against her skin. An old man guiding her gently about the dance floor, candles glittering, the smell of woodsmoke and pine.

And Ben. Ben standing in the snow, the collar of his navy pea coat turned up. His hand on hers in the little fishing boat and his face turned towards her, cheeks wet with rain. Moonlight breaking through clouds, and a pile of silver fish.

Jane shivered and drew her coat closer about her, sticking her hands deep into the pockets to warm them. As she did so, her fingers closed about something solid and round.

A pebble, from a beach in Norway.

Jane's Underground journey to the *Courier* on Monday was hot and crowded, made worse by the stench of stale alcohol smothered with aftershave. Christmas-party season was clearly in full swing. Everyone looked grey-faced and glassy-eyed, swigging coffee as though their lives depended on it.

On arrival, she was summoned immediately into Nadine's office to give her the full story. Jane was as brief as possible, sticking to the bare facts; but the bare facts weren't too edifying.

'Philip Donnelly really swiped the piece *you* were planning?' Nadine asked, her expression mildly impressed. 'I didn't know he had it in him.'

'He's a weasel,' Jane said. 'But I've got something better planned – you'll see.'

'So I *will* get a story out of all this,' Nadine said, her eyes narrowed. 'Because the Christmas edition goes to print in a fortnight and there's a big fat two-page spread with your name on it and zero copy.'

'You'll have it,' Jane promised fervently. 'Listen, Nadine. There's something else I need to talk to you about.' She took a deep breath. 'Something that I'm not sure you're going to like.'

Leaving Nadine's office half an hour later, Jane walked straight into Simon Layton.

'Oh, sorry,' she said, extricating herself. He looked irritatingly healthy and bronzed, as though he'd spent the last few weeks on a beach rather than watching films in the dark. Perhaps he and Emily had squeezed in a casual winter break to the Caribbean.

'That's OK,' he said, staring at her as though transfixed. 'Hi, Jane. Good to have you back. I heard your trip was, ah, interesting.'

'It was,' said Jane grimly, turning and heading back to her desk. If he wanted the gory details, then he wouldn't get them from her. 'It certainly was.'

Thank God for Margot, who met her in the tapas pub around the corner after work. She was already there when Jane arrived and had ordered handsomely. As Jane approached the table, she counted two plates of *croquetas*, *padrón* peppers, pork belly, tortilla, two baskets of bread, and two tumblers of pale rosé wine.

'Thank goodness you're here,' Margot said, as Jane kissed her on the cheek and sat down. 'I don't think they believed someone else was coming. The waitress virtually used air quotes when she asked if I wanted the extra bread *for my friend.* Is this enough? Shall we get some of that aubergine dip you like?' She peered at Jane, much as Simon had done earlier. 'You look different. All lit up and glowing and radiant. Like *I'm* meant to look.'

'I'm fine,' said Jane, clinking glasses. 'It wasn't the best first day, but that's to be expected. I promised Nadine a story to appease her – God knows what it will be. *And* I ran into Simon, who looks gorgeous and fit. Bastard. Thanks for coming and meeting me. Are you drinking?'

Margot took a dainty sip of wine. 'Under my midwife's instructions.' She squeezed Jane's hand. 'I'm sorry about what happened with Philip. I blame myself completely. Shall I have him killed?'

'Don't worry about that,' Jane said, tearing off a piece of bread. 'Like I said, I'm fine.'

'You are?' said Margot, sounding confused. 'I thought you were having a professional and personal crisis.'

'I was,' said Jane. 'My pride was hurt. It was obvious Philip was a bastard from the start.' She shook her head. 'But even if he hadn't abandoned me in a snowdrift and ripped off my story, we would never have been right for each other. He was always going to date someone with a triple-barrelled name while maintaining a sideline in hot twenty-somethings. He's not even a bad person – he just can't help himself. Anyway,' she said, sitting back, 'I've done some thinking and made some decisions. Big life ones.'

Margot dropped the pepper she was holding. 'I don't like the sound of this,' she said.

Jane set her elbows on the table. 'I realised something while I was in Norway,' she said. 'I realised I can carry on living my life here in London – which is a nice life – or I can leave and find myself a bigger one.'

'What do you mean, leave?' wailed Margot. 'Leave your job? London? *Me?*'

'Not for ever. But I keep thinking about Marit. She must have been so brave, to walk away from everything she knew and travel the world. She had everything to lose. But she did it, because she wanted to *live*.' She took a triumphant gulp of wine. 'Well, I want to live too.'

Margot looked at her uneasily. 'Can't you do all that living here, in your perfect apartment with your friends who adore you and the job you love?'

Jane shook her head. 'It would always be safe, though. And I've had enough of being safe.' She took another deep breath. 'I've taken that job as foreign correspondent with the *Washington News*.'

Margot gasped and her hand flew to her mouth. 'Jane! What did the *Courier* say?'

'Nadine's sorry to see me go, but she understands.' Jane grinned. 'She thinks I'll go on to do great things.'

'And you spring this on me at Christmas,' said Margot. She pushed her plate away miserably. 'In my condition.'

Jane lifted her friend's hands and squeezed them. 'I don't leave till the new year,' she said gently. 'I'll still be here for Christmas.'

Margot wiped her eyes. 'Well, that's good, because it's going to be amazing,' she said. 'We've ordered a crate of wine and a hamper from Fortnum's and Kate's cooking goose.'

'About that,' said Jane, taking another deep breath. 'Let's be realistic. I can't stay with you guys for Christmas, not this year. Everything is going to be different. You're going to have a *baby*.' Her voice wobbled slightly, but she carried on. 'You can't have me under your feet. Besides, what is Christmas really? It's just one day. I'll be busy packing.'

She looked up, to see that Margot's gaze had softened. 'Idiot,' she said gently. 'Do you think I'd let my best friend in all the world be on her own for Christmas Day?'

'But what about the baby?' asked Jane.

'The baby is exactly *why* I need you there, Jane. It's entirely selfish.' Margot's eyes were twinkling 'I'm hoping that the more people I can sucker into hanging out, the less nappies I have to change. Say yes.'

Jane smiled. 'Yes,' she said. 'If you're one hundred per cent sure, then yes.'

'One thousand per cent,' said Margot. She pushed the plate of peppers towards Jane. 'Eat something,' she said. 'They might not have tapas wherever you're going next. And let's talk about nicer things. Like . . . oooh, I don't know. Like Ben.'

'Ben?' Jane choked on her mouthful. 'Not this again?'

'Ben the dashing photographer.'

'He's not really dashing. He's just nice and kind. And handsome in a quiet sort of way. And tall. And capable and funny and smart. And brave.'

'He sounds dreadful,' said Margot, smiling.

Jane sighed. 'He thinks I set Thomas up for Philip's stupid story.'

'Can you not tell him that's utter bollocks?' Margot said. 'Politely ruining your life over a misunderstanding is very Jane Austen of you, but it seems like a shame. Especially if he's lovely.'

'He *is* lovely,' Jane said wistfully. She shook her head. 'Too lovely for me. I only go for callous bastards with cheekbones like razors and floppy hair. Besides, Ben's in Norway and I'm here. By the time he gets back, I'll be gone, and it'll go on like that for ever. Our jobs would mean we're never in the same country for more than five minutes.'

'Well, maybe that's why it would work. You *do* like him, don't you? I can tell.'

'No,' said Jane vehemently, although she was smiling. 'I mean it this time. I'm never falling in love again. I'm clearly not very good at it.'

Margot looked at her thoughtfully. 'As someone who has been married a whole six years, I'm going to give you some advice.' *Whether you like it or not* was the unspoken ending to that sentence.

'All right,' said Jane, picking apart a pepper and licking the salt off her fingers. 'Your advice worked so well last time.'

Margot pulled a face at her. 'It's awful having your heart broken. The worst. I mean, technically other things are worse – death and sickness and divorce – but it's pretty bad. Takes you ages to recover, if you ever really do. Agreed?'

'Is this going to make me feel better soon?'

'Do you remember when I married Kate? I thought she was so hot and smart and funny. Do I see those things now? Of course not! They're still *there*, I guess, if I look really hard, but they're buried under all the other things I can't stand – her filthy moods when she's hungry or her getting toenail clippings all over our new rug or the disgusting Garfield T-shirt she wears.'

'You're not really selling married life,' said Jane, smiling.

'I haven't finished yet.' Margot said. 'Despite this, though, I lucked out, because as well as looking like Jennifer Connelly, it turns out that Kate is kind and she makes me laugh. And there's the cooking, obviously. None of that would necessarily have been sexy six years ago. But it's the reason we got through three rounds of IVF and remortgaging our house without falling apart.' She put down her glass, her face serious. 'My point is that you're seeing Simon and

Philip as failures, when actually, you dodged a bullet. You don't want some whinging man-child at your side when things go wrong, when your kids get sick or you lose a job. It's a lottery, this relationship business, and you can't afford to pick the wrong person. You need to be a team.'

Jane chewed thoughtfully on another pepper. '*I always knew we'd be a team*' – that was what Sandra had said.

'You're making it sound like I have tons of men lined up and I'm just picking the crap ones,' she said.

'Nope.' Margot shook her head. 'I'm pointing out that you're looking at this all wrong. The point isn't to avoid all men – the point is to take this bitter experience and make it count for something. Simon, Philip – did you ever really *like* them?'

'Obviously. They're gorgeous and—'

'Right, but did you *like* them? Did they like you? Do you have any idea how sexy it is to be with someone who has seen you at your absolute worst and *still* likes you?' She picked up a *croqueta* and waved it for emphasis. '*That's* what you need in a man, Jane,' she finished triumphantly.

'Someone who's kind, even if they cut their nails all over the rug?'

'Absolutely. Kate had to tie my shoelaces this morning because I couldn't bend down.' She smiled, her lovely face suddenly dreamy. 'Someone who knows the bones of you and likes you anyway. That's probably the most important thing there is.'

29

Jane spent the next week at the *Courier* avoiding Nadine and keeping her head down. That Friday her colleagues assembled for their usual night at the pub, but she declined. She was sure they wanted the gossip from Norway, but she wasn't in the mood to laugh about it yet.

She went home instead, walking past brightly-lit shops, outdoor smokers and bustling restaurants, stopping off only at a deserted Marks & Spencer to buy a pizza and a large Christmas chocolate selection box. She got into her cosiest flannel pyjamas and she was watching Cameron Diaz tottering down a snowy country lane – wearing stilettos and expensive knitwear – and demolishing the last slice of overcooked pizza when the doorbell rang.

She stirred reluctantly, wondering whether she could get away with ignoring it. It would be her neighbour Jim with whatever packages he had taken in for her while she was away. She had meant to bring him a present back from Norway to say thank you, but amid all the drama, she had forgotten.

The doorbell rang again, for longer this time. 'All right, all right,' she muttered, pulling on a ratty cardigan over her pyjamas and trudging through the hall to the doorway. She opened the door.

It wasn't Jim from next door; it was Simon.

'Jane,' he said. Rainwater was running down his face, plastering his dark hair to his forehead, and he smelled faintly of beer. 'I was hoping you might be in.'

She stared at him. 'Simon? What are you doing here?'

He gave a shaky laugh. 'I'm not completely sure, to be honest. I was at the work drinks and I just . . . Look, can I come in?' He gestured at the lashing rain. 'I'm getting pretty wet out here.'

'No!' she said, more vehemently than she meant to. The thought of Simon in her flat, witnessing the pizza crusts and chocolate wrappers, was too much to bear.

'Fair enough,' he said, blinking. 'In that case, can I buy you a drink at the pub?' When she didn't answer, he leaned closer. 'Please, Jane. When I saw you the other day, I realised that— Look, let's not do this here. Please can we just sit down and talk? It's important.'

She sent Simon ahead to the pub at the end of the road – *their* pub, as Jane still thought of it – while she pulled on some jeans and a jumper. When she got there, she saw that Simon had managed to squeeze onto a free table, with two halves of Guinness in front of him. She hadn't wanted to commit to a whole pint. She wasn't even sure why she was here at all.

He waved at her and she walked over, pulling out a stool to sit down. They were sitting so close together that their knees were touching. She snuck a quick glance at him as she took a sip of her drink. He looked . . . himself. Gorgeous. High cheekbones, blue eyes fringed with curling, sooty lashes. A handsome, arrogant face. Although, she noticed now, less arrogant than usual. He looked ever so slightly unsure of himself.

'How are you?' he asked. He looked her over carefully, as

though trying to figure something out. 'You look . . . different. Did you get a tan in Norway?' He peered closer. 'Did you change your hair?'

'What do you *want*, Simon?' she asked.

He took several quick gulps of his beer.

'I heard all sorts of rumours while you were away,' he said. 'Did you really kiss Philip Donnelly in a hot tub?'

Jane took another sip of her drink. Perhaps the only good thing about the whole hideous episode was that it had clearly bothered Simon. 'Maybe I did. Maybe I didn't. What's it to you?'

'Nothing, nothing. Only I . . .' He ran his fingers urgently through his hair, so that it stood up on end. It was one of his characteristically extravagant, unconscious gestures when he was lost for words. Only – *was* it unconscious? Wasn't everything about Simon – from his artfully dishevelled hair to his frayed cashmere sweaters, to his love of old films and his boyish voice – carefully designed to seem bewildered and vaguely helpless?

'The thing is, Jane,' he said, his blue eyes wistful, 'I've missed you.'

'Have you?' she asked. 'That's weird – I haven't thought about you in ages.'

'Ouch.' He swirled the remnants of his Guinness around, looking into his glass. 'I suppose I deserve that.'

She looked at his downcast face. He sounded convincingly sorrowful; he had probably convinced himself.

'Look,' he said. 'I'll lay my cards on the table, Jane. I've broken up with Emily again.'

Jane's heart, which would once have leaped at this news, gave no more than a brief, dull thud against her ribs.

'You broke up with her just before Christmas?' she asked, thinking, *Of course you did.*

'Yeah, it just wasn't working. I realised I'd made a mistake.' His eyes met hers, wide and appealing. 'I've missed you, Jane. We were so good together and I was a fool not to realise it. It was hard, you know?'

'Hard?' said Jane.

'Yeah, it was.' He rubbed his hand across his face. 'I had to sit by and watch you be all clever, breaking that big story, and I admit I wasn't man enough to handle it.'

Suddenly, Jane could bear it no longer. A cheesy movie in her pyjamas and an M&S selection box was infinitely preferable to the loud, crowded pub with its sticky table and Simon sitting opposite her. She pushed her chair back and stood up.

'Where are you going?' he said.

'Look, Simon,' she said, buttoning up her coat. 'Can I save us both some time and guess what you're going to say?'

He stared at her.

'Tell me if I've got this right. You've broken up with Emily, and you miss me. It's Christmas, and you're lonely, and you and I are much better suited than you thought. Did I nail it?'

He nodded, still looking stunned.

'And,' she went on, winding her scarf about her neck, 'you'd like us to give it another try. Nothing concrete, mind – no solid commitment, let's not get carried away – you'd just like to *see how things go*?'

He nodded again.

'Mmm, thought so.' She pulled on her gloves and drained the rest of her drink. 'Do you even *like* me, Simon?'

'*Like* you? Jane, I-I think you're amazing. The smartest woman I've ever met. So strong—'

'Yeah, but do you *like* me?' She smiled at his confused face. They had spent a year together and he still didn't know her at all. Not really. 'Because I'm never going to stop working hard. I'm never going to stop striving for the big story. That's who I am.' She took a deep breath. 'I'll see you in the office on Monday, Simon,' she said, and left.

Jane's euphoria lasted all the way home, down her chilly Stoke Newington street, past the happy, giggling couples and Christmas-party escapees. She walked with gloved hands jammed in pockets, head held high.

It lasted through the hot shower, where she scrubbed the pub off her skin and hair, lasted as she sipped a cup of camomile tea and then brushed her teeth.

Even as she slipped between clean sheets and turned off her light, she was still beaming with triumph.

And then, quite suddenly, all of that euphoria drained away and Jane wanted to cry.

She lay there staring at the ceiling in the not-quite-dark, listening to the noises of the city outside and the bumps and scrapes as her neighbours moved around upstairs, getting ready for bed.

She had gone to Norway to write a story. And instead she had messed everything up.

Thomas and Marit's story would now never be anything more than a badly-written revenge job. Ben thought she was either a grasping journalist who had been willing to use a fragile old man's past for her own gain, or an idiot, hoodwinked by Philip's dubious charms. Jane wasn't sure which was worse.

Ben's face came unbidden into her mind, spattered with rain in the little rowboat in the middle of a loch. His grey eyes, calm and steady as he read Marit's letters. Their gazes locking across the crowded ballroom as she walked down the stairs in a flame-red dress.

She turned her pillow over, hoping to cool her burning

cheeks. Her sore ankle throbbed. Suddenly, impossibly, she wanted Ben to walk through the door right now. She wanted him to drop down next to her on the bed, stretch out his long legs and loop his fingers through hers. She wanted to rest her head against his chest.

She wanted . . .

She turned the pillow over again. Something else was bothering her and she couldn't figure out what. Something about Thomas's face as he had said goodbye that night at the ball, as he had pressed his worn love letters into her hands.

What was it that Simon had said in the pub?

'*I had to sit by and watch you be all clever.*'

Marit's words, their ink faded but jumping off the page still, after all those years.

'*I should like someone to know how clever I have been.*'

Jane sat up. What, exactly, had Marit meant by that?

What had been so clever about spending the war on a little island, feeding chickens and cooking her brother's meals?

Jane turned on her bedside light, pulled back the covers and got out of bed. She padded on bare feet through to the kitchen and put on the kettle, then took the packet with Marit's letters out of her bag. She shook them out onto the kitchen table. She stared at them as the kettle boiled.

Thomas, his dark eyes on hers in the glittering ballroom.

'*There might be, after all, more to Marit's story.*'

Jane ran her fingers across the letters.

It is hard, writing and getting no reply.

Jane closed her eyes.

All those letters and Thomas had never once replied.

Why not? thought Jane.

Marit had *known* she would never get a reply.

Because the letters themselves weren't the point.

Only one letter remained in its envelope, the last one Marit had sent Thomas towards the end of the war, the letter ending their one-sided romance. Jane drew it closer with the tip of her finger, then picked it up and held the envelope up to the light.

Perhaps you might save the stamp. I know you collect them. You are such a boy still.

The kettle was boiling, steam filling the kitchen. Jane held the envelope over the kettle, allowing little puffs of steam to make contact with the stamp. Ever so carefully, she peeled the bottom up with her fingernail, working quickly but gently, to detach first one corner and then the next, until the stamp was peeled back partway. And then she held it away from her, staring with disbelieving eyes.

There was something underneath the stamp.

30

Trafalgar Square, London, 11th December

The evening of the Christmas-tree-lighting ceremony was crisp and cold, with a definite promise of snow in the air.

Jane barely felt the chill. She had spent the last day poring over old newspaper articles and looking up all she could find about 1940s Norwegian spies and microfilm. She had found out enough to come up with a theory – but she needed to speak to Thomas to find out if she was right.

Now, she was waiting for Margot at the Trafalgar Square exit to Charing Cross Tube, vibrating with impatience. She and Margot had a dinner date, but Jane was hoping she wouldn't mind delaying it by just an hour or so.

Natasha had sounded only slightly surprised when Jane rang her that morning, telling her she'd come along to the tree-lighting ceremony after all.

'It'll be quite the reunion,' Natasha said. 'Sandra's coming, and Nick with his kids, and Lucy, Lena and Freddie are back – I've persuaded them to hang out with us ancient lot for one more evening.'

'Not Thomas, though?' Jane asked urgently, and Natasha hesitated.

'I'm not sure,' she said at last, and there was something odd in her voice. 'It would be a long way for him to come. But you never know – the old man is full of surprises.'

Jane was holding that faint hope close to her heart now. Thomas had *wanted* her to peel back that stamp, she was sure of it. That was why he had given her the letters, why he had involved her in the first place.

'Jane, sweetheart.' It was Margot, emerging out of the drab London night like a tropical bird. She was wearing a high-necked, brightly-coloured floral dress that skimmed her bump, along with tights, pink suede slingbacks and a pink coat. 'You look nice.' She eyed Jane suspiciously. 'Have you dressed up?'

Jane flushed. She had made an extra effort – a pretty blouse with her standard jeans. She didn't know why. 'Thanks,' she said. 'You too. Very festive.'

'I look insane,' said Margot wearily. 'I'm at the stage of wearing anything that fits.'

'Well, you make it work,' said Jane. 'Listen. We have to make a short detour.'

'Oh no. We're having Chinese food. It's our pre-Christmas thing.'

'I just need to do something first,' Jane said. 'They're turning on the Trafalgar Square Christmas-tree lights and I *have* to be there. I can't explain it all now, but it's important. Plus, it'll be a magical festive experience.'

'We're delaying dinner *and* you want to go to the hell-hole that is Trafalgar Square at Christmas, where I won't be able to sit down?' Margot scowled.

'Just for a few minutes,' Jane begged. 'If I'm right, then I might have got to the bottom of Thomas's mystery – and I can give Nadine her story, all tied up with a bow for Christmas.'

Margot raised an eyebrow. 'Fine, we can go for a bit. But then I get my dim sum.' She patted her shoulder bag. 'I brought the Gaviscon especially. Anything more delicious than a dry cracker is dicing with disaster.'

'I swear,' Jane promised, and took her arm.

As they neared the square, Jane caught her breath, stunned by the incongruity of it. There she stood, the Queen of the Forest, a world away from the snowy splendour of a Norwegian forest. Standing sixty-five feet high and strung with lights, in darkness now but waiting to blaze into life. There was a huge crowd, a mixture of tourists and Londoners, swaddled in thick coats, laughing and chatting.

The press party were waiting behind a cordoned-off area to the left of the tree. Natasha waved them over, gave Jane a brief hug and then, true to form, began taking photographs on her phone.

Sandra was there, muffled up to her eyes, wearing an enormous velvet hat, and Nick, with two excited small boys hanging off him. Freddie and Lena, managing to make bobble hats and mittens stylish as usual. Lucy, with a short, bearded man with a sweet smile, who she introduced as the mysterious Harry.

He was grinning and had his arm wrapped tightly around her. *Good*, Jane thought.

Jane opened her mouth to introduce Margot, but realised there was no need.

'Where on earth did you get those adorable boots?' Margot demanded of Lucy, and they were soon absorbed in conversation. Much like Ben, Margot had the gift of being able to find a million things in common with pretty much anyone.

Jane scanned the crowd frantically. She couldn't see Thomas. She caught Natasha's arm.

'Have you seen him?' she asked urgently. 'Thomas, I mean.'

Natasha's eyes were kind, but there was something in them that made Jane look at her more closely. 'He's all right, isn't he?' Jane said.

'I think . . .' Natasha said, and then stopped, her gaze sliding over Jane's shoulder. 'I think that someone else should explain,' she finished.

Jane turned in the direction of her gaze and there, standing before her, was Ben.

It was at once strange and absolutely right to see him there, in Trafalgar Square. He looked himself – the same shabby navy pea coat, rumpled dark hair. Her heart leaped into her chest and stayed there, fluttering uncontrollably.

'It's . . . it's nice to see you,' she said, smiling stupidly.

For half a second, she thought she saw her own happiness reflected in his face. But then something flickered in his eyes. He was still angry with her, she thought, about Philip and that stupid story.

She dragged him aside, aware that Margot and the rest of the group were watching them with interest.

'Ben, I need to speak to Thomas,' she said. 'The woman who wrote the letters during the war, Marit Elson – she wasn't his girlfriend. She was a *spy*. They weren't love letters; they were a way of getting information out of occupied Norway and into England. I steamed one of the stamps off and there was something underneath. I think it's a microfilm. The Allies used them during the war – spies sent maps and plans of German bases that way.' His expression was unreadable, and she felt impatience rising up. '*That's* why Marit spent the war on that island – because it was right next to a German submarine base. She was photographing it.'

He still said nothing.

'Look,' she said, 'I know I messed up, but if Marit was serving her country, then it's a story that should be told. Thomas wants me to, I'm sure of it. I'll do it properly this time.'

He said quietly, then, 'It's a story all right.' He drew her over to a bench, away from the crowd. 'Let's sit down for a minute, Jane. There's something I need to tell you.'

Thomas was gone, Ben said. He had died in his sleep two days ago, in his son's house in Oslo.

Jane thought about Thomas in the ballroom. All that advice, about grabbing love with both hands.

'He knew, didn't he?' she said quietly.

'He was seen by doctors when you were laid up with your ankle,' said Ben. 'That's when he told me. He was as well as could be expected, not in much pain. That's why he insisted on going on this press trip in the first place. Why he was so keen for you to read Marit's letters. It was his last chance, he said, to tell her story.'

Jane stared at her lap, unable to speak. For someone she had known only a brief time, Thomas had made a big impression.

'I wish I'd known he was sick,' she said at last, and Ben nodded.

'He didn't want anyone to know,' Ben said. He laid a package gently in Jane's lap. 'He asked me to give this to you.' Their eyes met. She longed to lay her palm against his cheek.

Jane opened the parcel. It contained a sheaf of old papers, folded neatly, and she turned them over wonderingly. Maps and photographs, on thin, faded paper. Diagrams. The original envelopes Marit had sent, the stamps missing and in their place the miniature microfilms. So here, on Jane's lap, was the fruit of Marit's labours, of all her years as a spy. A story, ready for the taking.

And one last thing – a letter, addressed to her, Jane Brook, in elegant script. She drew it out. It was from Thomas, dated three days ago.

Dear Jane,

I wonder whether by now you will have thought to look under the stamp. I rather think you will have – it was why I wanted you to have the letters. I wasn't sure what to do and I thought you might take that decision out of my hands. A coward's way out, perhaps.

We were never meant to be lovers, Marit and I. She was a secret agent and I was her contact, and that was all we knew about each other when we first met in Nybergsund.

Our mission was to get the king to safety, should he and the cabinet make the decision to go to war. And then I was to go to London, and Marit was to remain in Norway. There was a German naval base, off the coast of Otteroy, and Marit's objective was to photograph it and send me the plans. I was not to write back. I did not have an address for her, even.

The letters were to be love letters, they said – less suspicious. But then, that night, something unexpected happened. We really became lovers. Everything I told you about that was true. And those letters she sent me, which should have meant nothing at all, came to mean everything.

Madness, to spend your life loving a lie. To live for letters that were mere props in a war-game. Was it all in my own mind? I went back after the war to find out. I looked for Marit. And then I gave up. I left the letters in the chimney breast, like the foolish, nostalgic boy I was. I left a note with them that you might want to see – Ben can translate it for you.

I don't know whether she ever came back, whether she ever read it. It doesn't matter now. I had a good, happy, full life, and so, it seems, did she.

Spies are trained never to tell secrets. Not our own and certainly not those of a fellow spy. No matter how many years go by. That's the code. But there I stood, that day we cut down the tree, a local hero. Wealthy, lionised, honoured by my community. Famous, in my small way. While Marit, by far the braver of us, remained in obscurity.

I wanted to tell her story.

When you found her family for me, you did me a great service, my dear. I spoke with them, and they are happy to have Marit's story told. I am running out of time, so I ask you to do this for me. Tell it and tell it well.

One other thing, Jane. Remember that love is not worth waiting for. Grab it with both hands.

Your friend Thomas

Jane laid the letter down very carefully. She drew out Thomas's final note to Marit – faded, yellowed paper, thin in her fingers, and scrawled across it in a quick, youthful hand, *Marit.*

His last letter.

'Would you be able to read this to me?' she asked Ben.

Ben took it. Then, just as he had in Thomas's room, he began to read aloud:

Marit,

It feels strange to be writing to you. Out of the two of us, you were the writer. I don't know if you will remember me – a boy with a scar on his face, very serious and self-important. Boasting about how rich his family was. Easy to tease. A boy who made you a picnic of sardines and stale bread, terrible wine. A freezing cottage, and days and weeks and years of uncertainty ahead.

I lived for your letters, during the war. Can you imagine that? Even though they meant nothing at all. Or did they? I don't think I'll ever find out.

I am going to get married next month. I love her and she

loves me, and we will be very happy together, I am sure of it. I will have a good life. But will I always be thinking about a woman I left standing in the snow in Nybergsund?

I have knocked on every door in this village and the next and the one after that, and no one knows you. The cottage on the island is empty and shut up, covered in bird droppings. A fool's errand if there ever was one. But if you find this and you would like to write to me, this is my address.

A part of me will always remain,

Your Thomas

Jane and Ben sat there in silence for a while, watching the crowd – children shrieking and laughing, tourists stamping their feet.

At last, Ben spoke.

'His family were with him at the end,' he said. 'He was loved. He was right when he prophesied a good life for himself.'

'Marit was happy too,' said Jane. 'She travelled the world and did extraordinary things. She might have hated marriage and small-town Norway. Who knows what would have happened if Thomas and Marit had ever met again.'

Ben nodded. 'They might have been a sore disappointment to each other. Driven each other crazy.'

'Bickered like mad.'

'Divorced after a week.'

Jane laughed.

'Still,' said Ben. 'It's a good story.'

She looked at him, into his clear, serious grey eyes. 'It is,' she said.

Music struck up – the chords of a familiar carol. The choir singers began to sing, softly at first, barely discernible from the chatter of the crowd, and then, voices growing in confidence, soaring into the night air.

'*Silent night, holy night. All is calm, all is bright . . .*'

Norway seemed at once so far away and yet, with Ben at her side, distractingly close.

'And now,' called out a voice on a loudspeaker 'for the moment you've all been waiting for. The lighting of the tree.'

'This is it,' said Jane.

'About time,' Ben said. He glanced at her. 'This is the main reason I'm here after all,' he said.

'Oh, really?' Her heart knocked against her ribs.

'Absolutely. I can't get enough of this tree.'

Through the crowd Jane could see Freddie, Lena and Lucy, arms linked, cheeks ruddy beneath their bobble hats, camera phones trained on the tree. Natasha, standing a little apart, phone also raised. Nick, one child on his shoulders and another in his arms. Sandra, looking ironic and amused. And then, taking Jane almost by surprise, the tree blazed into life. Everyone began clapping.

'Now,' continued the announcer, 'for the English and Norwegian national anthems.'

Jane and Ben stood side by side as the music swelled. There she stood, the Queen of the Forest, ancient and majestic despite her gaudy finery. Only weeks ago, she had been in a peaceful forest in Oslomarka. Travelled miles across a chill sea. And now here she was, a Christmas gift born out of war, decked with lights.

'Well,' Jane said, breaking the silence between them. 'That was . . . nice. If I liked Christmas, I'd feel all Christmassy right now.'

He nodded. 'It's definitely arrived.' He glanced at his watch. 'I should get going.'

'Oh yeah,' she said, trying not to sound too desolate. 'You've got your next assignment, haven't you?'

'I'm leaving tomorrow. For six weeks.'

'Right.' She cleared her throat. 'I've got a new job too. With the *Washington News*. I'm going to be their foreign correspondent.'

'Hey,' he said. 'That's good news, isn't it? Congratulations.'

'It'll take me out of the country in the new year,' she said, tracing a pattern on the ground with the toe of her boot. 'And for most of the year, in fact.' She risked a look at his face. 'I'll be very, very busy and unavailable.'

He smiled, that slow smile that she realised she loved.

'It's the twenty-first century, isn't it? No one is unavailable. So you're moving across the world. What brought this on?'

'I decided life was too short to be safe.' She took a deep breath. 'And in that spirit, I wanted to tell you something. There is nothing at all going on with me and Philip Donnelly. No collusion on dodgy newspaper articles. Nothing.'

He grinned suddenly. 'I was prepared to take him out anyway,' he said, and she realised he was holding her hand.

She could feel her own smile spreading across her face, matching his.

'You were?' she asked.

'Yeah. That night on the deck, I lost it.'

'I noticed,' Jane said. 'I thought you didn't get angry about anything.'

'He's a patronising git.' Ben shook his head. 'But I can see why you fell for him. He's so dashing.'

'I didn't fall for him,' Jane said firmly. 'I just got distracted. Even though I didn't realise it, because I'm an idiot, I had fallen for someone else. Someone who always has to do the right thing even if it's inconvenient and drives under the speed limit and can't stop talking and has to make friends with everyone.'

'God, he sounds annoying,' said Ben. He drew her closer.

'He's the worst,' she said, and she kissed him.

They pulled apart at last. He held her face in his hands.

'Look,' he said quietly. 'It's snowing.'

He was right. Soft, fat snowflakes were drifting down and mantling their shoulders.

Jane grinned. 'I've been wanting to kiss you for weeks.'

'I've been wanting to kiss *you* for years. I'd finally plucked up the courage to ask you out last year, when I got back from Pakistan, and you'd started dating *Simon* of all people. I went to Aleppo.'

'I drove you to that?' Jane asked.

'And worse,' he said. 'But I couldn't help coming back. You're so gorgeous and amazing.'

'So are you,' she said. 'All of those things. Don't stop kissing me.'

'I've been bottling that up for weeks. God knows why.' His gaze darkened. 'Oh wait, I know why. Because you were wrapped up in a posturing, idiotic—'

She kissed him again. 'Hush. Let's never speak of Philip again,' she said breathlessly.

'Fine by me. Look, shall we just . . . go somewhere?'

'Where?' she asked.

'Anywhere,' he said. 'Anywhere I can kiss you for many, many hours before I get on a flight at the crack of dawn.'

'That sounds perfect,' Jane said, and then groaned. 'Margot! She's my best friend, and we're meant to be having our pre-Christmas dinner tonight – I don't think she'd like it if —'

'If you ditched her for some bloke?' came an amused voice to Jane's left, and she turned to see Margot, pink-cheeked and pretty under her hat. 'I'm Margot,' she said, sticking out a gloved hand. 'Nice to meet you. Ben, isn't it?'

Ben let go of Jane long enough to shake her hand. 'It is.' He gave her a puzzled look. 'How do you . . .?'

'I've heard a lot about you, although I had to read between the lines. I thought Jane would never realise.'

Jane's cheeks flamed. Ben turned to her, his face smug. 'Looks like someone was a bit slow on the uptake,' he said.

'Anyway,' said Margot, 'I overheard your conversation and I'm sorry to throw a spanner in the works, but Jane and I have a date. Unless,' she said slyly, 'you'd like to come along.'

Jane opened her mouth in protest and Margot held up a hand.

'Darling, he seems lovely,' she said. 'And I didn't realise he was going to be so handsome. But you have an awful track record and I want to vet this one.' She gave Ben a very sweet smile. 'Something tells me he might be around for a while.'

They walked through the streets of Chinatown to their usual restaurant and Ben poured them all tea, and agreed that three people absolutely needed to order half the menu, and he and Jane had held hands under the table and grinned at each other like idiots, and Margot grilled Ben relentlessly, but because Ben and Margot seemed to like each other very much, right away, it was all fine.

Better than fine.

And then Margot hugged them both and disappeared, after which it was just Ben and Jane in the booth, kissing, for hours, while the food grew cold around them.

At some point, they went back to Jane's flat on the bus, still kissing, and she found she wasn't remotely embarrassed about the front door she had to shove with her shoulder to open, or the pizza boxes and chocolate wrappers.

Eventually, they found themselves in the bedroom, Jane undressed down to her bra and pants – Marks & Spencer's finest. *Functional and plain*, she thought proudly.

'Look at you,' Ben said. 'Look at you.' He pressed a line of kisses across her collarbone. 'How did I get so lucky?' He kissed the tip of her nose. 'What a lovely face you have. That's the first thing I thought when I met you at the *Courier*.'

'You don't think I should smile more?' asked Jane, sitting up. 'You don't think I have a . . . face with the shutters down?'

'Shutters?' he said bemusedly. 'Not even slightly. What idiot told you that?'

Jane laughed. 'A prize one. Did you ever think . . . *this* would happen?'

He traced her bare shoulder with his finger. 'Why do you think I agreed to come to Norway? You were single at last. I hoped that all the fresh air and fjords would go to your head and I'd finally be able to make a move.'

'Oh no,' said Jane. 'And then Philip was there.'

He kissed her shoulder again. 'He was always hanging around smouldering and glowering, with his . . . cheek-bones. And you seemed to like it, so I gave up. But then he ditched you on the mountain that night.' His grip on her tightened. 'One of the worst nights of my life, that was, waiting for you to come round, hassling that poor doctor and holding your hand. I knew that I didn't just fancy you – I was besotted with you.'

'Why didn't you tell me at the ball?' asked Jane.

'I was about to leave the country. And I couldn't tell how upset you were over Philip. Both stupid reasons, I see now.'

'Did you think that was it?' Jane asked, pushing her hair out of her eyes. 'That I was gone from your life for ever, like Marit leaving Thomas?'

'Well, it was Thomas who said I should make one last attempt. Told me it was his dying wish that I should find you in London under the Christmas tree.'

Jane burst out laughing. 'That old devil. That's what he told me. Said you needed looking after.'

Ben pushed back her hair, cupped her cheek in his hand. 'Maybe I do,' he whispered.

Jane traced each of his lovely freckles with her fingertips. 'Maybe I do too.'

He smiled at her. 'In that case, I think this will work out nicely.'

31

The Following Christmas, Scotland

Snow lay all about, deep, crisp and, barring the lumps and bumps of the vast, rutted garden, even.

Jane leaned out of the window and breathed in. Miles away from the crisp air of Norway, but not half bad, she thought, staring out at the beautiful Scottish countryside. She had been delighted to see that there were Highland cows in the back field.

Downstairs, she could hear movement – Ben's dad, Martin, in the kitchen, preparations for Christmas lunch getting underway. Somewhere above them, she could hear the patter of excited feet, a door opening, a murmur of voices, and then the door closing again. One of the twins, being sent back to bed.

Jane thought back to last Christmas.

Margot had gone into labour on Christmas Eve morning, and Jane had spent the night lying in their spare room, staring at the ceiling and waiting for news from the hospital. And then the sound of a key in the front door, and, in the stillness of a grey dawn, the cry of a baby.

A Christmas baby was destined to always be very special, Margot had told her with glee.

Margot had breastfed the baby and Kate had somehow produced a Christmas lunch, and Jane had snuck out to have long, giggly, sexy phone calls with Ben in Turkey.

The Christmas issue of the *Courier* came out, with Jane's article as the main cover story. She had cleared it with Marit's family and they allowed her to use the microfilm Marit had hidden under the stamp in her final letter. A photograph, of a little cottage outside Nybergsund – one final memento for Thomas.

The story, Jane's last for the *Courier*, had taken off. She had a literary agent now and film rights had been bought. She was flying out to Norway later in the year to talk to Iacob and Susan and the production company. If they were going to tell Marit and Thomas's story, they had all agreed, it should be done properly.

She watched a robin hop from branch to bare branch. Kate, Margot and her goddaughter, Teddy, would be waking up soon in London. She would call them after lunch, she thought.

It was a treat to be in one place for a few weeks. The last year had brought more upheaval and more joy than Jane had ever imagined possible. She had moved across the ocean to a different country, where she barely had time to unpack before she had flown off again on an assignment. She and Ben lived out their romance in the margins of time differences and jet lag and snatched days. *Safe*, her new life was not. But it felt exactly right. Never had she felt so sure of anything in her life. And wherever she was in the world, there was a stone from a beach in Norway, solid and warm in her pocket.

Ben came and stood behind her, wrapping warm arms about her, pulling her close.

'You're freezing,' he said sleepily, against her hair. 'And it's too early. The madness will start up soon enough. Two sets of twins running purely on chocolate and adrenaline isn't pretty. Come back to bed.'

'I'm excited,' she said. 'I've never had a big family Christmas before.'

'Let's just say there's a reason we start drinking at nine a.m. Come on,' murmured Ben, dragging her back towards the bed. 'It's cold.'

'You grew up in Norway,' she said, allowing him to envelop them both in the duvet. 'You should be immune to the cold.'

'Norway has nothing on a Scottish farmhouse in winter with a father who doesn't believe in central heating.'

She lay against him, his lean body warm next to hers. 'Do you remember,' she said drowsily, 'that trip in the boat, over the fjord? God, I fancied you so much. I can't believe I didn't realise.'

'I wanted to push poor old Sven into the lake,' he said sleepily.

There was a thud on the landing outside, and a series of squeals and excited shouts as the twins thudded past their door on their way downstairs. Jane sat up.

'That's it. It's officially Christmas morning,' she said. 'Come on. I want to see what all the fuss is about.'

He grinned. 'Does this mean you're willing to give Christmas another chance?'

'Maybe,' Jane said. 'A lot is riding on today to convince me.'

He kissed her then, as though he couldn't look at her and not.

'Don't worry,' he said. 'I have a good feeling about this one.'

ACKNOWLEDGEMENTS

As an editor, I always wondered why authors got stressed writing their acknowledgments. Now I know – a lot of people go into making a book and you want to thank them ALL.

A huge, heartfelt thanks to Hodder and the awesome team there. Melissa Cox for asking me to write a comfort read in these miserable times, and for being so smart and insightful when we were plotting it. Lily Cooper, for her terrific editorial insights and for being such a champion of this book. I know full well how many people work on a book in-house and I wanted to thank, deep breath – Laura Collins and Barbara Roby for top-notch copyediting and proof-reading; Sarah Christie for a beautiful cover; Melanie Price in marketing; Jasmine Marsh in publicity, Melis Dagoglu in Rights and Susan Spratt in production. Being on the other side of the fence is very humbling – thank you for making it so easy and enjoyable.

Thank you to my agent, brilliant Jane Finigan at Lutyens Rubenstein – for your support, wise words, and the bacon naans – and Francesca Davies for all of your help.

I confidently thought I could write this book around my day job and childcare, during "nap time", ha. Easier said than done, and I owe the biggest thanks to all the people who helped me pull it off – this feels like the tip of a very large iceberg, but they include:

My parents, for so much, not only for making reading a part of everyday life for as long as I can remember, but – crucially – for sorting extra childcare so that I could finish a first draft. THANK YOU.

My in-laws, Sue and Steve, for much love and encouragement, and again – staying with the theme – for some seriously stoic childcare over one long weekend where I only came out for meals.

Cove Park, Birkbeck and the Sophie Warne Memorial Prize, for giving me the time and space to work somewhere so beautiful.

Sam Smith, for being the most supportive, hilarious and kind.

My two Eleanors, Eleanor Scoones and Eleanor Bindman, for being wildly enthusiastic about this book without having read a single word; Louise Lamont, wise, ruthless; Ellen Holgate, the absolute best; all the libraries and Glasgow cafes who let me nurse a lukewarm coffee in the corner for hours. Thank you to everyone who chatted to me about Norway and who kindly talked me through this new-fangled app called Instagram.

Writing the "com" part of a rom com concerned me because I'm not known for having the best sense of humour. Any sense of fun I've developed (questionable) is entirely down to my hilarious and amazing children, Florence and Theodore; thank you, you lovely maniacs.

And finally, this book quite literally could not have been written without my husband, Alex. I really did hit the jackpot. Thank you, for everything.